MASTERED BY MALONE

LAYLAH ROBERTS

Laylah Roberts

Mastered by Malone

© 2019, Laylah Roberts

Laylah.roberts@gmail.com

laylahroberts.com

Cover Design by: Allycat's Creations

Editing: Eve Arroyo

✾ Created with Vellum

LET'S KEEP IN TOUCH!

Don't miss a new release, sign up to my newsletter for sneak peeks, deleted scenes and giveaways: https://landing.mailerlite.com/web-forms/landing/p7l6go

BOOKS BY LAYLAH ROBERTS

Doms of Decadence

Just for You, Sir

Forever Yours, Sir

For the Love of Sir

Sinfully Yours, Sir

Make me, Sir

A Taste of Sir

To Save Sir

Sir's Redemption

Reveal Me, Sir

Old-Fashioned Series

An Old-Fashioned Man

Two Old-Fashioned Men

Her Old-Fashioned Husband

Her Old-Fashioned Boss

His Old-Fashioned Love

An Old-Fashioned Christmas

Haven, Texas Series

Lila's Loves

Laken's Surrender

Saving Savannah

Molly's Man

Saxon's Soul

A Mate to Cherish

A Mate to Sacrifice

1

D ead bodies were following her around.

Mia fought the insane urge to laugh. It wasn't funny, of course. Her next-door neighbor was dead. Very dead. Bullet in the head not gonna come back from this dead. Blood pooled under her body; her eyes stared lifelessly ahead. Mia stood frozen, staring down at Angel.

Move, Mia. It's not safe.

Trembles rocked her body. Her breath came in sharp pants. This felt like it was happening to someone else. Her body might be reacting, but on the inside Mia felt numb. Almost detached.

That was bad, right? She should feel something, shouldn't she? Horror? Fear? Sadness?

Run, Mia.

Okay, so admittedly, Angel was a pretty crappy person. She played her music too loud late at night. She had people visiting her at all hours. Mia wasn't certain if she was a prostitute or she just really, really liked sex. With lots of different men. But the things she'd heard through the thin walls of her apartment at night were enough to leave her blushing.

She'd also suspected Angel had been coming into her apartment and stealing stuff. Not that she could ever prove it. There was never any sign of a break-in.

Well, she'd been unable to prove it until now, since Angel was wearing Mia's bright yellow raincoat. She also had a hole in her forehead that Mia was pretty sure was supposed to be hers as well.

A bubble of laughter escaped. Aware of the note of hysteria, she forced her lips closed.

Angel had stolen her bullet. She was lying in the alley that ran along the side of their apartment building, dressed in Mia's favorite rain jacket, with Mia's bullet in her brain.

What wasn't there to laugh about, really?

Only everything. None of it was funny. It was terrifying and completely unfair. She'd always been a good girl. Worked hard. Paid her taxes. *She'd* never run a prostitution business out of her apartment.

And someone was trying to kill her.

She ran a shaky hand over her face. The numbness was fading. It wasn't safe. She needed to move. What if he was still around?

"If he was still here, you'd be dead," she muttered to herself. Had he checked to see whether he'd murdered the right girl? Maybe he thought she *was* dead. It was wrong to find hope in this situation, right? It was wrong to hope that Angel's death meant she was safe. At least for a while.

She sucked in a shaky breath and spots danced in front of her face.

Remember to breathe.

Her location had been compromised. He'd found her.

"I really loved that jacket."

Focusing on the wrong thing here, Mia. Get your ass gone.

Soon someone else was going to come across Angel's body. And if she was there, it wasn't going to go well. They'd probably wonder why she was just standing there, not reacting, not calling the cops, not doing anything.

Not her first rodeo. Not her first dead body.

She forced herself to turn away. She wouldn't go back to her apartment; she wasn't that dumb. Instead, she turned and walked out onto the sidewalk, moving away from the building where she'd lived for the last three months, leaving everything behind except her handbag and the clothes she was wearing.

"I NEED A FAVOR."

Alec Malone didn't bother looking away from the invoices strewn across his desk. How the fuck had Tanner and Raid destroyed a thousand dollars' worth of stuff at some trashy bar?

"What the hell were they doing in a place called Titties and Totems?" he muttered to himself.

"I'm sure I have no idea," his cousin drawled. "Doesn't sound like a place I'd want to visit."

Alec looked over at his cousin, who was sprawled in the chair across his desk, dressed in a three-piece suit. He looked as impeccable as always. Not a hair out of place. There was a knowing smirk on his face.

Alec snorted. "That's because you're a New Orleans Malone. The rest of us aren't fussy about where we have a drink."

"You say that like it's a bad thing to have standards." Jardin stood and leaned over Alec's desk, looking down at the invoice. "At least my brothers aren't racking up thousand-dollar bills in a place that sounds like it would make Hooters look classy. What did they do? Trash the place?"

Knowing Tanner and Raid, most likely.

"And this is why I'm going gray."

Jardin snorted. "So don't pay it."

"If I don't pay it, things escalate. People turn up here, demanding shit from me. I don't like when people do that," he said with a pointed look at his cousin.

Jardin just rolled his eyes. "I'm not people. I'm family."

"You're a New Orleans Malone, not sure I'd claim you as family."

"You're letting me live in your guest house."

"Must have had a momentary lapse in sanity." Malone glared at him. "You're evicted."

Jardin sighed. "Quit playing around, Alec."

He wasn't playing around. He'd meant every word. Too bad his cousin was shit at reading people. Not a great skill for a lawyer to be lacking.

"You need to get them in line."

"I don't have to do shit," Alec snapped back. Not that he didn't have the same thought several times a day. But he'd go to his grave defending his brothers. He could call them a bunch of dipshits, but no one else could. "Why the hell do I let you stay here?"

"Because you need someone with an ounce of sanity to help you rein that crazy family of yours in."

"I don't need help." And like he'd ask his stuck-up snob of a cousin to corral his brothers. The New Orleans Malones didn't get their hands dirty. They paid other people to do that.

"Yeah? Because the way I see it, someone is either going to end up dead or in jail."

He wasn't saying anything that hadn't occurred to Alec. Didn't mean he liked hearing a lecture on his family.

"You can't keep protecting them all their lives, Alec."

"I'm not protecting them."

"Look, I know what a bastard your father was—"

"Is this all you wanted?" Alec interrupted him. "To lecture me about my brothers?"

"One day, one of them is going to do something that you can't throw money at and fix."

"Why are you here?" Alec asked, his patience nearly gone. And it took a lot to make him lose his temper.

His brothers had always been a bit crazy. Wild. But who could blame them after the fucking hell life they'd all had growing up? Wasn't like his hands were clean. He'd done what he had to in order to survive. They were all alive and in one piece. Sort of. Beau was missing a finger and West had lost so much muscle in his right thigh after an infected knife wound that he walked with a limp.

But he'd done his best to instill some values. They might fuck with each other but no one outside the family messed with one of them and lived to tell the tale. Sure, they didn't always stick to the law, but he'd been the same when he was younger. That he tried to follow the rules now had more to do with not wanting to attract attention than any real respect for the law.

Something his cousin wouldn't get. The New Orleans Malones always did have a highly developed sense of self-importance. Thought they were better than their cousins because they were college-educated and lived in fancy fucking houses.

Go back far enough and all their money came from the same dirty place. Jardin and his brothers just had short memories. Of course, they hadn't been raised in a household with a monster. Or been made to do shit that would leave them screaming into their pillows at night.

Could he blame his brothers for blowing off steam? They were Malones. They had an abundance of energy, charm and a reckless disregard for authority. But he also knew Jardin was right. He couldn't protect them forever. And one day, he worried they'd go too far.

"I told you, I need a favor."

"I thought I already did you a favor by letting you live here."

Jardin raised his eyebrows. "You consider that a favor? I take my own life in my hands every time I come up that driveway."

"Drama Queen," he muttered.

"Raid shot out my front tire!"

Alec shrugged. "He thought you were that dickwad who keeps trying to buy the ranch."

"Osborne is fifty, balding, and drives a red Porsche. Are you seriously trying to tell me he mistook my black Audi for a red Porsche?" Jardin half-yelled.

"He's color-blind."

"God, give me strength," Jardin muttered.

"Stop moaning, it was relatively harmless."

"Relatively harmless? He shot out my tire. I could have had an accident. He could have hit me."

"Nah, those fancy cars practically drive themselves. It would have compensated for your crappy driving. And Raid's too good a shot to miss. If he wanted you dead, you'd be dead." Alec found himself having to hide a smile. Who knew Jardin would be so fun to mess with? Only good thing about having him come to live with them. There had to be an upside to having to listen to all his *advice*.

"Alec, he cannot go around shooting people."

"Ah, Jardin, you're not people, you're family, remember?"

Jardin's eyes narrowed. "And that's supposed to mean he gets away with shooting at me?"

"Again, he wasn't shooting at you. He shot the tire. You should be happy you're family, means he won't kill you."

"Does it?" Jardin asked. He sighed. "So, Osborne is still trying to buy the ranch?"

"Yep. He's got a real hard-on for this place."

"Gotta wonder why." Jardin looked around with a slight sneer.

"Not all of us need to live in McMansions with marble staircases and chandeliers."

"Oh, fuck you," Jardin said without heat.

"He thinks there's oil on our land."

"And is there?" Jardin asked.

Alec shrugged. "Who knows?"

"How do you know he thinks there's oil?" Jardin asked suspiciously.

Alec grinned. "You don't want to know."

Jardin ran his hand tiredly over his face. "Right. Look, will you help or not?"

"Help who? You in trouble?" Much as he liked to dig at his cousin, he was still family. No one messed with a Malone. Not even the stuck-up, prissy ones.

"Not me. I've got a friend who's a detective with the NYPD. His cousin is in trouble. She was a witness to a murder. Mob hit. Now she's got a hit man chasing her. Somehow this guy figured out where Mike had her stashed and killed her next-door neighbor, likely mistaking the neighbor for her since she was wearing his cousin's jacket."

"So? What has this got to do with me? Why should I care?"

"Nothing. Don't worry about it." Jardin stood. He'd looked pissed off before, but now he had completely closed down. Which meant he didn't want to show Alec how he really felt about this situation. But Alec couldn't see how this had anything to do with him ... unless ...

"Fuck, you want me to hide her?" Why the hell would he do that? Didn't he have enough going on? Did he really need to add in some woman with a target on her back? What the fuck was Jardin thinking?

A woman living here? With his brothers? He'd never be able to keep them off her.

That shit sounded too much like his old life. And he'd left that behind to become a rancher. He wasn't ever going back.

"This place is isolated, it's secure, there's a world-class security system, and you've got to admit you, more than most people, are equipped to handle something like this."

"Protecting a woman who has witnessed a mob hit? No way."

"Yeah," Jardin grumbled. "I'll help Mike figure out something else."

There was something he was missing here. "You know this girl? You want something from her?"

"No, I don't know her. Jesus, Alec, I can want to help her without having an ulterior motive."

Not in his world. Well, that wasn't true. That wasn't the world he'd grown up in. The world he now lived in was very different. When he ventured into Haven, the town closest to the ranch, he was surrounded by people who looked after one another, without any expectation of anything in return. It still baffled him. He found it hard to trust their motivation. This idea that the women of Haven would be protected and watched over at all costs. That people would turn up to help a neighbor in need without any expectation of payment in return.

His default setting was always to see the bad in people. When you'd lived the way he had, it was hard to see the good.

"Then what?"

"I like Mike, he's a good guy."

"So, you're asking me if I can house some girl with a huge target on her back just because her cousin is your friend?"

Jardin sighed. "He's found her once. She needs help or she's dead."

"That's a big fucking favor, putting my family in danger to protect a girl we don't know." He wasn't buying it. There had to be more to it. Jardin liked to act like shit didn't touch him, but he wasn't that much of a good Samaritan.

Family always came first. Before anyone or anything else.

Family . . . his blood ran cold. "How do you know this detective?"

Jardin's eyes narrowed. It was the only sign of emotion. But it was enough. "He's the detective who found Lottie."

Fucking hell. No wonder Jardin felt like he owed this guy something. Lottie was his only sister. Hell, she was the only Malone female to be born in three generations. She was special. And any one of them would die to protect her. About two years ago, she'd been kidnapped while on holiday. She'd been found, beaten and terrified but alive two days later. They all owed this detective.

Jardin looked him in the eye. "Forget I asked. It wasn't fair of me. I'll find some other way to protect her."

"I'll do it," Alec said. He could keep this girl safe. He had no ties to her. As long as whoever brought her here didn't have a tail on them, there was no reason anyone would come looking for her here.

"Yeah?" Again, there was just a sliver of emotion from the other man. Relief, this time. Tarred with a hint of worry. "You sure?"

"I'll have to tell them," he warned Jardin. "They'll need to be on high alert." Fuck, it just might be what they needed to keep them focused for a while and out of trouble. Give him a bit of breathing room to get some shit done around there.

Jardin grimaced. "Jesus, do we have to tell them?"

"Don't you think they'll notice a woman living in the house? Unless you expect me to keep her locked in her room." He pretended to consider that. "Not a bad idea. Easiest way to keep her safe." And out of his hair. Fuck. Why was he agreeing to this? Some strange woman in his house. A woman bringing trouble with her.

"You can't keep her locked in a room. How do we get them to keep their hands off her?"

"Guess that's up to her now, isn't it? My brothers would never force a woman."

"Of course they wouldn't. They'd just charm her into bed and then kick her out the next day when she started to bore them. Because they have short attention spans. And then where does that leave her? Stuck here for another two months with no way to get away from them."

Alec sighed. Why him? "Fine, I'll make sure they know she's off limits."

"Let's hope they'll listen. I'm starting to have second thoughts."

"Jesus, will you stop whining. You brought this up because you know I can keep her safe. I'll keep them away from her. So, just be grateful."

"And will they keep her presence here a secret?"

"They know how to keep their mouths shut. They learned that young. Especially when it comes to fucking family shit."

"You have such a way with words."

"Hey, we can't all have degrees from some fancy college, city boy," Alec said, putting on his best ol' boy Texas drawl. "We jus' be poor hillbillies here."

Jardin ignored his sarcasm. "You sure about this? I know I'm asking you to put yourselves at risk for a stranger."

"It's not for a stranger, it's for Lottie."

Jardin gave a nod. But there was a note of something in his gaze. Sadness. Fear. Gratitude.

"I'll keep her safe," Alec told him.

A sound like cattle stampeding could be heard through the house. Things rattled on Alec's desk and he sighed.

Jardin ran his hand over his face. "Maybe locking her in her room is a better idea that having her meet your brothers. They'll probably have her running for the hills in a day."

Alec shrugged. His obligation was to keep her alive. He'd do that however he needed to. It wasn't his problem to worry about her feelings.

"She's a good cook. She's worked in restaurants before. I thought you could tell people you'd hired a cook."

Alec just sent him a look. "I don't need to tell anyone anything. And the last time I hired a cook, he ended up running down the driveway, buck naked, screaming that the spawn of Satan was on his tail."

"Christ."

"Told those boys I wasn't hiring anyone else to take care of their asses."

"Which is why this house is always a disaster," Jardin muttered.

Alec didn't think that required an answer. Besides, it was true. The place was a cesspool. Wasn't so bad when Alice had lived there. The older woman had kept house for him. But she'd retired and moved to Baltimore to help her daughter look after her babies about a year ago. He'd hired a cook to help out and he hadn't even lasted a week. He'd given up after that.

Alec stood and left the office, walking into the kitchen and the chaos that was his family. Mounds of sandwiches, which is what they all basically lived on, were being created on the table in the center of the huge kitchen. This place had once looked like a showroom. And now, well, it resembled feeding time at the zoo.

He let out a piercing whistle and his brothers all shut up, looking over at him.

"I've got to learn to do that," Jardin muttered behind him.

"They won't pay any attention if you do it," Alec told him. "Listen up. Got a situation. We got a woman coming to stay, she's a witness to a mob hit. Now she's got a hit on her. We're gonna protect her."

"She hot?" Tanner asked.

"How old is she?" Beau asked.

"Can she cook?" Raid added.

Alec glared at them all. "It doesn't matter what she looks like, you're all going to keep your fucking dicks in your pants. Understand me? She needs protecting, not seducing."

"Why are we looking out for her? What's she to us?" West asked. West was the quietest of the lot. And the one least likely to get in trouble. Or at least any trouble Alec knew of. West was tight-lipped. And smart.

"Jardin's friend—"

"Wait," Jaret interrupted. "Jardin has a friend? By God, now I've heard it all."

They all laughed. Even West cracked a smile.

"For fuck's sake," Jardin muttered.

"Came as a shock to me too," Alec agreed.

"You're just egging them on," Jardin complained, sending him a look.

"But his *supposed* friend is this woman's cousin. He's been hiding her, but the hit man found her and killed her next-door neighbor, thinking it was her."

"Still don't see why we need to stick our necks out for her, especially if we don't get anything out of it," Maddox complained.

"You ever heard of being good Samaritans?" Jardin asked.

Alec just sent him a look as his brothers started to scoff at that idea. "Don't try to help." He turned to his brothers. "The reason we're going to help is because Jardin's friend is the one who found Lottie."

They all fell silent and looked over at Jardin.

"So, you all in? You got to keep this quiet, keep your dicks in your pants, and be prepared for shit to go down."

Raid smiled wide. "I'm always ready for shit to go down."

"That's cause you cause most of that shit." Beau gave him a dark look. "Not a chance in hell of you keepin' your fucking dick in your pants."

"You're just jealous because I had a taste of Lucy first. Fuck that woman could—" His words were drowned out as Beau jumped on him with a roar of fury.

Alec ran his hand over his face. He was too old for this shit. Knowing he wouldn't get any sense out of them until they'd worked off some steam, he turned and walked out.

"Christ, I think I've just made a huge mistake," Jardin said from behind him.

He glanced back. "What? Wearing a three-piece suit during summer in Texas, yeah, well . . . "

"I mean asking those louts in there to protect the only witness to a horrific crime. Her testimony is going to send Frankie Angelo to prison for a long fucking time—"

"Wait, Frankie Angelo?" Alec turned back sharply to gape at his cousin. "The Monster of Manhattan?"

"Yep, first time there's ever been a live witness."

"You didn't tell me it was Frankie Angelo who has a hard-on for her." Fuck. Shit.

"Problem? I didn't know you knew him."

"I don't," Alec said quickly. "Met his dad a few times." That had been enough. "He finds out she's here and he'll come after all of us. Not just me and my brothers, he'll come after the rest of the family as well."

"Then we need to make sure he doesn't find out," Jardin said grimly.

"I want her name first," Alec told him. "I want to do some checking before she gets here."

Jardin nodded. "As long as you can do it without raising any alarm bells."

Alec just shot him a look.

There was a loud yell from the kitchen. Jardin grimaced. "You sure they can be trusted?"

"They may act like overgrown children, but they're tough, they're loyal, and occasionally they even use their brains."

"Glad to hear they've got some."

"Relax. I have everything under control. But I won't be forgetting you owe me."

"I didn't think you would."

2

_____

She stared at the imposing gates looming in front of her.

"I think this is the place," her cousin muttered from beside her as he stared out the window. They'd been driving for days. Staying in crappy motels that didn't give a shit whether your ID was fake as long as your cash was real.

They hadn't taken the most direct route to get there. Instead, Mike had done a lot of backtracking, to ensure they weren't being followed. Neither of them had slept much over the past few days, Mike because he was in bodyguard mode, worried about protecting her. Her, because she knew if she fell asleep the nightmares would get hold of her.

Wrought iron gates hung between concrete posts. On one post was a small wooden sign: Lonely Horse Ranch.

"You don't have to do this, sunshine," Mike said quietly. "We can leave. I can protect you."

Mike was a warrior, a guardian, and it chafed not being able to look after her. Especially as this place and the man who owned it were unknowns to them both.

Alec Malone.

She liked his name. It was a strong name.

"I know you can," she told him. Not for the world would she ever say she doubted his ability to keep her safe. But if anything happened to Mike while he was protecting her, she'd never forgive herself.

Oh, but it's fine to put a stranger at risk?

"But we'd be running for the next two months trying to stay ahead of this hit man. This is a better solution." *I hope.*

Mike reached over and took hold of her hand in his. Drat, she'd been tapping her fingers against her thigh. Something she only did when she was feeling nervous or scared. He gave her hand a squeeze. "If you hate it here, if you want to leave, if you need anything, you call me, and I'll come."

Tears filled her eyes and she blinked them away before looking over at him. "I love you." He was her everything. Her only family. She wouldn't risk him for anything.

"Love you too, sunshine." He gave her hand a final squeeze and let it go. Then he drove forward and opened the car window, reaching out with his hand to press down on the buzzer.

Here goes nothing.

"WHAT THE HELL IS TANNER DOING?" Jardin asked.

Alec studied the dusty sedan making its way slowly up the driveway. It hit a pothole and bounced. It wasn't made for country driving. Of course, he kept his driveway purposely rough in order to dissuade anyone from visiting—or returning. Tanner was sitting on the trunk, his arm resting along the roof.

"I sent him down to greet them."

Jardin turned to give him a look. "You did what?"

"Someone had to go."

"Yes, but Tanner? He doesn't have a filter on his mouth. Polite isn't in his vocabulary."

Alec shrugged. "Figured she should know what she's in for."

"Or you were hoping she'd call things off and then you wouldn't have to take her in," Jardin muttered.

Alec sent him a look. "Either works."

The sedan came to a stop. Yeah, it had probably been a dick move. Tanner wasn't a jerk; he didn't have a nasty bone in his body. But there was little he took seriously, and he was an incorrigible flirt.

He jumped off and raced over to open the passenger door to the car. That didn't surprise Alec. His brothers didn't have many manners, but they knew how to charm the pants off a woman. Fuck. Maybe he'd made a mistake in sending Tanner. Knowing his luck, the woman in the car wouldn't take offense and refuse to stay, she'd fall in love and follow his brother around like a lovesick teenager.

Alec sighed. Then she stepped out and raised her hand to her face to shield her eyes as she stared up at Tanner. Her gaze dropped to the ground and his stomach clenched. Then she turned and looked up to where he and Jardin stood on the porch and it felt like he'd been sucker-punched.

She was gorgeous. Her long, wavy, red-blonde hair was pulled back in a ponytail. If she were his, he'd want that hair down when they were playing. He'd wrap his hand around it and use it to control her movements as she went down on him.

Shit. He needed to stop thinking like that.

She was his responsibility for the next two months. Not his plaything. Getting involved with her would be a terrible idea. He'd warned his brothers away, he couldn't turn around and invite her into his bed.

"You didn't tell me she looked like that," Alec grumbled. The photo he'd dug up on her background check had done her no justice at all.

A big bruiser of a man climbed out of the driver's side. Her cousin. The cop. He couldn't believe he was letting a cop onto his land voluntarily. It was a wonder lightning wasn't striking him down. Every time Jake, Haven's sheriff, came out to the ranch he got a case of acid reflux.

The man stared around him, his eyes not missing a thing, his body tense and ready. Tanner must have said something to him, because he turned to his brother with a glare hot enough to fry a lesser man. Tanner just grinned and sent him a salute.

"Like what?" Jardin asked innocently.

"Don't try my patience. You know what the hell I'm talking about. How the fuck am I supposed to keep them off her?" As soon as they saw her, they'd descend. And the one thing standing between her and them was him.

"Problems? I thought you had them under control," Jardin shot his own words back at him.

"Fuck you," Alec muttered. "I can control my brothers and protect her. But you damn well owe me." The headache her presence was going to give him for the next two months was not something he was looking forward to.

He watched her move forward, pressed against the side of the big guy and felt a surge of protectiveness that shocked him. He didn't feel protective towards anyone who wasn't family. Sure, he pretended to tow Haven's rules, that every man was supposed to look out for the women in town. Protect them. All so he could go to Saxon's a few times a year.

Otherwise he'd have to drive several hours to get to a decent BDSM club and he didn't have that sort of time to waste. So he paid lip service to the rules, while not really believing in them. So why did this woman stir the Dominant inside him? The part of him that said *protect, possess, play.*

Oh, she would be fun to play with. With those curves and her fuck-me eyes, he could see her tied to a cross, naked, his whip biting into her back and buttocks. Him licking his way along each mark until he reached down between her pussy and—

"Alec. For fucks sake, Alec." Jardin poked his elbow into his side.

"What?" he snapped.

"You're staring and it's freaking her out."

As she got closer, he could see how pale her skin was, the dark crescents under her eyes. She had a haunted, fragile look. And, just like that, he shut down those instincts to take and command. This woman had been through hell. And she didn't look like it would take much to push her over the edge.

No way could she handle what he would want.

And no way he should want it with an innocent like her. His background check had unearthed very little of interest, other than the fact her parents had died when she was a kid and she'd moved in with her aunt and uncle. She hadn't even had so much as a parking ticket. She was a veritable saint and he was anything but.

"Hey, Mike, Mia," Jardin said stepping forward. "Drive here uneventful?"

"I wasn't followed, made sure of that," Mike replied, looking Alec up and down. He had a tense look on his face as he glanced over at Jardin. "You sure this is a good idea?"

"Nope," Jardin replied. "But right now, it's the best option I can think of to keep her alive."

Mia sucked in a sharp breath, and Alec turned his gaze from Mike back to her. Her expression hadn't changed, but he saw a shudder run through her body.

Yep, fragile.

"What makes you think he can protect her?" Mike asked, ignoring him. A deliberate insult. Rude considering he was opening his home to protect a stranger. "Sure, you've got a fancy gate, cameras, and some high fencing out by the road, but you can't tell me this place is entirely secure. What's to stop someone coming in the back?"

"It's not impossible to get onto the ranch," Alec admitted. "But there are no back roads. We're surrounded on two sides by other ranches and the mountains at the back. They'd have to come in by foot or horse or bike. Then they'd have to get past the cameras and my security system. As long as she stays inside or near the house it's going to be damn hard for anyone to get to her. And, provided you held up your end and weren't followed, no one should know she's here."

"I wasn't fucking followed." Mike took a step forward and, surprisingly, it was the girl who stopped him from exploding. She moved in front of Mike, between the two them.

What the fuck? Had no one taught her she shouldn't get between two aggressive men. She was supposed to stand behind the muscle. He narrowed his gaze, shifting it down to her, unsurprised when she looked away.

"Mia, get behind me." Mike tried to shove her behind him. But, for some reason, Alec didn't like him touching her. Especially when she stumbled slightly as he pulled at her.

"Easy," Alec growled.

Her eyes widened as she stared up at him.

"Maybe everyone could just calm down a bit," Jardin said, giving Alec a look that clearly said he needed to remember they owed Mike. Big. He hated owing anyone anything. But Jardin was right. He needed to play nice.

He just needed to remember how.

Jardin turned to Mike. "Mike, I get that you're feeling protective of Mia. You guys have been driving for hours, you probably haven't slept properly or eaten, why don't you come in and have a coffee and something to eat and we'll talk, all right?"

Mike continued to glare at him. Mia peered around the wide

man and he could see the exhaustion in her gaze, the slump of her shoulders. She needed rest, not to be in the middle of a pissing contest.

"Come inside." There, that had been nice, right? Although from the look Jardin sent him, maybe not.

"Who are all the guys sneaking around out there?" Mike asked, his shoulders tense as he glanced out around the yard.

Alec's opinion of him went up. "Those would be my brothers."

"How many of them are there?" Mike asked.

Alec shrugged. "Enough."

"ENOUGH?" Mia asked, finally finding her voice. She stared up at the large man glaring down at her. What did that mean? He didn't want to tell them how many brothers he had? Why wouldn't he want them to know? If she was going to live here, she assumed she'd meet them. And if they were anything like the one she'd already met then she was in trouble.

He turned his gaze to her, and she wished she hadn't drawn his attention once more.

"There's five."

"You've got six," Jardin said with a note of exasperation.

"I do?" He shrugged, seemingly indifferent. Didn't he know how lucky he was to have just one brother let alone six? "Figured they would have murdered each other by now."

She couldn't tell if he was joking or not. It had to be an act, surely. She'd already met one brother. Tanner had greeted them at the front gate, going over Mike's car with a machine he said would search out any tracking devices or bugs. Mike hadn't been too happy with that; he'd been even less impressed with the way Tanner had flirted with her the entire time. She hadn't read anything into it. He struck her as the type of guy who flirted with

all women, be they eight or eighty. It wasn't like she was the type to
attract someone as gorgeous as Tanner Malone.

Alec Malone was just as stunning. But he certainly didn't have
Tanner's easy nature. As he glared down at her, she found herself
wondering if she'd be better off facing the assassin, because Alec
Malone certainly didn't seem pleased to have her here. Not that
she could blame him. She didn't know why he'd agreed to any of
this. She was putting his entire family in jeopardy with her
presence.

Tall, with broad shoulders, his dark hair was kept neat and
short. His jeans were a faded blue, his shirt stretched across his
wide chest, tight around his arms. He wasn't the biggest guy she'd
ever seen. He didn't look like a guy who worked out at the gym for
hours each day. He looked like a man who knew how to work hard
for what he wanted.

There were hints of gray in his dark hair, but they just added to
his appeal. Those dark brown eyes pinned her, as though he'd
sensed her studying him. She stood there, frozen as he held her
with just his gaze. This man . . . he was dangerous, potent, and so
gorgeous it took her breath away.

She needed . . . she needed to get her act together. He was the
guy who was opening up his home to keep her safe. She didn't like
this plan any more than Mike did. But she liked his alternative
idea even less. The one where he took a leave of absence to protect
her.

Yeah, that one sucked. Because in that scenario she was pretty
certain her only family was going to get himself killed.

"Look, Mike," Jardin said. "You don't know Alec and his
brothers but they're solid. They'll protect Mia."

"I called in a favor from you," Mike stated. "I only trust you."

"Even though he's a soul-sucking lawyer, Jardin doesn't have
the resources I do. Besides, he's here half the time and in New
Orleans the rest. You hardly want her moving around, do you?"

Alec ground out. "Or are you planning on taking her back to New York with you?"

She trembled. She never wanted to go to New York again.

While he said all this, his gaze was on her. Mike didn't miss that. His glower was hot enough to scorch.

"Maybe that would work. Last thing that he would suspect is for her to be hiding right under his nose."

"That will never work," Alec spat out dismissively. "Stupid idea."

She could sense Mike bristling. Alec Malone didn't seem to have much of a social filter.

"Mike." She placed her hand on his arm as she stepped forward so she stood beside him. "I don't want to go to New York."

"If it's the best way to keep you safe—"

"It's not," Alec Malone interrupted.

She resisted the urge to scowl at him. Couldn't he see she was trying to smooth things over? And he was just making it all worse. And she had to live with this guy for the foreseeable future?

"Mike, I can't go back to New York. I can't." She stared up at him, willing him to understand. A hint of softness entered his gaze and he nodded. She breathed out a sigh. Sometimes, when he got an idea in his head he couldn't let it go.

"All right, sweetheart. New York is out."

"Good," Jardin said to them both. "She'll be safe here, I promise."

She looked over at Jardin, who appeared to be the sane one. Although she didn't know how sane it was to be standing there in a Texas summer dressed in a three-piece suit.

"Aren't you hot?" she blurted out, without thinking first.

Alec Malone snorted out a laugh. Okay, the man was just plain rude.

Be nice, Mia. You need him.

She hated having to rely on other people. Hated creating this headache for her cousin. She rubbed at her forehead.

"I'm fine," Jardin replied smoothly, shooting Alec a look he missed since his gaze was still on her. What was with that? Why did he keep staring at her? She was no great beauty. She wasn't even interesting looking. She was plain. Most interesting thing about her was that someone was trying to put a bullet in her head. And she'd really rather not be that interesting.

"Do I have something on my face?" she muttered, scrubbing at her cheek.

"What?" Mike turned to look at her with a frown and she flushed. Drat. Hadn't meant to say that out loud.

When she risked looking at Alec Malone, his eyes were dancing. He was laughing at her! She turned her gaze away before she said something totally inappropriate.

You need him. Play nice.

She let out a deep breath.

"Still not happy you're only here part of the time," Mike said to Jardin. "Thought I was giving her to you to protect."

"Like Alec said, he's better equipped to watch over her."

"Yeah? How's that? Who even is this guy? All I know about him is that he's your cousin, he owns a ranch, has a lot of brothers and he likes to tie women up and whip them," Mike snapped.

"Interesting that you know that." Alec sent Jardin a look.

Jardin frowned. "Don't look at me, I didn't tell him."

"Your brother did when he was going over my car with a bug detector. I asked him if he thought his brother could take care of my cousin. He said you were uptight, cautious and liked to be in charge. He also told me that you hardly ever leave the ranch so you could keep a close eye on her, except when you go to the BDSM club in town."

She gaped up at him, she hadn't heard any of that conversation, but her cousin wouldn't look down at her. Instead his gaze was on Malone, who had his arms crossed over his chest and an amused look on his face.

"While I like to use the whip on occasion, it's more Jardin's preference than mine. I like a nice paddle. I have quite the collection."

"Thanks very much, cousin." Jardin glared at Malone. But his gaze was back on her. He couldn't tell, could he? That her body had heated at his words? That her nipples had hardened? That she had to bite back the urge to ask to see that collection.

What was wrong with her? Sure, she liked to read books about that stuff, but she'd never gone to a club. She was pretty certain she never would. Because she was chicken shit. And with her luck, she'd walk in, trip over something and end up with her hoo-ha on display. Mind you in a place like that there was probably a lot of hoo-ha and cock on display. But knowing her, she'd make an absolute spectacle of herself, probably get herself kicked out and—

"Mia! Mia, you okay?"

She blinked, looking up into Mike's concerned face.

"What?" she asked.

"She's exhausted," Alec said sharply. "She needs to rest. You done with your posturing yet?"

Mike scowled at him then Jardin. "You're into that dominance bullshit as well?"

Jardin sighed. "Well, we don't go around calling it bullshit. But if you're asking if I'm a Dom, yes, I am."

"You go to clubs and tie up girls then whip them?" Mike asked using the same tone of voice that one might ask someone if they had a shrine to Hitler in their basement. Disgust, horror, and anger.

"Mike, please," she said quietly

"I won't have my cousin exposed to any of that shit."

"Mike!"

"Damn, there goes my plan to lock her in the basement and

keep her there, naked, bound, and fucked," Alec said in a low voice that sent a wave of need washing over her.

What was wrong with her? She didn't want that. But she could picture it. All too clearly.

Mike took a step forward and she stepped in front of him. Suddenly, all three men frowned down at her.

"Mike, he was joking."

"Mia, stop stepping front of me like that." Mike reached out for her, grabbing hold of her arm with the clear intention of pulling her back.

"Let her go," Alec said in a low voice.

Mike's jaw clenched. But to her shock, he let her go.

Alec turned that hard gaze on her. "That's the last time you step between two men like that. Your job isn't to protect. Your job isn't to be a diplomat. He can do that." Alec nodded over at Jardin. "Your job is to do as you are told, understand?"

"Jesus. Fucking. Christ," Mike said.

"Alec." Jardin sent his cousin a frown.

"What? You both disagree? Tough shit. I'm the one being charged with keeping her alive. She needs to obey me." He turned his gaze on her. "Mia, come here."

Her body immediately leaned towards him, but her mind brought her to a stop. She had to be loyal to her cousin. The only person in the world who loved her. Just because this guy had a face that could stop a woman in her stride and a voice that could command an army did not mean that she had to do what he said, right?

"All right, enough," Jardin said in the firmest voice she'd heard from him. "You're scaring her."

"I don't think she's scared. I think she's torn. And this is why he needs to go. There can only be one person in charge here. One person she obeys."

"And you think that one person is you?" Mike snarled. "Bullshit. Forget it, Mia. I'm not leaving you here with this asshole. Come on."

"You can take her if you want," Alec said to Mike. "But you're going to get her killed."

"I got her away once."

"And he found her. He nearly killed her. Murdered someone else he thought was her, isn't that right?"

She trembled as she recalled the sight of Angel lying on the ground. Pale and still. Nausea bubbled as an anxiety attack loomed. No, not here. Not in front of these alpha males. She couldn't.

"Mia, you all right?" Jardin asked in a soft voice.

At least someone cared to talk to her instead of speaking about her like she wasn't even there. Her mind raced, trying to figure out a way to make everyone happy in this scenario. She looked back at Mike then over at Alec.

"She's exhausted," Alec said quietly. "And you're not making this any easier on her. You need to leave. Don't contact her. Don't contact me. You have anything urgent to tell us, call Jardin. But make sure you do it from a secure line."

"I've been an NYPD detective for fifteen years. I don't need you to explain this shit to me."

"Then let me explain this. You want her kept alive? I'm your best shot at that. But things are done on my terms. I'm putting my life—my brothers' lives—on the line to keep her safe because we owe a family debt. But that's all I owe you. I don't need to give you an explanation about what I do in my private life. I don't need to listen to your bullshit judgment. I'm not fucking going to force her to submit to me. I have plenty of women eager for me to do perverted shit with them, I don't need to force anyone. She's not my type anyway."

Ouch. Well that didn't hurt. But it wasn't anything she didn't know already. Plain. Boring. Still, people didn't usually say that stuff to her face.

"Jesus, Alec," Jardin muttered.

"You do anything she doesn't want, and I will make the rest of your life very short," her cousin threatened.

"Understood," Alec said calmly. God, he was cold. "Mia, I'm going to be in my office. You have ten minutes to meet me there. I'll take that as you agreeing to my protection and the rules that come with it. Including cutting ties with your cousin. You're not there in ten minutes, I expect the two of you to get off my land and never return."

She watched with no small amount of shock as he turned and walked away. That was it? Ten minutes. Ten minutes to decide whether to turn her life over into this a stranger's hands? But then what other choice did she have? And for his faults, of which she was certain there were many, she really did believe he would protect her.

"Mike, you gotta trust me on this," Jardin told her cousin. "I owe you. You need some help. You can't protect her on her own and he really does know what he's doing."

"How?" Mike snapped. "He's a rancher."

"I can't tell you about Alec's background. That's his business. But I wouldn't leave her with him if I didn't think he was our best shot at keeping her safe."

Mike let out a frustrated noise. "If I could think of any other way..."

"I know, man. I know he's not an easy man to get along with. I get why you worry about leaving her here. But the fact that you don't agree with what we enjoy when it comes to women doesn't make it wrong. Or mean that any of that will touch Mia."

That was almost disappointing. She bit her lip. Crap, she needed to keep thoughts like that on lock down. Last thing she needed was to blurt that out.

Mike looked over at her and she cleared her throat. "I'll be all right, Mike. I want to stay here."

"Mia, you don't know—"

She put her hand up on his chest. "Mike, I know when you look at me you see the kid you've looked out for all her life, but I'm an adult now. I can't go back with you and put you in danger. I'd never forgive myself if something happened to you. Please, just let me stay."

He looked away with a sigh. Then nodded. "Fine, but I don't care what the fuck he says, you call me if you need me."

"I will." She wrapped her arms around him. "I love you."

"Love you too, sunshine."

"All right, good. Mia's tired. She needs to go see Alec then get some rest and settle in. Mike, you need to get out of here and get back to your job. I know you don't trust my cousin or like him. Believe me, very few people do. But he knows what he's doing and when he says he'll repay the family debt, he will. This really is the best place for her."

"It better be."

SHE WALKED THROUGH THE HOUSE, following Jardin. She was almost too nervous to look around, but curiosity got the best of her. From the outside, the two-storied ranch house was impressive. One of the biggest houses she'd ever seen, it dominated the land-scape. It was a gorgeous house with a large porch that ran along the front with French doors leading inside. But it almost looked out of place. The landscape was rugged and bare. There was nothing to soften the place. But then, it seemed to suit Alec Malone to a tee. He wasn't a soft man. He was as hard as the land around him. And she was completely out of her depth.

Fuck. What have I done?

The inside of the house was no less impressive with its high ceilings and gorgeous wooden floors. But the house felt a little unloved. It wasn't messy exactly, although it wasn't particularly clean either. It felt a bit bare. Cold. There was no art on the walls. No furniture in the huge foyer or anywhere along the hallway.

"Here you go, sweetheart." Jardin stopped in front of a large wooden door. He put her small bag down on the floor. She didn't have much, just what Mike had quickly grabbed for her from a Walmart when they'd had a brief stop to rest. She was going to need to get some more stuff. How, she had no idea. Online shopping would be easier, if she had a damn credit card. Being on the run sure was hell on the pocket.

"Just don't let him bully you. Stick up for yourself, but do it respectfully," he advised, before turning away.

"Wait. You're not coming in there with me?"

Jardin turned, shaking his head. "This next part is between the two of you. I can't help you with that other than to tell you that his bark is worse than his bite." He turned away, probably not expecting her to hear the next part. "Mostly, anyway."

Great. Awesome. He was leaving her to enter the monster's den all of her own. What kind of a gentleman did that? And what kind of wimp did that make her that she needed someone to protect her? She could do this. She took one calming breath then another. But still her hand trembled as she reached out to knock.

Nothing.

Okay. Maybe he wasn't there. Maybe she should just . . . what? Wander around a strange house? Stand out there until he came?

She reached out and knocked louder.

"Yeah."

Right, she guessed that was all the greeting she was going to get.

She stepped inside and couldn't decide whether to shut the

door or leave it open. In the end, she left it open a few inches. That way, someone might, possibly, hear her screams for help.

Melodramatic much?

But that feeling of walking to her doom increased as she stepped further into the room.

"You're three minutes late," was all he said, not even bothering to look up at her.

She resisted the urge to fidget like a naughty schoolgirl brought in front of the principal. What was the worst he could do? Kick her out? Order her to bend over his desk, pull down her panties, and smack her bottom with one of those paddles?

Okay, get your act together, Mia. You are losing your mind.

"Sorry, I knocked on your door but there was no answer."

"Knock harder next time," was all he said in reply.

She waited for him to say something else, but he didn't even look up. Jesus, was he the rudest man on the planet? Well, she'd met a few in her time. She'd worked for plenty of them. She could put up with his attitude for a few months until the trial.

And then she had a whole new set of things to worry about.

Finally, he looked up at her. Studied her.

"Let's get a few things straight, shall we? Rule number one, I am in charge. My word is law."

She nodded shakily, though he didn't seem to require an answer from her.

"Two, you don't go anywhere without my permission. You don't call anyone without my permission. Do you have a phone?"

"Mike got me a burner phone."

"I'll take it. Credit cards?"

"No, I got rid of those when-when it first happened. Mike said it was a good idea not to have anything that could be traced back to me."

"So he does have a brain," he said dryly.

"Mike is a good guy. He takes care of me. He's the only family I have. He loves me."

"You cannot contact him without my permission," was all he said.

She longed to ask him if he was this cold with everyone or if it was just her. But she wasn't ready to die today.

"All right," she agreed. She dug the phone out of her bag and handed it over. He didn't reach for it, so she just put it on the desk.

"Hand over the handbag too," he told her.

All right, the phone she kind of understood even though it was a burner phone so she didn't see how it could be traced. But why would he need her handbag?

"Why do you need my handbag?"

"Because I said so."

"Look, I really appreciate you letting me stay here and everything—"

"I'm not letting you *stay here*," he interrupted her. "You are here because you need protection from some mob boss who's trying to kill you. I'm offering that protection in return for a favor owed. You are my responsibility. We're not friends. This isn't some polite arrangement. You are under my protection. You are under my rule. Now, give me your bag."

Fingers trembling with a mixture of fear and anger, she passed over the bag putting it on his desk again as he didn't reach for it.

"Fine. You want my tampons and twenty bucks in change, it's all yours. Gonna need the lip-gloss back though. Chapped lips, you know."

Holy sugar balls. She needed to get away from him. Before she completely lost her mind. She wasn't going to have to worry about an assassin taking her out, because she wasn't leaving this room alive.

Malone just stared at her for a long moment. Then he went through her purse. He pulled out her wallet, opened it and rifled through everything. Then he pulled out her lip gloss, inspected it. Next came the tampons. Jesus he even opened up the box and looked inside. Then he went through every inch of her bag, searching.

"What are you looking for?"

"Any bugs or trackers."

She swallowed heavily, feeling ill. "Your brother used that gadget thing to search the car earlier, he didn't find anything."

He didn't reply.

"Surely if there was a tracker or a bug, this guy who's after me would have taken me out already." That was a sentence she'd never thought she would say. "And when would anyone have put anything in there?"

"Will need to go through your luggage too, including what you're wearing."

What? Did he intend to strip her where she stood? She flushed at the thought.

"Everything I have is brand-new. Except for the clothes I was in when I . . . when I found Angel's body."

"Unlikely he was using those to track you, since he shot the wrong person." There was a note of derision in his voice.

He put her stuff back into her bag. "You're gonna need more stuff. Write a list and the boys will get it for you. Including lip gloss and tampons."

Do not blush. Do not blush. He's just trying to get a rise out of you.

"I can go and get it myself. I just need a vehicle to get there. And some directions."

He pierced her with his cold gaze. "Don't you remember the rules I just gave you five minutes ago?"

Of course she did. She wasn't stupid. "You said I couldn't go anywhere without your permission."

"And I'm not giving it to you."

She breathed in . . . then slowly out. Trying to calm the fear coursing through her. Another panic attack loomed on the horizon; she could feel it low in her gut. But it couldn't happen. She couldn't show weakness around this man.

"I'm a prisoner here?"

"Of course you're not. You can leave anytime you want. But the minute you leave without my permission, my protection ends."

She had to remind herself that he was putting his life on the line for her. She needed him. And when it as all over she didn't have to see him again.

"Understand?"

She nodded "Understood."

"Good. I'll get West to show you where you're staying. Get me that list and I will get the stuff to you in a few days."

And, with that, she knew she was dismissed. But she wasn't quite ready to go.

After a few moments, he let out a deep breath. "You can go."

"I can cook," she blurted out. "And clean."

He stared up at her impassively. "Not why you're here."

"Yes, but I thought I could make myself useful while I'm here." It would make her feel better, that was for sure. She hated the imbalance of knowing he was taking all the risk and she was giving nothing in return. Even if he was a jerk.

"Just do what I tell you and stay out of the way, that's the most useful thing you can do. You can go now."

Great. She was starting to think that New York might not be such a bad option. Maybe facing a mobster would be preferable to living here with Alec Malone.

3

She lasted two days.

Two days of sitting in her room, being bored out of her mind. She'd managed to find a few books to read in the smaller, second living room downstairs. In fact, she'd started to treat that like her own space once she'd figured out nobody else used it. When Alec wasn't working out on the ranch, he holed up in his office. Often with West, his not-very-talkative brother. In fact, West took taciturn to a whole new level.

After showing her to her room when she'd first arrived, West had gone over her luggage with that little device again, then left. All without a word. At least he hadn't pawed through her underwear. Mind you, he would have been pretty disappointed if he had. It was all plain cotton and there wasn't much of it.

Jardin had left for New Orleans the day after she'd arrived. She'd figured if she just stayed out of everyone's way, she'd been fine. But when she'd woken up this morning, she'd decided she couldn't stand to live there for two more months like this. Sitting around, doing nothing just wasn't who she was. So she'd headed into the kitchen and gotten to work. The Malone brothers all ate in the main house, even though they slept in a large bunkhouse.

They all ate in the larger living room at the front of the house. And left it in a pigsty each time. She'd spent most of this afternoon cleaning the kitchen. Those boys seemed to live on steak, sausages, and bacon. And nothing else.

She braced herself as she heard a door open. Right on time. It sounded like a runaway herd of cattle was headed towards her. If cattle could talk. And the majority of what came out of their mouths was profanity. She was blushing even before they hit the kitchen. The first brother came to a fast stop, the rest of them pushing against him as they tried to get through the door at the same time.

She resisted the urge to check that her hair was tidy or to wish she had something nicer to wear. The plain, white T-shirt she wore was a bit baggy and wouldn't have been her first choice. White didn't really look good against her pale skin. And if she didn't start eating better, the dark jeans she was wearing were going to slip right off. Malone had told her to make a list of what she needed, but it didn't feel right to ask for anything.

Only she really needed to get her prescription for her anti-anxiety meds refilled. But she didn't want Alec Malone to know how weak she was that she couldn't cope without being medicated. Nope, not happening. She'd just figure that shit out later. Somehow.

"Well, hello there, darlin'," the first rogue drawled at her. He looked her up then down and by the time he was finished a blush had engulfed her entire body. "I thought my brother had you locked up in your room. Now I can see why."

"Beau, get out of the damn way," one of the others growled. "I'm fucking hungry."

The one at the front, Beau, didn't answer but he did take a couple of steps forward and headed straight towards her. She backed up a step, she knew it was cowardly, but she couldn't fight instinct.

His grin just widened. She looked behind him, to find the other brothers had entered the kitchen, all but two staring at her like she was a piece of prime beef steak.

Beau, who still had his hat on and wore dusty, ripped jeans and a faded checked shirt, leaned in close. He hadn't shaved in a few days, and his bright, blue eyes stood out against his deeply tanned skin.

He was gorgeous. And dangerous. Her heart raced.

She was trapped. Trapped. Trapped.

She could feel the scream inside her rising. Then he reached down and grabbed her hand, raising it to kiss the back. Her breath came in sharp pants even though he did nothing more than hold her hand and smile down at her.

"Beau!" A sharp voice barked from the doorway, and she jumped.

Beau didn't look worried. He just turned slowly, letting her see past his wide chest to where Alec stood in the doorway. He stared at his brother then his gaze moved around to the rest of them.

"Having dinner with us tonight, brother?" one of the others asked. There was a note of something in his voice she couldn't quite decipher.

Alec's gaze settled on her. Shit. She had nowhere left to retreat to.

"What are you doing in here?" he barked.

"Jesus, Alec, she's allowed to eat." One of them glared at his brother. She wished she knew all their names, but she'd only met Tanner and West. Well, and now Beau.

"I just thought . . . I was bored . . . I cooked dinner," she said lamely.

"You cooked dinner? Hot damn." Another one rubbed his hands together.

"I know what I'd like for dinner," Beau said slyly, giving her a long, hungry look.

Oh, shit. She was in such trouble.

"Beau!" Alec snapped again. "Give us a minute."

It took her a few beats to realize he was speaking to her. She nodded quickly, feeling like a complete idiot.

"I'll just go finish setting the dining table."

"The dining table?" Another of the brothers asked her. He scowled. "We don't eat at the dining room table. Don't even know why we bought that damn thing."

"Because it came with the house, dickhead," another brother said.

Her eyes widened. But the one who'd first spoken didn't seem offended. He just shrugged. "Should have used it on a bonfire a long time ago."

She had seen the dining room table earlier. It was beautiful and made out of walnut. It obviously cost a lot of money. And they wanted to use it as firewood?

Not my place. Not my home.

She looked up at Alec, wondering if he'd say anything. But he just stared at his brothers. As she slipped by him, he grabbed her arm. "I thought I told you that you weren't to cook."

"I can't sit in my room for two months; I'm going to go insane. I'm sorry if my presence offends you. I'll try to keep out of your way."

He let her go as she tugged at her arm.

Asshole.

DAMN IT. He hadn't meant it like that. He just wanted to keep her out of the way of his brothers. Plus, she wasn't here to work as their unpaid cook. Maybe they could come to some arrangement though, if her food tasted as good as it smelled.

He ignored his rumbling gut and stepped into the kitchen, closing the door behind him. As soon as she left the room, his brothers started grabbing plates and lifting the lid on the dishes sitting on the counter.

"Want some of this?" Raid asked him around a mouthful of food. "Damn this shit is good."

"Good?" Maddox said. "Its best fucking whatever it is I've ever tasted."

"Stop," Alec commanded in a low voice. They all stilled and looked at him. "Do you not remember me telling you all that you need to keep your hands off her?"

They all looked at each other, except for West and Jaret. Jaret had a girl in town. The only one of them that had had a steady girlfriend for longer than a few weeks. And West, well, he'd never shown an interest in any girl except Lana.

"We just figured you were saying that in front of Jardin," Tanner said.

"If Jardin doesn't want us touching her, he should have taken her to his brothers," Raid said. "Don't even think they have a dick among them that works."

They all laughed except West and Alec. "This has nothing to do with Jardin. She's here for our protection, not to cook and clean, and definitely not to be your fuck toy."

Now everyone stared at him.

"You want her?" Maddox asked.

"Hey, man, if I knew she was yours, I never would have—" Beau started to say.

Alex scowled at him. "She is not mine. I'm not interested in her. She's my responsibility while she's here. We've got to keep her alive until she can testify. Keeping her alive, doesn't mean having her in your beds. Just keep your hands off her. Got it?"

He turned and walked away before any of them could say anything. Mia was waiting anxiously outside the dining room.

"You can cook for them if you want. I'll work out a wage for you. It will have to be cash. No paper trail."

"No need to pay me," she replied quietly. "You're already doing so much. I want to do something in return."

"You'll get paid." He stomped away, down towards his office, ignoring the urge to turn back—to take her in his arms and demand that she not even think about going near one of his brothers. But he forced himself to keep walking. He didn't want to think too closely about why he cared whether Mia ended up in one of their beds. Probably because he didn't want any more problems. He intended to carry on with his life and ignore their house guest as much as possible.

THE MALONE BROTHERS WERE MAD. Crazy. Reckless. And she was fast falling in love with them.

But they also had absolutely no manners. She still couldn't believe they never used that dining room. They'd all rather fight over the furniture in the huge living room, so they could sit in front of the TV and shovel her food into their mouths. All the time grunting, talking over each other, and trying to snatch food from each other's plates. By the time they were finished eating, the place was a pigsty. After a few nights of sitting through that, she'd had enough.

She been there for a week. At first, she'd jumped at just about every loud noise or blushed with each rude innuendo, but she was coming to know them better now and most of what they said and did was in good fun. They were charismatic and full of energy and life, so much so, they made her feel exhausted just being around them.

She'd managed to work out who was who. Alec, of course, was the oldest. And he never joined them to eat. Neither did

West, who was the second oldest brother. Next came Jaret. He was her favorite. He wasn't around as much because he had a girlfriend in the next town over. He was the one who always took a minute to ask her how she was doing and he often helped clean up.

Then came the twins, Maddox and Beau. They were a handful. They were identical, and at the beginning the only way she'd had of telling them apart was that Beau was missing part of a finger, but it was becoming easier as she got to know them. Maddox tended to be less of a flirt, just a tad more reserved than his twin brother. Then came Butch. She'd figured that was a nickname—it wasn't. And he suited his name. He was the biggest of all the brothers, with wide shoulders and a booming laugh that she was certain could be heard in the next state over.

Then there was Raid. Boy, could Raid eat. She'd never met someone who loved food as much as he did. Almost as much as he enjoyed creating chaos wherever he went. The youngest was Tanner. He was just a couple of years older than she was, and quite possibly the wildest of the lot, which was saying something.

But eating with them was an exercise in self-control. She didn't have any right to tell them that they had horrible manners and they needed to clean their shit up. That was kind of her job now. Even if she didn't intend to take any money from Alec.

Living there was payment enough. Sure, she hadn't been at all certain in the beginning, but the longer she stayed, the safer she felt. There was no reason for the mob hit man on her tail to look for her here. She hadn't felt a panic attack looming since day three. She was still having nightmares, but thankfully, all of the brothers except Alec slept out in the bunkhouse. And Alec's bedroom was down the other end of the house.

Keeping busy helped. And cooking and cleaning for these guys certainly kept her occupied. This was a huge house. She wasn't sure why the brothers all slept out in the bunkhouse, although that was probably a good thing, since spending time with them was an exercise in self-control.

She knew they were just teasing her, of course. They didn't really want to sleep with her. But sometimes it was hard to remember that. They were all freaking gorgeous. With varying shades of dark hair, muscular bodies, tanned skin, and that glint they got in their eyes when they were about to say something cocky was just about more than she could take.

All of them except West, Jaret, and Alec that was. Jaret was the only one with a girlfriend. West never even spoke to her. And Alec, well, he was never around. He never ate meals with them. West usually took a plate to him in his office. He was often gone before she even got up. In the beginning, she'd worried it was because of her. That he just didn't want to be around her. But Jaret had reassured her that he never ate with them.

She didn't even know if he liked her cooking. But at least the other boys seemed to. They'd certainly given her enough praise and they ate every meal like it was their last. Unfortunately, they all insisted that she eat with them.

That first night she'd cooked for them, she'd decided to eat at the kitchen table. Not that she had much appetite. She'd just settled down with a plate of food in front of her when Tanner and Butch had stormed into the kitchen.

Fear had held her paralyzed. Even as she'd tried to tell herself they wouldn't hurt her she still couldn't help her reaction. But they didn't seem to notice or, if they did, they ignored it. Tanner came straight to her and pulled her up into his arms.

Tanner had carried her into the living room, set her on the couch, and Butch had put her plate of food on her lap. Apparently, they'd just expected her to sit there with them, eating in front of the television, which had been blasting with re-runs of the *Dukes of Hazard*.

But no more. She might not have the right to tell them to take their messy boots off at the door or to stop yelling at each other every time they spoke. But she wasn't sitting through it anymore. Tonight, she was sitting at the dining room table. And if one of them dared try to pick her up and carry her to where they thought she should be then she was fully prepared to stab him with her knife.

Okay, she wouldn't do that. But she was going to make a fuss. And the offender wouldn't be getting any more of her desserts, that was for sure. Tonight, she'd carried all the food out to the dining room table. She'd put out all the cutlery, plates, and napkins. She'd wished there were some flowers she could pick, But, then, she figured they wouldn't really appreciate flowers anyway.

She could hear them coming. Tramping their way through the house.

She heard them yelling something when they got to the kitchen.

"Mia? Mia! Where are you?"

She popped her head out of the dining room. "Here!"

Raid moved towards her, as usual, leading the pack when it came to food. "Where's dinner? I'm starved."

"You're always starving," Maddox said. "Better watch out you're going to end up with flabby gut and a double chin. "

"Not with the way I work out." Raid winked at her as he strode past her. She figured she didn't want to ask about what sort of workout he was talking about.

"Oh, yeah?" Tanner asked, coming in next. "When was the last time you got any sort of workout?"

"Last weekend, moron," Raid replied as he started to fill his plate. When he had a mound of food piled high, he walked towards the door. As the passed her, he looked down and smiled. "Good you found a use for the dining table, sweetheart. But we're happy to come to the kitchen to get our food. No need to go to any extra effort."

And then he disappeared into the television room. Along with the rest of them.

Okay, so Rome wasn't built in a day, right?

"I'M BUSY, what do you want?" Alec demanded as he picked up the phone in his office.

"Hello, nice to talk to you too, cousin," Jardin replied. "I'm doing well, thanks for asking."

"What part of 'I'm busy' didn't you understand?" Alex growled. He knew he shouldn't have picked up the damn phone.

"We're all busy," Jardin said patiently. "I'm calling to check up on our house guest."

His gut tightened. "What about her?"

"Is she doing okay? How's it going with your wild pack of brothers?"

"Why are you asking me?"

There was a moment of silence. "Because I left her with you. You're supposed to be taking care of her."

"No. The deal was I would keep her alive. She's alive."

Truth was, Alec was avoiding having anything to do with Mia directly. He kept tabs on her, of course. He couldn't have her wandering off the ranch and getting herself killed. It would make his life easier, sure, but they owed her cousin a favor. And that was the only reason he cared about her. How the fuck was he supposed to know how she was doing?

"That's it? That's all you have to say about her?"

"You want to know more, then why don't you come here and see for yourself?"

Jardin sighed. "I can't. Stuck in the middle of something.

Mike's been calling me for updates about her. He wants to make sure she's doing okay."

"Well, why don't you talk to her yourself?"

"Because I thought I'd call you and ask. I thought you were keeping an eye on her."

"Not her babysitter. Talk to her yourself or come here." Alec hung up. But there was a little kernel of guilt that had started to grow.

Fuck.

～

Mɪᴀ sᴀᴛ down at the dining table again to eat. Alone.

Three nights of this and no change. She sighed. But after a moment of staring at a plate of pot roast she had no interest in eating, she suddenly became aware of the silence. She glanced up to find them all standing there staring at her.

She glanced up. "Yes?"

"You planning on eating in here alone again, darlin'?" Tanner asked.

"Yes. And don't even think about trying to move me anywhere, Tanner Malone, I am not in the mood."

"Learned that after the other night when you smacked me around with your fork."

"I did not smack you around." She blushed; a bit ashamed of her behavior. They were turning her into a crazy person.

"Wasn't anything you didn't deserve," Raid muttered around a mouthful of food.

"Why you want to eat in here so much?" Maddox asked.

"Because it's civilized and normal. It's what a family should do. And I'm tired of watching you make a mess in the living room while you fight over food and insult each other at the top of your lungs."

"Well, sorry we offend you," West said, surprising her. What was he even doing here? Mostly, he ate with Alec in his office. "Didn't realize you were the manners police."

"I'm not. It's just . . . " Okay, she'd started this, time to finish it.

"Manners?" Tanner looked around at all his brothers "We have manners. Don't we always say thank you for cooking?"

"Never. You've never once said thank you. You traipse through the house with your dirty boots on, you don't take your hats off, and you make a pigsty of the living room every night when you eat."

All right. She hadn't meant to say that.

"You're exaggerating," Maddox told her. "We're not that bad."

She pointed a finger at him. "You bit Beau's hand this morning when he tried to reach for the last biscuit."

"Yeah, and I think it's infected. Where the hell has your mouth been?" Beau turned to him.

She knew she needed to take back control or they'd start to argue and not listen to a word she said. "I just think we need a few house rules is all."

"This ain't your house," West pointed out. "You don't get to make any rules. You're just the cook."

She sucked in a breath. Pain stabbed at her. He wasn't saying anything she didn't know. She'd forgotten her place. They'd lulled her into thinking she was a part of them. But she wasn't. She didn't belong here. Or anywhere.

She pulled away from the table. "You're right. Excuse me." She knew it was cowardly to flee but she also didn't want to burst into tears in front of them all. To her surprise, Jaret grabbed her arm, pulling her close to him.

"Apologize," he insisted, glaring at West.

Oh, shit. She hadn't meant to start an argument. Why hadn't she just left things alone? Was it so bad that they got their muddy footprints everywhere and liked to yell at each other constantly?

"What?" West snapped.

"Apologize. She's not just the fucking cook. She's a friend. Apologize now."

The rest of them had all stilled, looking back and forth between West and Jaret.

She pressed a hand against Jaret's chest. "It's okay. I'm going to go lie down now. I have a headache."

She moved out of the dining room without looking at anyone. She was such a fool. She'd overstepped her bounds. She was there to hide and cook and clean. Nothing more. This wasn't her family.

She walked up the stairs, feeling a little numb as she got ready for bed. She left the bathroom light on before climbing into bed. She took a deep breath and let it out slowly. No way would she be able to get to sleep as tense as she was. Not that she slept much anyway. And when she did manage to get off, she was usually woken by nightmares.

She closed her eyes. She had sedatives, but she was too scared to take them. Even here, where she felt safer than she had in a long time. She couldn't be completely out of it if something happened.

Then again, that could be a mercy if the thing that was about to happen was her getting a bullet in her brain. An image of Angel flashed through her mind.

Okay, thinking about that wasn't going to help her get to sleep.

Her aunt's face flashed in front of her then. Angry and twisted. Fuck. Fuck. She rolled over. Tried to reach for some calm deep inside her as she took in another deep breath. She felt kind of stupid, but she whispered good night to different parts of her body, imagining them growing heavier.

Nighty-night foot.

Yep, total idiot.

But gradually, her body grew heavy and she slipped off to sleep.

~

THE NIGHTMARE GRIPPED her by the throat, stealing her breath. She sat up, her heart racing. Fighting for each breath. Her pulse raced. Her whole body shook.

She glanced around frantically, staring into the shadows of the room. Searching for something. Anything.

No one was there.

No one had come to kill her. She was on her own. She curled her legs up to her chest, rested her forehead on her knees and concentrated on calming her breathing.

I'm safe. No one is here. I'm safe.

As her heart rate dropped and her breathing came easier, she uncurled herself, and climbed slowly out of bed. She whipped off her T-shirt, which was damp with sweat. She threw it into the bathroom to wash tomorrow. Then she pulled on another one. She grabbed the lamp, turning it on. Soon after she'd arrived, she'd found an extension cord in the storage room and claimed it so she could have the lamp in the wardrobe with her.

She walked to the wardrobe, opening the door and setting the lamp down at one end. She'd also found some spare blankets and a pillow, which she'd used to set up a second bed. She climbed in and closed the doors of the wardrobe behind her, wrapping herself up in the blankets.

She knew it was weird. She didn't get why this made her feel safer. It certainly wasn't that comfortable. The floor was hard. The wardrobe wasn't going to give her any protection against a bullet. But when she slept in here, the nightmares stayed away.

So she snuggled down, trying to tell herself that one day this would all be over. She'd be better.

One day.

~

THE NEXT NIGHT, she left all the food in the kitchen. No one said anything to her as they grabbed some food. She wasn't in the mood to eat. But as she headed towards the smaller living room, she came to a sudden stop as she heard noise coming from the dining room.

With no small sense of amazement, she stepped inside. They were all in there except for Alec and West. And they were loud. They were talking over one another. And they were snatching from each other's plates. But not one of them wore a pair of boots. Or a hat. And they were eating in the dining room.

Jaret turned to her. "About time you got here." He pointed at the head of the table where there was an empty plate and cutlery. "Sit. Eat."

She sat. "So," she asked when there was a lull in the yelling. She had to admit she was getting used to the way they roared every word. At least it was lively, unlike dinner at her aunt and uncle's place which had been somber enough that someone could be forgiven for thinking they lived in a funeral parlor. "What's your favorite dessert?"

They all looked at each other. "You bake?" Maddox whispered.

She blinked, surprised by the reaction. "Well, yes. I figured tomorrow night I'd make dessert. What would you like?"

They all yelled out their favorite treats, none of which were the same, of course. She held up her hand with a laugh. "All right, one a night. Tomorrow night we'll start with lemon meringue pie." Which had been the one Jaret had called out.

He winked at her. "You've done it now, babe. They'll never want to let you go."

She found herself wishing that were true. Even if the two oldest Malones didn't like her, this was the closest she'd had to a home in years.

And wasn't that just sad.

4

"What are you doing?"

Mia let out a screech and dropped the tray of brownies she'd been transferring from the oven to the counter. The tray landed on the floor, thankfully, missing her toes and the brownies flew everywhere.

Shit. Shit.

She turned to stare at Alec, her heart racing, her breath coming in pants. She tried to calm herself, but she could feel herself trembling. Nausea bubbled.

Calm.

"Fuck. Mia, you okay?"

Suddenly, he was looming over her and it did nothing for the panic swirling through her stomach. She took a step back, flinching.

Immediately, he froze, and a look of awareness crossed his face.

"Baby, easy. I'm not going to hurt you."

It was the gentlest he'd ever been with her. And she could feel herself starting to calm as he simply stood there.

Not moving, not threatening, no hint of cold disdain on his face.

"Easy, now. Just breathe with me. In, then hold for two then out for two. That's it. Good girl. That's a good girl, Mia."

Oh, God, those words. They sent a wave of warmth through her blood.

"S-sorry," she said. "You just g-gave me a fright."

His gaze narrowed and he opened his mouth to say something, so she slipped to her knees to avoid the questions looming. She didn't want to talk about the panic attacks that had plagued her since she'd come across the dead bodies of her coworkers. The fact that not a night went by where she didn't wake up shaking and sweating from a nightmare.

She hadn't had a good night's sleep in months. And couldn't see that changing anytime soon.

But even worse than all that would be talking to Alec Malone about it. What was he even doing up? He'd managed to avoid her for nearly two weeks now, why couldn't he have kept doing that?

She started gathering up pieces of brownie and placing them on the tray. Well, that batch was ruined.

She felt him kneel across from her but ignored him.

"Mia."

She hoped he didn't see the way her hands were trembling.

"Mia, look at me."

His voice was still gentle. How long was he going to kneel there staring at her? Couldn't he see she was busy?

"Mia. Eyes on me. Now."

The command in his voice was impossible for her to ignore. She raised her eyes to his.

"Should have known that would work," he muttered.

"What?"

"Nothing." He stared into her eyes. "Mia, what are you doing?"

"Cleaning up the brownie," she replied. She dropped her gaze back to the mess.

"Mia. Eyes."

Damn it. Why couldn't he let her hide? She opened her eyes, stared into his brown orbs, and wished she'd just hidden in her closet tonight instead of coming down here to bake.

"Why are you making brownies at two in the morning?"

Fuck. Shit.

"Because they're West's favorite."

He blinked at her answer, looking more than a little surprised. "And why are you making West's favorite?"

The rough note to his voice made her flinch.

He sighed. "Damn it, will you stop looking at me like I'm going to hurt you?"

"I didn't . . . that wasn't . . . " she took a deep breath, "I'm not scared of you."

"Then why did you flinch away from me?"

"I'm not sure." And she couldn't believe she was having this conversation. "I just . . . I guess you intimidate me a little. I'm making it because it's his turn. I've made all of your other brothers their favorite desserts and it's West's turn. Even though he can be a jerk."

He didn't say anything to that. Just stood and held out his hand.

"I have to clean this up."

"No, you need to get to bed. It's two a.m. You're pale and tired."

"I can't just leave this mess here." She gave him an appalled look.

"You can't?" Did his lips just twitch? Was he laughing at her? "I'll clean it up, little worrier. Come on. Up you get."

"I'll help you," she said, surprising herself. She should be taking the out and getting the hell away from him. He was far too much for her. Too scary, too handsome, too dominant. And yet she couldn't help but stare at his hand and wonder what it would feel like to have him touch her. To have him run that hand down her body, over her stomach to squeeze her breast.

"No."

"No?" What was he saying no to? Oh, shit, she really should be paying more attention.

"No, you're not helping me. You're going to bed as I just said. Now get. Before I decide to tuck you in myself." There was a dark note of promise in his voice.

Oh, yeah, that really wouldn't be a good idea. She grabbed hold of his hand without thinking and a shot of electricity ran through her, making her gasp.

As he pulled her up, she stumbled and fell into him. She rested against his chest, staring up at him, her heart pounding and for a crazy moment she thought he was going to kiss her. Then he quickly stepped back, letting go of her.

And that was as good as being thrown in a cold mountain lake. He wasn't interested in her. And she needed to find a way to get past this weird attraction she felt towards him.

She made her way towards the door.

"Oh, and, Mia?"

She paused and looked back. "Yes?"

"My favorite is apple pie."

"What?"

"My favorite dessert. It's apple pie. You're making everyone else's, so I get a turn, right?"

"Um, right. Sure, apple pie. I can do that." She forced herself out of the room before she made more of an idiot of herself. When she got to her room, she hastily shut the door then leaned back against it and slid down so her butt rested on the floor, her legs up against her chest.

His favorite was apple pie. Holy hell. Here she was, wondering if it was possible to self-combust because she was so turned on and he wanted to talk about apple pie.

She was so out of her depth.

"Something smells good, darlin'."

She turned to see Tanner and Butch walking through the kitchen door. She pointed a finger at them. "Boots off."

Alec might still intimidate the hell out of her. And West seemed to dislike her as much as ever, even after she'd made him a new batch of brownies after that first lot had ended up in the garbage, but she'd stopped being daunted by the other brothers.

Butch gave her his best puppy dog look. "But we're just coming in for a minute," he implored her.

"Take those boots off now or you don't get in my house." As soon as she said the words, she wished them back. She blushed bright red. It wasn't her house. She might clean it, take care of it, feed the people who lived in it. But it wasn't hers.

But neither man said anything to contradict her. And she knew she had to stand her ground with these guys, or they'd walk all over her. Not meanly, but they were definitely used to getting their own way.

Tanner and Butch walked back in, this time in just their socks with their jeans rolled up. She gave them an approving look. Tanner leaned over her shoulder, sniffing. "What you got cooking there, darlin'?"

She moved to try and put some space between them, but he pressed closer. "Of course, nothing smells as good as you do. What do you call that scent you're wearing?"

"Soap," she said dryly. "Will you give me some space? I've got to get the cookies out of the oven."

He backed off immediately, practically jumping for joy. "Butch! She's got cookies."

"Yes." Butch raced over. "Please tell me you made chocolate

chunk ones like last week."

"The two of you are overgrown children, you know that, right?" She pulled out the tray and Tanner immediately reached for one and she slapped his hand away. "Get off, they have to cool and they're for everyone. Now if you don't have anything better to do, get!"

"Jeez, so grumpy. No one has to know if you give us one now. Go on," Butch wheedled her.

"No. Go away."

"Please." Tanner gave her another puppy dog look. "We're growing boys."

"You're that, all right. You keep eating like this and you'll definitely be growing boys." She patted his slim stomach.

"What are you trying to say? That I'm getting fat? Butch, she called me fat," Tanner complained.

She rolled her eyes. "You know very well you're not fat."

"Here, look, I'll show you just how much I'm wasting away." He reached for the bottom of his T-shirt, pulling it off before she could stop him. And the body he revealed was definitely not going to fat. He was chiseled. Muscular. Tanned.

"See?" He ran his hand over his stomach, pinching at the skin. "Not an inch of fat on me."

"I don't know. You kind of look like you're getting a little soft here." Butch poked at his gut and she rolled her eyes.

"Yeah? Don't notice you taking your shirt off, ashamed to show Mia your gut?" Tanner dared.

Oh, hell. Why hadn't she just given them a cookie and sent them on their way? Now they'd be here all day, competing with each other.

Butch whipped off his shirt. She now had two shirtless men in her kitchen. And it wasn't the warmth from the oven making her cheeks flush.

"Will the two of your put your shirts back on?" she demanded with exasperation. She needed both of them out of her kitchen. Then, maybe, she'd go take a cool shower or something. It would take a stronger woman than her not to be affected by the two half-naked men standing so close she could feel the heat coming off their bodies.

"Who has the better body, Mia?" Tanner demanded.

Oh, no. No way was she getting into that.

"Yeah, Mia, tell this dipwad that my body is way better looking than his scrawny ass." Butch held up an arm, flexing the muscle. "Look at these biceps. Feel them, Mia. Touch them." This little display of testosterone had gone on long enough.

"Both of you get your shirts back on now." The snap of an icy voice coming from the doorway made her gasp and jump. Her heart raced and she automatically cringed back, looking for a way to flee.

Fuck, she hated feeling this way.

"Just having a bit of fun, Alec," Butch told him with an unrepentant grin.

"Fun?" He said the word like he didn't understand the meaning of it. Maybe he didn't. He seemed to work all the time. "You two get back to work. Mia, you stay where you are," he demanded as she tried to make her way towards the door.

Drat.

"We're going," Tanner told him, putting his shirt back on. "We just came in for a snack."

"Get a snack and go."

"All right, no need to get all heated up," Tanner grumbled. But he reached out to grab a couple of cookies. Butch did the same as he slipped by, giving her a sassy wink.

"We'll take up where we left off later, sweet Mia," Butch called back at her.

She gulped and looked at Alec's hard face. Jesus, was Butch trying to poke the beast? Tanner obviously had more sense than his brother because he reached back and grabbed his brother's shirt, dragging him out through the mudroom.

Alec turned that icy gaze on her. Shit. She licked her lips. "Look, I—"

"Seems I missed a rule," Alec said in a low voice. Shit. Shit. Her heart raced. She had to remind herself he wasn't the enemy. Since the brownie incident, he'd gone back to ignoring her. Meanwhile, she spent most nights recalling the feel of his hard body against hers, imagining what it would have been like if he'd kissed her.

"What do you mean? I haven't left the ranch or contacted anyone." Hell, she hadn't even left the house, other than to hang the washing out on the line. This place felt safe. Out there did not. And she was so tired of being scared.

As she stared into his hard face, she felt her insecurities rush to the foreground. She hadn't broken any rules. He had no reason to look at her like that. He wasn't going to kick her out, was he?

"You haven't broken any rules. I didn't think you would, knowing the consequences."

Yes, that she'd lose his protection.

She still worried that being here was a mistake. What if the hit man found a way to get to her? What if he hurt these guys? She couldn't stand it if any harm came to them because of her.

"I'm talking about a completely new rule. I told them but didn't think I'd have to warn you. My brothers are off-limits."

Off-limits? What did that mean? Suddenly it hit her, and she sucked in a deep breath. "You think that I . . . that I want . . . that I could ever . . . " She couldn't get out the words, she was so flabbergasted at his insinuation.

"I came in here, you standing between them with their shirts off, face flushed, arousal in your eyes, those stupid grins on their faces meaning they were teasing you about something, and you think I don't have to warn you that they're off-limits?"

She straightened her shoulders. She hadn't done anything

wrong. She wouldn't be ashamed.

"I am not interested in your brothers."

He didn't look like he believed her. Her short burst of confidence started to dissipate.

"And even if I was, would that be so bad?" Why didn't he want her to get involved with one of his brothers? She wasn't a terrible person. She was kind, polite, hard-working. Boring.

Yeah, she was definitely that.

"Yeah, it would." He pointed at her. "Do not encourage that shit I just saw again."

She took a step back, unable to help herself. She hadn't encouraged them, had she? What if it happened again? Would he send her away? Of course, he would. He wasn't the type to not follow through on his threats.

Where would she go? She liked it here. She felt safe here. Could breathe here.

She felt a wave of dizziness wash over her and reached back, accidentally placing her hand on the still-hot oven tray. She pulled it back immediately, hissing. Thankfully, it wasn't as hot as when it had first been taken from the oven, but it still stung.

"What did you do?"

She gasped as she realized he'd moved without her noticing. He now loomed over her, glaring down at her. She tucked her throbbing hand behind her. It was probably a childish reaction, but she didn't need him berating her for messing up yet again.

"Nothing. I have to start getting dinner ready."

"Give me your hand."

He held his out imperiously. He didn't move any closer. Didn't try to reach for her. Just held his hand there like he expected her immediate obedience. And weak fool that she was, she gave it to him.

His hand engulfed hers. For a moment she couldn't help but wonder what that hand would feel like against her naked ass.

What need did he have for paddles when he had one at the end of his arm?

Mia. Stop being an idiot.

"Little fool, you burned yourself."

The insult rushed through her. And she rocked back. All right, so he got to boss her around. He got to make all the rules. He even got to be a cold asshole. But there was no need to call her names.

"It was an accident."

"Notice you've had a few of those."

She gaped at him as he led her over to the sink and turned the faucet on, sticking her hand underneath.

"What do you mean?" She turned to look at him as he moved away.

He turned back with a firm look. Two steps back and he was next to her once more, his front against her back as he leaned over her, grasped hold of her hand and firmly placed it under the water again. This time he held it there for a beat or two. And as her body reacted to having him so close, she berated herself for having drawn his attention back to her. She should have let him leave. Then they could have just gotten on with their days.

But, no, she had to prod the beast.

"It means I've noticed a lot of things seem to go wrong around you, Calamity Jane."

She gasped in an insulted breath. She thought she preferred being called a little fool.

"They do not!" she protested, trying to turn to look back at him. But he kept her firmly pressed against the counter. And she couldn't help but react to his closeness. Her whole body went into hyperdrive, she felt like her insides were melting, her knees growing weak.

She needed to get past this weird attraction she felt towards him.

"Yeah? Tell that to my grandmother's lamp."

Oh, God. He would have to bring that up.

"I was dusting it. It was an accident. I'll pay to replace it."

"Its value was in its sentiment," he replied, making her feel even worse. "Of course, it also had a monetary value of around two thousand dollars."

Two thousand dollars! No way could she find that kind of cash. "For that ugly old thing?"

Whoops. He stiffened behind her.

"Um, sorry. Really, I am. I know it was your grandmother's and I feel terrible about what happened. I didn't mean to knock it over."

"Just like you didn't mean to flood the laundry room?" he asked in a low voice.

"I didn't realize the plug was in the tub. I cleaned it all up."

"The floors need replacing."

"I'll pay for that too." Shit. Shit.

"Bill's mounting up."

Didn't she know it.

"Then there's West's bruised ass."

She tried to turn again. He held her still.

"I apologized to West. I didn't mean to flood the laundry and I thought I'd cleaned up the water well enough. I didn't think it would still be so slippery." The quietest Malone brother had slipped on a wet patch of tile in the mudroom, which doubled as the laundry room. He'd fumed all day yesterday. And the scowl he wore whenever he saw her . . . she shivered slightly.

"Do you think he's still mad at me?" she whispered.

He narrowed his gaze at her. "You have nothing to fear from West."

"I'm not scared of him." *Liar. Liar.*

"Lying isn't allowed."

"Just how many rules are you going to make?" she demanded, fed up with him and his high-handed ways.

"Many as you need."

"As I need? All right, I'll make it easy on you. I'm a grown woman. I'm reasonably intelligent. And I don't need any rules."

He just huffed out a laugh. "You forgot that you have a good sense of humor."

"I wasn't joking," she said through gritted teeth. Although it was nice that he thought she had a sense of humor.

"Whose house you living in?"

She figured that was a rhetorical question and didn't answer. Her hand was about to freeze off, and she reached for the tap to turn off the water.

"Don't even think about touching that," he told her in a low, commanding voice.

She froze. Fuck. She hated when she did that. Just obeyed him like some mindless fool.

"Whose house are you living in?" He repeated the question. Okay, maybe he wanted an answer.

"Yours," she spat out.

"And whose protection are you under?"

"Yours."

He leaned in until his lips were practically touching her ear. He wrapped an arm around her waist, pulling her back against him. "And so you are going to obey my rules, are you not?"

"Yes."

"Yes, Sir."

She froze. He couldn't mean that. He was just doing it to mess with her head. Finally, he backed away from her.

"Keep that hand under the water. I'm going to go get the first aid kit. You move, and you'll be in trouble."

There was some idiotic part of her that wanted to ask what sort of trouble he was talking about. But she hadn't lost all sense of self-preservation. He returned quickly and turned off the tap himself. Then he gently dried her hand.

She looked down at the palm of her hand. It was red, but the throbbing pain had pretty much disappeared.

"It feels much better now. I should be fine without anything else."

He didn't even acknowledge her. He just pulled some burn cream out of the first aid kit, along with a bandage.

"It's just a small burn," she insisted. "I've worked in kitchens for years. I've had plenty of burns. I don't need burn cream or a bandage."

"Don't recall asking you what you thought you needed." He proceeded to gently rub cream on her burn then he wrapped her hand up.

"Just how am I supposed to cook dinner with this on my hand?"

"You'll get by."

"I'll get by? I've got potatoes to peel. Veggies to chop. I can't do this with this great big monstrosity on my hand." She reached for the bandage and he grabbed hold of her good hand.

"Do not take that bandage off your hand, understand me?"

Damn it. She knew when she wasn't going to win an argument. And she didn't much like arguing anyway. Finally, she nodded. "Fine, but don't blame me if there are no veggies with your dinner tonight."

"Doesn't make any difference to me. I'm going out. Try to stay out of trouble."

He gathered up the first aid gear and walked out of the room without so much as a backward glance, leaving her standing there like a fool.

SHIT. Fuck.

He walked into his office and went immediately over to pour

himself a glass of whiskey. He took a deep sip, hoping it would erase the scent of her from his memory. The feel of her against his body. He reminded himself she wasn't in the lifestyle.

Getting involved with her would be a mistake. She wasn't a sub at the club he could just walk away from. She lived with him. There would no way of keeping her feelings out of it. That female was a ball of emotions. Mia wasn't someone you just played with and then walked away from. She deserved happy ever after. She was sweet and kind.

And he'd been an ass. He didn't much care what people thought of him. He lived life his own way. He felt bad for being so cold to her, but it was the best way he knew to keep a barrier between them. There was just something about her that called to him.

Underneath her fragile exterior, there was a tough core. He hadn't seen it in the beginning, not with the way she tended to bite her tongue and pull in on herself, but a few times now she'd shown him the real Mia. The one she kept hidden. Sure, she was someone who liked to keep the peace, but push her hard enough and she'd bite back.

He hadn't thought he would find that appealing. But he was glad to know she was tougher than she looked. She had to be to have lived through what she had.

He ran his hand over his face. The jealousy he'd felt when he'd walked into the kitchen and seen Butch and Tanner shirtless and standing so close to her, it didn't make him feel good. He didn't want to be jealous of them. He didn't want her to mean anything to him.

Which is why he'd snapped at her that his brothers were off limits. Damn it. Mia was everything he wanted in a woman. Soft, sweet, beautiful inside and out.

And totally off-limits. For him as well as his brothers.

5

She carried the dirty linen from her bed and Alec's down the stairs. She probably should have made two trips, but she couldn't be bothered walking up and down the stairs all the time. She was feeling tired as hell these days. She knew it was because she wasn't sleeping—or eating. The nightmares were still plaguing her. And, even worse, she was about to run out of her meds. Which meant having to go to Alec to talk about getting more. Shit. She really didn't want to do that.

Maybe it was time she went off the meds anyway. Surely, she could do without them. Perhaps. Oh, hell. She wished she could talk to her cousin. She'd spoken to Jardin a few times and he'd told her Mike was worried about her but otherwise fine.

She heaved up the pile of linen, determined to wash it all today. Most of it smelled a bit musty. She wondered how long it had been since it had all been washed.

Mia took a step and stood on the hem of her pants. She immediately dropped the linen, trying to grab for the railing to keep herself from falling, but her fingertips slid off the wooden banister as she flung forward. She tensed, letting out a cry of alarm as she waited for her body to hit the stairs. But instead of slamming against wood, she came up against a hard chest. The person who caught her, let out an oomph as they braced themselves against the banister to keep them both from flying.

She took in a shaky breath. Then another one. She didn't want to look up. She knew it wasn't West or Jaret or Tanner who'd caught her.

She knew it was *him* and she did not want to look up.

He just held her against his chest for a long moment. Her feet weren't even touching the ground, they just dangled in the air. She had the crazy thought that she could just snuggle in against him as though they were cuddling.

Then he set her down. Disappointment hit her hard.

Stupid.

She took a step back. "Sorry about that. Thanks for catching me." She tried to move around him, but he grabbed hold of her shoulders, holding her there. "Umm, Malone? You okay?"

Why wasn't he saying anything? She risked a look up into his face, saw how tense his jaw was. He was glaring down at her. Was he mad?

"Uh, is there something wrong?"

"Something wrong?" he repeated.

"Yes, is there something wrong?"

Silence.

"You're. . .um. . .acting odd. Did I hurt you?"

"Hurt me?"

Why was he repeating everything she said? "Did I hurt you? When I fell against you."

"Did you hurt me? Hurt *me*? Fuck." He stared down at her. Then he moved one hand to cup the side of her face, wrapped his arm around her back and pulled her in to kiss her.

And, oh, boy, what a kiss it was. Her body sizzled from the tip of her toes all the way up to her hair. He didn't just kiss her, he possessed her. He took complete control and all she could do was hang on for the ride.

When he drew back, she couldn't help but make a small sound of protest. She wanted more. Needed it. But instead of kissing her again, he swung her into his arms, one under her legs, the other around her back, and he turned, carrying her downstairs.

"What are you doing?" she asked. She wrapped her arms around his neck, terrified he was going to drop her. But he didn't even show a hint of strain as he carried her straight into his office and then set her down on the leather sofa that lay in front of the fireplace. He started to pace back and forth, and she just sat there for a moment, watching him, taking him in.

Her lips still tingled, and her clit throbbed. Damn, if that's what it felt like to kiss him, what would it be like to take things further? To have him touch her, taste her, take her?

She cleared her throat. She got that he was angry. She just wasn't sure why. She inched her way forward on the sofa, ready to stand. He must've seen her movements because he turned around and pointed a finger at her.

"Stay."

She ground her teeth together. She wasn't a damn dog. Her heart was still racing from her near miss. And that kiss. What the heck did that kiss mean? She had no idea. All she knew was that right now, the last thing she wanted or needed was an Alec Malone lecture.

"Thanks for catching me," she said. "But I need to go tidy up the mess I made. I've got to get the sheets in the wash. And I'm gonna be late getting dinner started if I don't get a move on."

He moved closer, his hands on his hips as he loomed over her. "You fell down the stairs."

"Yes, well, I just tripped. I'm sure I would have been all right. Sure, I might have had a couple of bruises—"

"You tripped halfway down the stairs," he interrupted her.

"You could have broken a leg or an arm or hit your head or anything. This has to end."

"What has to end?" she asked.

"This habit you have of getting yourself into trouble," he snapped back at her. "Why the hell were you trying to carry your weight in linen down the stairs? You couldn't see anything. You didn't even see me coming up the stairs."

"I thought I could get it all down in one go. And I tripped because my pants keep slipping down. And I don't make it a habit of getting into trouble, you know. Do you think I wanted to fall? Do you think I want all these things happen to me?"

How could he go from kissing her to scolding her like a naughty teenager caught out after curfew?

He blew out a deep breath. "You need to take more care. No more carrying heavy things down the stairs. Got it?"

"This a new rule, is it?"

His jaw was tense as he glared down at her. "Yes. Another rule. And why are you even doing the washing? Your job is to cook. It's not to clean my grandmother's lamp. It's not to hang out the washing. It's not to wash all the linen. It's to cook. And it's to do as I tell you. I am in charge of your safety and I will get you to that damn trial in one piece, even if no one told me the biggest risk to you would be you."

She looked up at him for a moment. All right, so obviously that kiss hadn't meant much to him. Certainly it didn't mean he cared about her.

She stood. Not her home. Not her family. She needed to remember that. "Fine. Sorry for overstepping my bounds. I'll get out of your way."

She got to the door when he called out to her.

"Yes?" She turned back to look at him. Maybe he was going to apologize for being a jerk. Miracles did happen, right?

"Your pants are slipping because you've lost weight. You need to eat more. You need clothes that fit better."

"Is that it? Nothing else you want to add that you find lacking about me? Maybe my hair? Or my makeup?"

"You don't wear any makeup."

Awesome. She guessed he liked curvy girls who dressed with style and were made-up from the minute they got up until they went to bed. Not walking disasters who tripped over their own pants.

He moved over and sat at his desk. "If that's all, I have work to do."

Damn, he was an ass.

ALEC WALKED over to his whiskey and poured a drink, taking a sip. At this rate, by the time the damn trial rolled around, he was going to be an alcoholic. His hand shook and he looked down at it in shock. After the things he'd seen and done, he thought it would take much more than this to make him tremble. To make his gut clench in fear. But seeing her stumble, watching her flying through the air, the worry that he wouldn't make it up there in time to catch her, yeah, he'd realized he did have something to fear.

He feared failing to keep her safe.

And it wasn't even the hit man who was the biggest threat to her health at this stage. It was her. He sat on the sofa and took a deep breath. She was going to be the death of him. He could still feel her lips against his, still had the taste of her in his mouth.

Fuck. What had he been thinking, kissing her? He knew as soon as he'd kissed her that it was the wrong move. But he'd been scared. Scared he wouldn't be quick enough and she'd fall and hurt herself. Fear wasn't something he was used to, and he didn't cope well with it.

He should probably apologize. He also needed her to stop staring at him like she wanted him to fuck her. His control had slipped, and he'd kissed her, if it happened again who knew how far things would go. So, instead of chasing after her and apologizing for being the world's biggest ass, he sat on his sofa and sipped his whiskey, wishing like hell he'd never agreed to this in the first place.

6

Mia sat in the small living room she'd commandeered as her own. This house was just begging for a family to live in it. To have kids running around, filling up the eight bedrooms. For some reason it felt like the house was as lonely as she was.

It was crazy to feel alone when she could walk over to the bunkhouse and have plenty of company. It was poker night. She could join in. She had an open invitation. But she just didn't think she could handle all of them right now and Jaret was with his girl-friend in town.

She wished she could call Mike. Her cousin was the only person she had left in her life. The only person who loved her. After her parents had died, she'd gone to live with her aunt and uncle. Her uncle had been away a lot and her aunt, well, calling her cold was an understatement. She'd always done her best to remind Mia that she was a burden. A responsibility. That she wasn't family.

The only person who'd ever treated her like family was Mike.

She'd often wondered how such a kind man had come from such a mean woman. Not that she'd ever said that to Mike.

She worried at her lower lip. Maybe she should ask Alec if she could call him. He never said she couldn't call, just that she couldn't do it without his permission.

Except she'd made a vow never to talk to him again. Okay, that wasn't going to be possible, but she was going to do her best to stay away from him. She tapped her pen against the pad of paper in her hand, looking down at her list with a frown. The only reason she was making one was because she didn't want him sending one of his brothers to pick up whatever they thought she might need. She'd probably end up with twenty pairs of G-strings.

"Warning: the next story contains some disturbing images of the victims of a mass bombing in the. . . " The rest of the announcement faded out as she reached frantically for the remote. But she was too late, the images flicked up on the screen.

She sucked a breath in, trying to stave off the black creeping into her vision. Spots danced in front of her eyes. Her hand fumbled the remote. Her fingers and toes grew numb, her lungs were starved for oxygen. She slid down, off the couch and curled in on herself, her head on her bent legs, her arms over the back of her head.

She couldn't breathe.

"Mia! Fuck, Mia." The words barely penetrated. She flushed hot then cold. "Mia, it's all right. You're okay. You're safe. Just breathe. In and out."

She tried. She really did. But her throat was so constricted, air didn't want to make its way in.

Then she felt herself being moved. And her stomach instantly protested.

"Breathe for me, baby. You're safe. You're safe."

But it wasn't lack of air that was the problem now, it was the nausea bubbling in her gut. Vomit. She was going to vomit. She opened her mouth to warn Alec, right as she threw up all over herself and him. Immediately, she started to sob. That breath she'd been fighting for entered her lungs then left on a huge wail.

"Oh, God. I'm so sorry. Oh, God."

"Sh, baby. Hush. Don't cry. Fuck. Please, don't cry. It's all right. I've had worse."

"W-worse?" she asked in a trembling voice as he carried her out of the room and down the hallway. Instead of heading for the downstairs bathroom he carried her upstairs. "How could there be w-worse?"

"Hush, Mia."

"You're going to get vomit everywhere—"

"Hush, Mia."

"You should put me down and strip. I'm so—"

"Hush, Mia. I'm not going to tell you again." His voice was soft but there was a hint of steel running through it.

And so she hushed. After all, she'd just vomited all over the man, the least she could damn well do was shut up.

Another quiet sob left her mouth as he carried her into his bedroom. The scent of him was stronger in here. Not a bad scent. Not at all. It was masculine. He smelled like the outdoors. Sometimes she wished she could wrap herself up in that scent.

Mortification warred with the lingering traces panic. Oh, God, he'd seen her in the middle of a panic attack. And she'd vomited all over him.

How was she ever going to look him in the face again?

He sat her on the counter in his bathroom. It was done in gray tile with white fixtures. It was simple, masculine, and it suited him.

"Wait there," he told her. Then he moved over to the huge, walk-in shower, turning on the water. She took the opportunity to slide off the counter. She knew he didn't really want her here. She'd just go back to her room and clean herself off, climb into bed, and try to forget that this ever happened.

Yeah. Good luck with that.

"Mia. Freeze."

She stilled at the doorway.

"Jesus, I have never met a sub who had a harder time following direct orders."

She got the feeling he was talking to himself, but she couldn't help but comment as he grabbed hold of her and started to pull off her sweatshirt.

"I'm not a sub."

"You spend your days trying your best to keep everyone happy, to give them what they need, usually at the expense of yourself."

He had her sweatshirt and T-shirt off quickly and was crouching in front of her to remove her pants. She was so caught up in thinking over what he'd just said that she didn't even notice him stripping her down to her bra and panties.

"That doesn't mean I want to . . . that I'm interested . . ."

"You practically salivated when I talked about my paddles."

"I did not!" *Fuck. I almost did.*

He just gave her a knowing look. "Don't try to fool me, little girl. We both know you're very interested." He shook his head. "This is a damn stupid idea."

"What is?"

He just studied her for a moment. Then he took off his shirt and shook his head. "Doesn't matter. Got to do better than this."

"I don't understand anything of what you're saying," she wailed. "I've just had a panic attack, vomited all over us, and now I'm standing in your bathroom in nothing but my underwear while you're distracting me with all those abs and skin and what-ever . . . so if you want me to understand what you're saying, you're going to have to lay it all out."

He cupped her face between his wide hands, and she realized she was trembling. After effects. Mostly after a panic attack, she crashed into bed exhausted. Of course, she was usually alone. And she'd never thrown up on someone in the midst of one.

First time for everything. Yay.

"Sh, Mia. It's all going to be okay."

"It's not. It's really not. My life is shit."

"Don't swear, baby."

"Don't call me baby."

He pulled her close and kissed her forehead. Then he did the best thing ever. He held her. Just held her. Even though the shower was steaming up the bathroom.

He held her.

He ran his hand up and down her back. A quiet murmur of reassurance reached her ears every so often, but for the most part they just stood there. And gradually she became aware she wasn't shaking as much. The coldness that usually engulfed her during one of these attacks was being replaced by heat. So much heat.

She tried to pull back. To her surprise he let her move.

"I should ... I should go use my bathroom." She shouldn't be there. With him. Both of them partly naked. It was a bad, bad idea. A man like Alec Malone wasn't for her. He'd chew her up and spit her out and they both knew it. In fact, he already kind of had. Several times.

He didn't pull punches. He could be a little mean.

And she really wanted to bury her head against his chest and feel his arms wrap around her again.

"You should. But you're not going to."

"What?" She stared up at him in surprise. Her brain wasn't working properly. It was full of cotton, something that was pretty normal for her after a panic attack. What wasn't normal was ending up half-naked with a man.

"Mia, you just had a panic attack. You couldn't breathe. Then you threw up. I can't leave you on your own right now," he answered her patiently.

Oh. Right. He just wanted to make sure she was all right. That was nice, she guessed.

Too bad she didn't really want nice. She'd rather have hot. Have him declare he couldn't resist her. That he'd been wanting to do this ever since she'd arrived on his doorstep. He needed to ravage her. Possess her.

Damn, you've got an overactive imagination.

"It's okay, I'm used to being alone after an attack. I'll just have a shower and go to bed." She looked around the bathroom then down at herself. "My clothes."

"Are in the hamper. They need to be washed."

"Right . . . right . . . do that tomorrow."

"Mia, look at me."

She couldn't quite figure out why she wasn't moving. She should head to her own bathroom, shower then sleep. Or maybe just sleep. She wanted a shower, but she didn't know how she was going to manage it.

He grabbed hold of her chin, raising her face so he could look at her.

"You're really beautiful," she told him.

Whoops.

He smiled. Actually smiled. Alec Malone didn't smile much. Not that she ever saw anyway.

"You shouldn't smile."

"What?" he asked, looking surprised. Why wouldn't he? She was making absolutely no sense.

"When you smile you go from beautiful to irresistible. Shit. Didn't mean to say that out loud."

"Honey, you're not yourself. And I'm not leaving you alone like this. So your choices are a shower with me then bed or I run you a bath and you have one while I shower then bed."

Some choices.

She didn't want to wait until the bath filled. "I want a shower by myself."

"That wasn't one of your options, now was it?"

Shit. His voice had turned to steel. And she was weak. Weak because she couldn't resist when he used that tone.

"What's it going to be, baby?"

"Please stop calling me that." Because she couldn't resist him when he called her that in that low tone of voice. As though they actually meant something to one another. As though they had some sort of relationship. When, in reality, she was just an obligation. A debt to be repaid.

Tears stung at her eyes and she blinked, shoving them back. Nothing good came from crying. She'd learned that.

"This is going above and beyond, isn't it?" she asked. That fatigue was really hitting her now and it was making her feel melancholy. Because the only reason he cared about her was the obligation his family owed her cousin. No other reason. And while his brothers might be friendlier, she was still just a guest. When she left she'd just be a memory. Hell, mostly, they were more interested in her cooking than anything else.

But sometimes she could pretend she was part of this crazy family. It made her feel less alone.

"You're really not with me, are you?" he murmured. "Okay, sweetheart, I want you to just relax. I'm going to make all the decisions right now and all you have to do is what you're told."

"You like to boss people around, don't you?" she mumbled.

"It's what I'm good at."

With that, he pulled off his jeans.

She immediately slammed her hands over her eyes. "You have no underwear on. Why don't you have any underwear on?"

"Mia," he laughed. "Jesus, in all my years, me stripping has never made a woman cover her eyes and ask me about my habit of wearing underwear."

She got that her reaction was maybe a little childish. And probably more than a little insulting. But he was naked. Alec Malone, the man who centered in so many of her dreams was standing there naked.

And she . . . she was standing there in her underwear, covering her eyes like an idiot.

"This . . . I . . . shit."

"Second time I've ever heard you swear," he commented. "Not sure I like it."

She removed her hand from her eyes, looking straight up at him. "Fuck."

THE LITTLE GIRL had just challenged him. Well, he wouldn't be ignoring that.

He cupped her chin, lifting her face up to him. "What did you just say?"

"I said, fuck."

"Careful, little one, you're playing with fire."

Her eyes were wide in her pale face. Shit. He was an asshole. She'd just had a panic attack. She was exhausted. She was swaying where she stood and he was screwing around, making her stand there when he could already have her tucked into bed.

Question was, which bed?

He wrapped his arm around her waist and steered her towards the shower. He debated whether to try and get her bra and panties off. But he figured that was just going to create more of an argument, and, right then, he wanted to get her clean and into bed.

He opened the door to the shower. "In you go."

The bra and panties were cheap cotton. He frowned. About as crappy as the rest of her clothes. He knew she probably didn't have much money. Being on the run cut into funds quickly when you couldn't hold down a regular job. But why the hell hadn't her cousin taken care of her?

Screw waiting for her to tell him what she needed, he'd send one of the boys down to get her more clothes and shit.

When she didn't move, he wrapped his hands around her waist and lifted her in. She let out a small squeal. But he stepped in behind her before she could try to escape.

"Malone!"

"Easy," he soothed. "We're just going to get clean then I'll put you to bed." Might kill him. His cock was already hard and aching, even though she hadn't seemed to notice. Probably a good thing. Even if it was a bit of a hit to his ego.

He snorted. This was the first time he'd ever been in a shower with a woman who he hadn't or didn't intend to fuck. He guessed maybe he was a bit spoiled when it came to women. He'd never really had to work at it. He'd never had one try to escape as Mia was trying to do.

She brushed against his dick as she tried to turn towards the door, and he gasped in a sharp breath. Fuck, it would be so easy to take her. To push her against the wall and lift her onto his cock. Okay, maybe he was arrogant as fuck, but it was obvious that Mia had little experience with sex. She was innocent. Sweet. Not for him at all— she would be all too easy to seduce.

She's an obligation. A responsibility. And she obviously had PTSD, a fact nobody had seen fit to share with him. If he'd known he'd have been keeping a closer eye on her. Aside from a few issues, she'd pretty much been a model guest. She hadn't disobeyed him once. Hadn't tried to murder him in his sleep, even when he'd been a complete ass. She'd stuck to the ranch. She liked to please people. And she tended to put everyone else first.

That needed to stop. Damn woman needed a keeper.

And that can't be you.

"Oh my God, you're hard." Her horrified voice cut through his thoughts.

He sighed. "If I wasn't such a confident person, you'd be well on your way to giving me a complex."

"What?" She couldn't move her gaze from his dick.

"You've seen one before, right?" he asked, a bit more impatiently than he'd intended.

"What?"

"Mia. Eyes. Now."

She shot her gaze up to his then groaned and winced, her hand coming up to her temple.

"Headache?" he murmured, turning her around so she faced away from him. Having her stare at his dick wasn't helping him regain control. He reached for some shower gel and started washing her shoulders. He then massaged the tight muscles in her neck and shoulders.

She let out a low groan of pleasure that went straight to his cock. Yep, seemed like he was in for a case of blue balls tonight. He washed down her back and undid the clasp of her bra.

"Malone," she said in a low voice.

"Just washing you, baby. Nothing more. I promise." Even if it fucking killed him, he'd keep that promise.

Obligation. Responsibility. Fragile.

Yeah, that last one really got to him. Because while there was a core of steel at the heart of her—she couldn't have gotten through what she had without it—there was also an air of fragility about her. He didn't do fragile. Or needy. Not that she clung in any way. Or demanded anything of him, which for some weird reason pissed him off. But he felt a need to provide for her.

Obligation. Responsibility. Fragile.

He needed to get that tattooed on his brain. He left her panties on. That was just one step too far. Okay, it might be argued that he'd already stepped way over that line, but it was a last line of defense.

He turned her around. She held an arm over her breasts, keeping her bra pressed against them.

"I can wash myself," she told him quietly.

"All right."

He saw a flare of surprise in her eyes. He kept a close eye on her. He didn't want her keeling over on him. She slowly reached for some gel and half-heartedly rubbed it over herself, keeping one arm over her breasts.

He sighed and turned his back. "Wash yourself properly. You have thirty seconds before I turn back around.

"O-okay."

He waited, listening to the sounds coming from behind him and took that moment to try and calm himself. He needed a trip to the club. Hell, he'd spent more time at the club these last two weeks that he had in the last four months.

When he turned, she had her bra in one hand, her arm back over her breasts. She was swaying again, and he knew she was going to crash.

Yeah, the club was out tonight when she was in this state.

"I'm sorry to be such a nuisance, Malone."

"I'm used to dealing with nuisances," he replied.

She frowned up at him, a hint of red entering her pale cheeks. That was better. He turned away to hide the grin trying to form. Teasing her was fun.

Teasing her? Was that what he was doing? He never teased anyone.

"Thanks a lot," she muttered as he turned off the water and stepped out of the shower, quickly grabbing a dry towel. He held it out to her. She quickly took it while he turned away to get another towel. When he turned back, the towel was wrapped around her,

her panties and bra in her hand. He took them and threw them into the hamper.

"You're welcome."

She huffed out an irritated breath. "You know, sometimes I can't tell if you're really obtuse or just trying to annoy me."

"Come on. Time for bed. You're exhausted." And he was willing to bet that headache was getting worse.

"Okay, sure."

Yep, she was really gone. Her eyelids were drooping. He took her hand and led her out into his bedroom. When he stopped, she did the same and just stood there. He searched through one of his drawers and pulled out a T-shirt, popping it over her head then pulling the towel down. He turned down the bed.

"In you go."

"Into your bed?" She looked up at him quizzically, although she didn't appear alarmed or like she was going to bolt. Definitely out of it.

"Yes, Mia. Into my bed." He made his voice deliberately hard. She needed rest and he wasn't fucking around with her anymore. He was fully prepared to tie her to the bed if necessary. Although probably not a good idea considering what she'd been through.

Fortunately, she didn't argue, just climbed up into his huge bed and settled down on her side, facing him. She drew her legs up to her chest and held them there. He didn't like that she had curled up into a defensive position.

He grabbed some underwear, in concession to his bedmate since he liked to sleep naked.

"Baby, you got any painkillers for that headache?"

"Yes, in the top drawer in my bathroom."

"All right, I'll be back in a minute. You stay right where you are."

"Uh-huh." Her eyes remained closed; her face even more pale than before. That headache had to be a killer. He walked out of the room and down to the other end of the hallway to her bedroom. The alarm for the house was already on. He'd do another check of the house once he got her settled though.

He walked through her bedroom which was neat as a pin. She sure did like things tidy. The house had never been so clean, not even when he'd employed someone to do it.

He shook his head as he moved into the bathroom. She was getting to him. Kicker was, he knew she didn't even mean to. She wasn't doing anything deliberately. Wasn't being anyone but herself.

Just as he suspected, there wasn't any feminine shit strewn around. Just a toothbrush and hairbrush by the sink. He opened the top drawer and grabbed the three bottles in there. All of them prescriptions. One a strong painkiller for headaches and migraines. The other was a sedative.

His gut tightened as he looked at the third container. An anti-anxiety drug. He opened the lid, and saw it was nearly empty. Shit.

Why the fuck hadn't her cousin told him she had anxiety? Not that it wasn't understandable. Did she have PTSD? She should be having therapy. But, then, she couldn't do that without a paper trail, could she?

Except, he knew a shrink who would help him out without any paperwork. Part of this was his fault. She was his responsibility now. He should have asked her when she first came here if she had any medication. Anything he needed to be aware of. That was on him. He'd been too busy avoiding her and he hadn't taken care of her the way he should have.

Of course he'd expected her to come to him if she needed anything. The fact she'd kept all this hidden pissed him off. And he'd be letting her know that. Once she was feeling better.

He grabbed both containers. She had a bottle of water by the bed and he got that too before returning to his bedroom. He'd left the light on by the bed. It looked like she hadn't moved at all.

"Still awake?" he asked quietly.

"Hard to sleep when there's a jackhammer trying to crack a hole in my head," she told him.

"Got your painkillers and the water that was beside your bed." He put the anti-anxiety drugs on the bedside table then shook out a couple of the strong painkillers and handed them to her. She took them and swallowed some water before laying down again.

"I'll turn the light out."

"No, wait—" she said urgently, trying to sit up, then groaning with obvious pain.

"Easy, lie still." He placed a hand on her shoulder.

"I . . . the light . . . I should go to back . . . to my room."

Yeah, that wasn't happening. But he got the gist of the problem.

"You don't like sleeping in the dark."

"Not anymore. Not since . . . "

His jaw tightened at the reminder. Not since she'd discovered a bunch of dead bodies and found herself on the run from the fucking mob. Yeah, he should have guessed the dark wasn't her friend.

"Bathroom light be enough?"

She looked up at him. "You don't think I'm being ridiculous? I know it's childish and silly, but I—"

Yeah. Enough.

"Babe, you've been through more shit in the last six months than most people go through their whole lives. You need the light on, the light stays on. Now, bathroom light? It enough?"

"Yes, thank you."

He turned on the bathroom light, leaving the door partially open. He wasn't used to sleeping with the light on, but he could put up with it for one night. Tomorrow night, she'd be back in her own bed. He switched off the light by the bed then walked out to do a check of the house. He took his time, hoping she'd be asleep by the time he got back. He was also hoping that his hard-on from hell would go down.

When he walked back into his bedroom and saw her lying there, curled up under the blankets, he knew the likelihood of getting his dick to rest was pretty much nil. He sighed. Sure, he could go take care of matters himself, but that held pretty much zero appeal.

He climbed up into his side of the bed.

His side. The whole damn bed was his side. He needed to get his shit together. He pulled the covers up and rolled over, facing away from her.

"Malone?" she said in a sleepy voice.

"Go to sleep, babe," he growled at her, hoping to scare her into doing as she was told. He needed to get back to her avoiding him and him ignoring her. Yep, that would be the best idea.

And he had very little chance of that happening. His protective instincts were well and truly stirred. He wasn't used to feeling this protective of a woman. But then he'd never had one live with him.

"Thank you."

Fuck. She was killing him.

7

"**M**ia, wake up."

She slowly drifted out of the fog of sleep and blinked up at the blurry face of Alec Malone looming over her. She let out a gasp and tried to sit up, but he placed a hand in the middle of her chest.

"Easy, babe. Sorry, didn't mean to startle you."

How could him in her bedroom not startle her? But wait . . . this wasn't her bedroom at the ranch. Where was she? Oh, shit. Oh, no.

"Fuck," she muttered to herself.

"Again with the swearing. I don't like it."

"I've heard you swear plenty."

"Don't like it on you. Someone who looks like you shouldn't have filth spilling out of their mouth."

"That is a horrible double standard."

He sighed. Glared down at her. "I've gotta get going, got work to do, but I need to talk to you first. And not about my double standards."

Wait. What time was it? She looked around for a clock, spotting it.

"Oh, no, I'm late. Breakfast!"

"Boys have already been and gone."

"I'm so sorry!" Her one freaking job. The only way she had for paying him back—she knew it was a pretty shitty payment—and she'd slept in.

"I'm so sorry. It won't happen again. It's just . . . I don't . . . hell." She tried to get up and once again, he held her back.

"Stop apologizing. I don't have time for it."

She frowned up at him. "Are you always this grumpy when you first wake up?"

"I've been awake for hours." He stared down at her for a long moment. "How often do you have panic attacks?"

"Not very often," she lied.

His gaze narrowed. "What was the rule about lying, little one?"

She heaved out a much-put-upon breath and tried to move so she was sitting, since she felt at a decided disadvantage. To her surprise, he arranged pillows behind her back as though he cared about her comfort.

Don't let it lull you into a false sense that you mean anything more to him than you do.

"Fine. I have them every now and then."

"Anti-anxiety medication helps you control them?"

She stiffened. What? How did he know about that? She looked over at the bottle he picked up off the bedside table.

"You snooped in my drawers?" she snapped.

He raised an eyebrow and she could clearly see the disapproval in his gaze. Shit. How did he manage to make her feel like a surly teenager with just one look?

"I went and got your painkillers last night for you. Remember? You told me where to find them and this bottle was next to them. Along with some sedatives that barely looked touched."

"I don't like to take them. I don't like to feel out of it," she explained, hating the knowing look in his eyes."

"Why didn't tell me that you were on medication for anxiety. How long you been taking these? Since you witnessed that hit? Anything else going on other than anxiety attacks? Was last night a typical attack?"

"You sure have a lot of questions."

"Which I wouldn't have if you'd come clean from the start."

"Didn't know I had to give you a rundown of my medical history."

To her surprise, he nodded. "And that's on me. Should have asked you that when you first arrived here. But I'm making up for that now. These the only medications you have? What about birth control? Anything else I need to know about?"

"I don't think you need to know about any of it," she snapped. "I need to get up. I'm running late. Were the guys pissed off that breakfast wasn't ready?"

She felt terrible about that.

"They're capable of frying some eggs and making toast. Don't let them fool you into thinking they're helpless, they're not."

"I know that," she said. Way to make her feel like she wasn't important at all.

Alec sighed then surprised her by sitting on the bed, facing her. "I didn't mean that they didn't miss your cooking. Moaned about it something fierce. But you're allowed to sleep in. Especially when you're not feeling well."

She was silent.

"Calamity Jane? You know that, right? You're not our slave. You can have a damn day off."

"And do what?" she whispered. Shit. She hadn't actually meant to say that. "Forget it. Cool. Day off. I can do that. And stop calling me Calamity Jane. I know there have been one or two issues, but I don't cause chaos wherever I go."

"That's debatable." He watched her carefully. "I want to know more about these anxiety attacks and this medication. It's running low. You supposed to get a refill?"

"Hard to do when I can't leave a paper trail."

"How'd you get them and the other shit in the first place?" He looked down at the label.

"Mike knew someone who owed him a favor. I guess I could call him, and he could organize some more." Hope filled her.

"No can do. Too risky to use the same person. And I don't want you getting more pills without talking to someone in person first."

She ground her teeth together and tried to remind herself that she couldn't tell him where he could shove his orders.

"First, it's going to be kind of hard to talk to anyone when I can't leave the house. Second, what pills I do or don't take has nothing to do with you."

"It does when you're having panic attacks that make you curl into a ball and throw up then pretty much pass out in exhaustion on my watch."

"I'm not on your watch."

He just stared at her. Fine. She got it. She was on his watch.

"You're in charge of keeping me alive. You don't have to keep me sane."

"Actually, I've got to do both. You think the defense attorneys won't use this against you?" He shook the container.

She sucked in a breath; she hadn't even thought of that. Just the idea of being in front of a bunch of people, of seeing that monster again . . . her breath came in short, sharp pants.

"Shit. Fuck. Babe, stop it. Slow your breathing. Come on. In then out. That's it. Do it with me. Fuck. That's it."

She focused in on him as she managed to fight back the impending panic attack. He held her hand to his chest but, as she calmed, he dropped it down onto her lap, still keeping hold of it.

"How often do you have these attacks?"

"N-not usually one after another like this," she reassured him. She concentrated on her breathing. Slow and steady.

"How many have you had since you've been here?"

She didn't really want to answer that.

"How many?" he demanded in a voice she couldn't ignore. Damn him.

"Four, not counting last night."

"I don't like that you kept that from me." His voice was a dark warning.

She narrowed her gaze at him. "Far as I was aware, your protection only regards my body, not my fucked-up mind."

He shook his head. "Again with the swearing."

"Again with the arrogant commands."

He eyed her. "I'd like to know what you planned to do once these pills ran out."

"Hadn't really thought that far ahead."

"Medication should have been at the top of the list I told you to write. The one I still don't have."

"You just said that I can't get hold of more," she pointed out.

"No, I said I didn't want you getting more without talking to someone. You need to be talking to someone on a regular basis."

Not something she didn't know. "Again, how?"

"I know someone. She'll keep quiet about you. And she can assess if you need more of these. Not good that you have a panic attack just thinking about testifying when you've got to actually do it in a few weeks."

Again, he wasn't saying something she didn't know.

"You trust this person?"

"Much as I trust anyone who isn't family, yeah. Molly's good people."

Molly. Was she an ex-girlfriend? And why did she feel so jealous at the idea of him seeing someone? She bet Molly was curvy and gorgeous and put together. Not a freaking mess.

"Didn't you say you had somewhere to be?"

"Got plenty of places I need to be. But right now, I'm trying to sort this mess out."

Okay. That stung. She knew that she wasn't important to him —not even close—but being called a mess was never something someone wanted to hear.

"Fuck. Shouldn't have put it like that." He reached over and cupped her chin. "But you've got to know this is a mess, right? You on the run for your life, having to hide here, not being able to sleep in the dark, panic attacks. It's a mess."

"Yeah. My life, right?" She tried to smile. Didn't work. "But it's not your mess to figure out. It's mine."

"Afraid it is. You're living in my house, under my protection." He looked down at her. "Right now, you're in my bed."

"Yes, but not like that. I mean . . ." Why had she slept in his bed last night? "You were just watching over me."

"Was that what I was doing?" he muttered. "Wasn't quite sure."

What the heck did that mean? Before she could question him, he looked down at the bottle of pills. "You have to take these with food?"

"Um, best to, yes."

"All right. You get up and dressed. I'll make you some breakfast."

"I don't need you to make me breakfast. You need to get to work."

He just studied her. "Fine. Make yourself breakfast. Then get some more rest. No housework today. No baking. You rest. You take your meds and you rest."

He stood and set the bottle down. "You never answered me before. Anything else about your health I need to know? There was no birth control in that drawer."

"I really don't think that's any of your business."

He just stared at her.

"I get a shot twice a year, all right? I can't remember to take those little pills."

He nodded. "I'll call Molly, see if I can get her out here to see you. Sooner the better."

Right. Because she wouldn't want this to happen again. Even if she didn't particularly want to talk to some stranger about what she'd seen, it had to be better than living like this, surely.

8

Mia stood beside Alec on the porch and watched as the small car drove up the driveway, bouncing along the potholes.

"You should really get those holes filled in," she told him. "They nearly knocked out all my fillings when we were driving up here."

"That's the idea," he told her.

"What? Do you get kickbacks from a local dentist if you send them a certain number of customers each month?"

He just sent her a look. "No, they're there to make people uncomfortable. So they don't come back."

She didn't really know what to say to that, so she just fell silent. The whole time she'd been here, there had only been one visitor to the Lonely Horse Ranch, and he'd been stopped at the gate. She only knew because Jaret had been cursing up a storm about someone called Osborne who wanted to buy the ranch and wouldn't give up.

So she guessed he was right, the potholes did the job. As did the gates. And the fact that there were always a couple of Malones around at all times.

"Why do you have such security measures?" she asked.

All she got in reply was another look.

Right. She got it. He wasn't going to answer that. There were a lot of things he wouldn't answer. Nerves bubbled in her tummy. She couldn't do this. Couldn't talk to a stranger. But she also didn't want a repeat of the other night. Nope, she could puke on someone once but twice was just taking it too far.

Oh, hell. She really was losing it.

A woman climbed out of the car, and the sunlight caught her gorgeous, red hair. She had a killer figure. All curves. Mia was kind of surprised that she was dressed in just a pair of plain, black jeans and an oversized, bright-blue shirt.

She clenched her hands around the porch railing. Her knees went weak. "I've changed my mind."

He didn't say anything, but she could sense his gaze on her. Then he moved closer, not touching her, but his scent surrounded her. Mia felt the desire to lean back, just to lean into that strength for a while. But she held herself tensely. It was bad enough he'd seen her at her weakest. He wasn't her boyfriend, he wasn't even a friend, he was just the poor guy who was unfortunate enough to have to deal with her.

"It's going to be okay, Mia." His breath whispered against her neck and she shivered slightly. The last two nights she'd dreamed about him, when she wasn't having nightmares. Dreamed of him touching her. Tasting her. That instead of sleeping that night in his bed, he'd rolled over her, pressing his weight against her, telling her he couldn't spend another moment in her presence without taking her.

She didn't know whether to be peeved or relieved that hadn't happened.

"How do you know? Do you talk to a lot of shrinks about your personal shit?"

"One, don't swear. Two, what makes you think I've got any shit to talk about? Three, the shit you've got going on is more than most people could take without having a breakdown. There's nothing to be ashamed of, Mia."

"One, I'll swear if I want to. Two, I may not know you well, but I do know that there's a lot you don't talk about. Three, that's exactly why I don't want to talk about it. I don't want to bring it up. I don't want to think about it."

"Burying stuff doesn't make it disappear. Believe me."

And then she had to shut up, because the pretty redhead had stopped talking to Tanner, who had somehow miraculously appeared out of nowhere, and was coming up the steps.

Right. It seems she was doing this whether she wanted to or not.

TURNED out Molly was nothing like she'd expected. For one thing, she'd kind of thought she might hate her. Mostly because of the hint of fondness in Alec's voice when he talked about her. But Molly was warm and funny and kind. She was also married to the Sheriff of Haven; which Alec had left out. The ass.

"Thank you for coming all the way out here, Molly," she told the stunning redhead. "I'm really sorry to be a nuisance. Alec wouldn't let me go to you."

"Understandable. Best no one knows you're here. Even though I trust everyone who lives in Haven, there are all the tourists and people driving through. You never know who might be around."

"There's little chance he'd have anyone here." But the thought of it was enough to keep her from protesting too much. Actually, from protesting at all.

"But better safe than sorry," Molly said softly.

"Am I putting you in a tough position, with your husband being the sheriff? Alec never told me that and I wouldn't want to make things awkward."

Molly waved that away. "Doctor-patient confidentiality. No reason for Jake to know." Molly smiled. "You don't need to worry about me."

"I know . . . it's just . . . what about the medication? You can't prescribe me anything unless you fake my name. Is that even possible? How does that work? Won't you get in trouble?"

"Mia. I can call you Mia?" Molly leaned forward in her chair. They were in her small living room.

Not hers. Not her home.

"Yes, of course."

"Mia, I knew what Alec was asking of me when he called. You don't need to worry about me. But if you don't want to talk to me, if you're being forced to see me—"

"No, it's not that," she said quickly, not wanting to seem ungrateful. "Well, it's not only that. I guess a part of me is scared to talk about it. I want to forget; I don't want to relive it."

"I understand. But honestly, sometimes the best thing you can do to break free of the things that scare you is to talk about them."

"Yeah that's kind of what I'd expect a shrink to say." She slammed her hand over a mouth as she said, looking at Molly and horror. "Oh my God, I'm so sorry."

Molly waved that away. "Oh, don't worry, I know exactly what you mean. It does sound like a typical psychiatrist thing to say. After all, I wouldn't have much of a job left if everyone stopped talking about the things that scare them or worry them or keep them awake at night. But I'm not insulted, believe me I've heard everything coming out here. These boys don't hold back."

She wouldn't exactly refer to the Malones as boys. But she thought it best not to say that. She kind of figured she'd insulted

Molly enough as it was, and she was just doing her a favor. Or, rather, doing Alec a favor.

She wondered just how well Molly knew Alec.

Don't ask. Don't ask.

"How well do you know Alec Malone?"

Well, that whole don't ask thing lasted all of thirty seconds.

Molly looked slightly surprised. "Well, to be honest, not that well at all. Alec tends to keep to himself. I see him sometimes at the club, of course."

The club? Did she mean a BDSM club? Okay, this time she definitely couldn't ask.

Molly grinned. "I can see you're dying to ask. Go ahead."

Mia bit her lip. "What sort of club are you talking about?"

Molly tilted her head to one side. "You know what sort of life-style Alec is into?"

"Yes, I do."

"Haven is a small town," Molly told her. "You pretty much know what everyone else is doing, although Alec Malone tends to be a bit of a loner. Of course I guess it's hard to be a loner when you have a heap of brothers."

She wasn't sure. It seemed that even here, on his ranch, surrounded by family, Alec was still a loner.

But she nodded anyway. Alec's secrets were his own. And she wasn't about to divulge anything. After all she owed the man big time.

"So while I don't know that much about Alec, we do belong to the same BDSM club. My husband Jake, is also a Dominant."

"He is?" She blushed. "Sorry, I'm being really rude. I shouldn't be asking you about your private life."

Molly shrugged. "Like I said, Haven is a small town. Wouldn't have been long until you found out anyway. And I don't have anything to hide."

What would it be like to have nothing to hide? She didn't even know how that would feel.

"Mia, again, anything you say to me here is confidential. I won't tell Alec, unless you want me to. He's given me some background information about what's happened. He also said you had a panic attack the other night. Do you want to tell me about that?"

"The panic attack?" She didn't know what there was to say, really.

"Do you get many of them?"

"Not as many as I used to get before I started taking medication." She looked down to see she was pressing her fingers together so tightly they were turning white. She forced herself to let go. Then she looked over at Molly. "They started almost immediately after . . . after you know what."

"Have you talked to anybody about what happened?" Molly asked her.

"I told the police. I told my cousin."

"Anyone else? Another friend? The psychiatrist that wrote this prescription for the anti-anxiety pills?"

She shook her head. "The psychiatrist owed my cousin a favor. I had a couple of panic attacks around Mike and he knew I wasn't going to be able to function unless I got them under control."

"Drugs can be really helpful," Molly said to her gently. "But they can't fix the crux of the problem. They can't help you process what happened. They can help manage the symptoms. How are you sleeping? Eating?"

"Sleeping and eating have become harder," she admitted.

"Harder?" Molly said thoughtfully. "I bet they have. Nightmares?"

"Yes."

"Every night?"

"It had gotten to the point where they weren't coming every

night, maybe every second night. And then my neighbor was shot dead instead of me."

She suddenly realized that sometime while they'd been speaking, she'd pulled her feet up onto the sofa and had her arms wrapped around her legs defensively. Shit. Fuck.

"Do you know anything about PTSD?" Molly asked her gently, watching her. She bet the other woman didn't miss much.

She shook her head. "A little. I know it's what soldiers often get after they've been to war."

"You're right. People often suffer from PTSD after they've been through a traumatic experience. They've seen something, experienced something that's out of the norm for them. It can make them anxious, ill, can make it hard to sleep. It can make it hard for them to leave their home."

"And you think I have PTSD?"

"Yes, I do. There're a few things you can do to help. Talking like this can help. About what happened. About how it made you feel."

"I don't think I can do that."

It sounded like a form of torture. She didn't want to talk about what happened. She just wanted to forget. "I know it's scary but keeping everything locked down isn't healthy. Sometimes going back to the scene can help."

"What? You mean going back to the restaurant?" She wasn't doing that. Not ever.

"Well, maybe not going back to the actual scene, physically. But going back to it in your mind. Hypnosis can help with that."

She shook her head. "I don't want to do that. I can't do that."

"All right," Molly told her calmly. "What I'll do for the moments is get you some more anti-anxiety medication. But I want you to think about what I've said. There are exercises you can do. And I'd really like to see you again, Mia."

Yeah, she was pretty sure she didn't want to see Molly again. She felt terrible for thinking that. Molly was here to help her. Just because she had suggestions that sounded like Mia's worst nightmares, didn't mean she got to be a bitch to her.

But her pulse was racing as she thought about having to confront what had happened that night. Having to relive it.

"Mia, can I take off my professional hat now and ask you something woman to woman?"

That was unexpected. Mia looked over at her and nodded slowly. "Sure."

"How on earth are you resisting the Malone charm?"

Charm? She guessed Alec had a sort of charm about him. If you found overbearing, dominant men who think they're always right charming.

"What do you mean?" she asked

"It's well known through this county and into the next that those Malone boys just have to look at a woman and she has an orgasm."

She let out a bark of surprised laughter. "Molly!"

Molly grinned good-naturedly. "What? I'm just telling you the rumor. And I've met them." She fanned herself. "Why do you think I leapt on the chance to come out here? Not only are they a pack of lovable rogues, but there are also completely insane. Coming here is like winning the super bowl for a psychiatrist. I could write papers for the rest of my life on this bunch."

Her eyes widened. "They'd let you do that?"

"Good Lord, no. But it's still a hell of a lot of fun. Riles Jake up something good though. I've stopped telling him when I'm coming out here. Last time, Tanner shot a hole in his hat and he locked him up. Alec was not happy."

"I can't believe Tanner did that. He didn't shoot at you, did he?" She'd kill him if he had.

"Oh, no. Although one time they disabled my car and told me they were keeping me. I had a date that night, so I wasn't very amused."

She shook her head. "I'm sorry about that. If anything like that happens again, you tell me."

Molly gave her an interested look. "They don't scare you at all?"

"No. They don't scare you, do they?" she asked Molly.

"No. But I have a poor sense of self-preservation, as my husband likes to say."

"They're not dangerous. Well, not really. They're just a bit, um, impetuous. They're good guys."

Molly laughed. "I did wonder when Alec called me what state I was going to find you in. Three weeks out here on your own, I worried I might find you in a fetal position in the corner, slowly losing your sanity."

She shook her head. "You make them sound completely feral—"

Molly laughed. "Feral. That's exactly the right word. Honey, the whole town thinks they're feral. They're the wild Malone boys. They've been known to incite bar brawls, riots, they've been called the scourge of the state. They live up here, with little regard for things like the law, yet they're hardly ever held accountable. And do you know why?"

She shook her head.

"Because they're the most charming, gorgeous pack of demons you've ever met. That's why. And you, honey, are the only woman under the age of ninety who seems to be immune to their charms."

"I'm not immune to their charms," she denied.

"Well, you're not naked and in one of their beds. What did you do? How are you keeping them at bay?"

She could feel herself growing red. "Maybe they don't want me."

"I don't think that's it. You're gorgeous. You're tiny, like a little doll. Hmm, maybe that's it? Is it because they feel protective of you? They're helping to guard you."

"Really, Molly. I don't know what you mean. Sure they joke around, but they're just having fun."

"Honey, they are not having fun. Believe me. It's not a joke. The minute you give them the go ahead, you'll be in their bed. And when I say *their* bed, I mean it in the plural sense. Not sure how many of them like to share, the last tally I heard was five, but make no mistake, you will be very, very satisfied."

"Wait…what…" It was hard enough to wrap her head around the idea they might actually want her and not just be teasing her, but five?

"When you say a tally of five, do you mean … "

"Five Malone brothers, one very lucky woman. Yes, I mean exactly that. It's happened once that I know of. I have no idea how that woman managed to walk the next day. Mind you, she wouldn't have had to, would she? They could have just carried her around. Not that they're known for sticking around. They're more the love 'em and leave 'em smiling and satisfied type. Hmm, wonder if that's why they haven't touched you. Because they'd have to see you the next day, then the next."

"Or maybe they're just joking around and all these rumors are just rumors. They're flirts, that's all. They don't really want me, and I don't want them."

Five of them at once? Yeah, even if she was interested, there was no way she could live up to that.

"It's rumored that Maddox once winked at a woman and her panties fell down. Just fell to her ankles, she tripped over them and whacked her face against the pavement."

"Oh, come on, you don't really believe that."

Molly grinned. "No, but it's a fun story. But the Malones aren't used to following anyone's rules. Except Alec's. They'd probably do what he says. Maybe he warned them off you."

"Or maybe they're worried about being cut off from my cooking. So what do they say about Alec? Does he make women's panties drop?"

Molly stopped smiling. "Alec is a different story. He only comes into Haven to visit Saxon's and that's not very often. I've never heard any rumors of him seeing a woman outside of Saxon's. He tends to stick to the ranch. Guess taking care of this place takes up a lot of his time."

"Yeah. I guess." Why did she feel so depressed to learn that Alec never dated? That he never got involved with anyone who wasn't a sub?

Stupid Mia, were you actually hoping for something to develop with him? That kiss was just a mistake. He's so far out of your league it's not funny.

"Molly, do you think we could talk about something else?"

"I'm sorry." Molly immediately looked contrite. "They're one of my favorite topics, and I tend to get a bit carried away."

Did she? Mia wasn't so sure. Molly was a smart lady. She'd no doubt seen how upset Mia had been earlier. And now, she was caught between wanting to laugh and shaking her head in despair. She'd also unwrapped herself from that protective ball and was sitting with her feet down on the floor.

"It was really nice to meet you, Mia. I'm glad you found your way here. Haven is a pretty special place. The men here are, well, overprotective and dominant and bossy, but they always, always put the women first. The Malones do tend to stick to themselves. But they are still citizens of Haven."

"It sounds like an amazing place."

"It is. And the people are very open-minded. There's a lot of different types of relationships here."

"Different, how?"

Molly looked her over then seemed to come to some decision.

"Well, a lot of Doms and their subs live in Haven. There's also a number of ménage relationships."

She blinked. "Ménage?"

"Men or women who are married to more than one partner."

She took a moment to wrap her head around that. "That's not legal, though, right?"

"No, not technically. The official marriage is just between two people and they have a ceremony to include the others. Haven is a place for people to be themselves. Everyone has to agree to the rules when they move here."

"I didn't agree to any rules."

"No, but yours is a special circumstance. Besides, you're under Alec's protection."

"That matters?"

"Around here it does. All women are protected in Haven. But particularly by the men they live with or are related to. If they're single and alone, well, Jake and his deputies tend to keep a close eye on them as well."

"And none of them feel smothered? Controlled?"

Molly seemed to think that over for a moment. "The men of Haven like to be in control, I'm not going to deny that. But they try to do the best they can for those under their protection. And there's a difference between control and controlling. Do you know what I mean?"

Oddly enough, she thought she did. "I had a boyfriend once, in college, I thought he was just protective. That he wanted to know where I was going and what I was doing all the time because he cared. But it got to the point that if I went anywhere without his permission, he'd get mad. He started to tell me who I could talk to and what I could wear, and he didn't want me going out anywhere without him. In the end, I was actually scared of him."

"What did you do?"

"I tried to break up with him, but he wouldn't listen. He threatened that if I tried to leave him, things were going to get nasty. I already thought things were nasty. So I went to the only person I knew who would have my back. My cousin Mike. He went over to where he lived in a frat house and had a chat with him. I never heard from him again."

"This Mike sounds like a good guy."

"Yeah, he is. I think he believes that all Doms are like my ex-boyfriend. Controlling."

Molly shrugged. "There's a lot of misinformation out there. But, personally, getting involved with Jake was the best thing to ever happen to me. I'm happier, more centered, and I always feel safe and loved. Of course, sometimes I don't sit well depending on how naughty I've been." She grinned.

Mia couldn't help but grin back. It was hard not to. It was clear Molly was very much in love. "You don't sound too worried by that."

Molly leaned forward. "Don't tell Jake, but sometimes I act up just to get punished."

Mia's eyes widened. "I didn't think a Dom would like that."

Molly shrugged. "It's not a one size fits all kind of a deal. There're lots of different sorts of Doms and subs. Some who are hard-core, twenty-four-seven. Some are just like a bit of bondage and maybe a spanking or two. Others who don't like pain at all. Personally, though, I find it can be a damn good way to get rid of some stress. There's nothing like a spanking or an orgasm to clear your head, to help you have a good cry, to get rid of everything that's bottled up inside you."

"Are you suggesting that I . . . " She couldn't even finish that sentence. And she could feel herself blushing bright red.

"Before I came here, I had a number of patients who were involved in the lifestyle. I'm not saying it's for everyone. And I wouldn't suggest it to just anyone. But I don't think you're just anyone, Mia. Of course, I wouldn't just suggest that you turn up at a club and choose just anyone to play with. You'd need someone who knew at least a bit about your past, to be aware of any triggers that might come up. Jake and I would be happy to act as monitors if you wanted to do a scene at Saxon's."

Okay, somehow, she'd ended up in this alternate universe, where her shrink was seriously suggesting that she go to a club, get tied up and spanked, while she and her husband watched.

Molly stood up. "Okay, I can see I may have shocked you into silence. Just give everything I've said a bit of a think. I'll drop your prescription off at the pharmacy and one of the boys can go and pick it up for you since you're not leaving the ranch. Might be an idea to get out for a walk every once in a while, though. Exercise is a good way to relieve stress too."

She winked and then turned and left. "Nice to meet you, Mia. I'll be in touch."

"Yeah, nice to meet you too."

"MOLLY, WAIT UP." Alec walked up to Molly where she stood by her car. He wouldn't admit it, but he'd been waiting around for her to finish with Mia. In fact, he'd now wasted two hours of his day waiting around. He told himself it was just because he was responsible for Mia. He needed to make sure she wasn't going to freak out and do something crazy. That was all.

It wasn't that he actually cared or anything.

"Hey, Alec. You going to Saxon's this weekend?"

It was a slightly odd question since he never interacted with Jake or Molly at the club.

"Perhaps," he allowed. "How is she? Everything okay?"

"You know I can't talk about what was said in there. Doctor-patient confidentiality."

Alec gave her an impatient look. "She is my responsibility, Molly. I need to know if she's going to do anything stupid."

Molly raised her eyebrow, looking unimpressed at his speech. "If you're asking me if she's going to hurt herself, then I would tell you it's highly unlikely."

The relief hit pretty hard, but he just gave her a nod. She looked at him thoughtfully. "She's pretty closed off, wouldn't talk about much. I think she's buried it all deep."

That didn't sound healthy. He should know, he was the king of burying shit.

"This isn't something you get over easily, certainly not just with one session."

"You coming out here regularly might garner attention."

She nodded. "I can do Skype sessions if need be, you can talk to her about that. Do you know what triggered the panic attack?"

"Triggered it?"

"Often there's a trigger. Something that sets them off. Maybe a loud noise or an image of something that reminds the person of their trauma. For some it's a certain scent."

"No. I don't know." But he could try and figure it out, prevent it from happening again.

"I can prescribe drugs to help with the symptoms. And hopefully she'll continue our sessions. Mia went through something horrific. She needs help to cope with that. To learn to live with it. She's lonely. She's scared. She could do with a friend. And considering she's a sub, she could also use a Dom."

"Who says she's a sub?"

"Don't play that game with me. We both know she is." Molly gave him a look.

"Don't you think she has enough going on right now?"

"Maybe it could help her cope with everything."

"She can't go to the club to play. She's not leaving the ranch." And he didn't like the idea of her going anywhere without him.

"Hmm, too bad there's no one around to help her explore her submissive side," she said.

He narrowed his gaze. "I don't teach inexperienced subs."

"We all started somewhere. There was a day when you didn't know anything about being a Dominant. Someone taught you, right? Maybe you could teach her about being a sub."

"That's not my job here."

Molly studied him for a moment then nodded. "Fine. I get it."

Oh, he doubted it.

"Just, treat her kindly, all right? She's strong, that's clear to see. But she's dealing with a hell of a lot. Her tendency is to put other people first, and I don't think she's very good at asking for what she needs. She could really use someone looking out for her."

Before he could say anything else, she got in her car and closed the door. He found himself staring after her as she drove away, her little car banging up and down over the potholes. She was driving too fast and he shook his head. He hoped she got pulled over by one of Jake's deputies and got her ass reddened by her husband when she got home. But he knew, like with most of the woman in Haven, that wouldn't deter her from doing what she thought she had to do.

The men in this town might think they were in charge, but it was the woman who had the ultimate control.

He ran his hand over his face, thinking over what she'd said. Hell. Like he didn't have enough going on in his life to worry about. He wished he'd never waited around to talk to Molly. What the hell was she trying to get him to do? Enter into some kind of BDSM therapy with Mia?

"Malone?" The low voice came from behind him.

He turned and saw her standing on the porch. He didn't really think about it, just raised his hand and cooked a finger at her.

"Everything okay?" she asked him as she got closer. He noted the way her shoulders had tensed. Molly was right. She was wound up tight. No wonder she couldn't sleep.

"Of course it is."

She's lonely.

And for some reason, he couldn't stand the idea of her being lonely. Or scared. Or locking everything down in order to protect herself.

"Did she tell you I'm a basket case?"

He scowled. "What did you say?"

Her eyes widened in surprise and she took a few steps back.

"Freeze."

She immediately stilled. Crap. He didn't want Molly to be right. Not that it was anything he didn't already know. He knew Mia was submissive. He also knew how delicate she was. He didn't deal with fragile. He wasn't a teacher. He didn't take new subs under his wing. He didn't heal lost little lambs who looked at him with big, wide eyes like he could fix everything.

"I don't want to hear you speaking about yourself like that again, understand me?" The temptation to add an "or else" was right there, but he couldn't do that unless he intended to follow through. "You went through something traumatic. It's all right to need help."

"Right," she said disbelievingly. "Got a lot of experience asking for help, have you?"

"We're not discussing me. Molly wants to continue your sessions via Skype. Have a think about it and let me know. You look tired. Why don't you go rest? I have to get to work."

He turned away, knowing he was being abrupt. But he had to get out of her presence before the temptation to take her into his arms and kiss that look of confusion and pain on her face became too strong to ignore.

What the hell was happening to his control?

9

Mia sat curled up in the corner of the sofa, the TV was muted with some romantic comedy playing on it. She wasn't really interested in watching it. Three days had passed since Molly had visited and she had barely seen Alec.

Maddox had gone into Haven and picked up her prescription. Raid had grabbed the things on her list while he was in Freestown getting supplies. She'd kept the list as small as possible.

It was best that Alec was keeping his distance. It wasn't like she needed him; she was fine as she was.

Sure, you are. Fine and lonely.

Molly had called, wanting to set up some Skype sessions, but she'd brushed her off. The last thing she wanted was to talk about what had happened. Bad enough she had to relive it each night in her nightmares.

Real healthy way to live, Mia.

The phone rang just as she was trying to decide if she was tired enough to go to bed. Not that it really mattered, she wouldn't actually be sleeping. She knew she shouldn't answer it. She'd been warned against doing that.

She let the phone ring. It stopped. She sighed. She'd actually considered answering just to have someone to talk to. Pathetic, huh?

It started up again. She frowned at it. Then it stopped. What was going on? It started ringing a third time and she knew she couldn't just sit there and ignore it. Alec was going to kill her, but she picked it up. She attempted to disguise her voice, making it low and gruff. "Hello?"

"Hello? Who's that? Mia, that you?" Jaret asked. Relief filled her.

"Jaret? What are you doing calling?" He was supposed to be with Gloria, his girlfriend tonight.

"Mia? You ill? You sounded funny before."

She sounded funny? He was slurring his words.

"Are you drunk? Jaret?" Alarm filled her. What was going on?

"Yeah, it's me." She glanced over at the clock on the wall. It was only ten. But then who was she to judge?

"You're not supposed to be answering the phone, darlin." He made a tsking sound.

"Jaret, did you just call to tell me that I shouldn't be answering the phone? Or did you actually want something?" She was damn sick of Malone men telling her what she could and couldn't do.

There was a beat of silence. And she could practically feel the surprise coming through the phone. No one was really used to her biting back. She just wanted to do what she had to in order to fit in. Do what she had to in order for them not to kick her out.

But she was growing tired of doing what everyone else wanted of her.

"You're gonna get in trouble with Alec."

"He'd have to be talking to me for me to get in trouble with him."

"Don't gotta talk to you to spank you. You know that's what he does, right? Spanks women. I'm thinkin' of takin' it up. Maybe if I'd spanked Gloria, she wouldn't have cheated on me."

Oh, hell. Gloria cheated on him? No wonder he sounded so awful.

"Is Alec there?" Jaret asked her.

"No, he went out about two hours ago. Did you try his cell?"

"Shit. He doesn't usually go to the club this early. I was hoping to catch him. Can't get hold of him there unless I go through Saxon. Fuck. Darlin', do me a favor and call one of those useless, bonehead brothers of mine. Get one of them to come to Freestown and pick me up, 'cept don't call West. He won't come. And don't bother with Tanner or Butch, they're pissed at me. Just call one of the others, okay?"

"Jaret, what happened?"

"Fucking Ron Bergman happened, that's what. Now I gotta get out of here before someone finds out what I did."

"What you did? Jesus, Jaret, what's going on?"

"May be in a spot of trouble. I'm usin' the phone at the 7-Eleven. Mine's busted. Jus' get Maddox or Raid, will ya?"

"I can't. They've all gone out." And she didn't have anyone's phone number. "West is here—"

"Not West. That fucker won't come. Shit. Goddamn, imma end up in jail. I hate jail. Nobody gots a sense of humor there. Come visit me, will ya, darlin'?"

Panic swirled in her gut. What had he done? "Stop being an idiot. I'll try to reach one of them. Where's the 7-Eleven?"

"It's the one two streets over from the main road. They'll know the one I'm talking about."

"Okay, just stay there, all right?"

"Okeydokey."

She hung up. Alec was out. He'd told her to call West on the short-wave radio if she needed something. Right. She walked into the kitchen where the short-wave radio was kept and picked it up.

"Yeah?" West's voice crackled through.

"Um, I just got a call from Jaret. He needs a lift back from Freestown."

"Tell him to call a taxi."

"Well, I think—"

"He dying?" West asked abruptly.

"No, I don't bel—"

"Then I don't care."

She knew it had been pointless to try. West never left the ranch. She guessed she could try the bunkhouse on the chance someone was home.

She walked into the mudroom and grabbed a flashlight then turned off the security system before making her way out to the bunkhouse.

As she drew closer, she could see there was a light burning in the main living room. She knocked loudly. She just hoped they were all dressed, unlike last time when she'd walked in to find Maddox streaking his way through the living room. Of course, she'd been the only one embarrassed by that. He'd stopped as soon as he'd seen her, then just stood there in all his naked glory and grinned at her.

She pushed the door open slowly, while keeping one hand over her eyes. She called out, but there was no reply.

Damn it, what was she going to do? She couldn't just leave Jaret at the 7-Eleven. But she had no way of reaching anyone but West. And he was no help. Anger at Alec filled her as she made her way back into the mudroom. This was all his fault, if he'd given her everyone's number then she wouldn't be in this predicament.

She made her way back to the main house and as she put the flashlight back on the shelf, she looked at the keys hanging there.

She could take one of the ranch trucks. She bit her lip. Alec would kill her if she left the ranch. But she'd only go to Freestown, pick up Jaret and then drive home. Maybe he wouldn't even know. She wouldn't get out of the truck and she'd wear a hoodie. No one would see her.

Trying to ignore the voice screaming at her that this was a bad fucking idea, she snatched up a set of keys.

And if Alec did find out, well, she'd just point out how it was all his fault.

Yep, there was a failproof plan if ever she'd had one.

It was a really stupid idea.

She knew it was. And yet as she approached the gates at the end of the driveway, she knew she wasn't going to turn back. Shit. What if she needed a code to get out? But, as she got closer, the gates opened automatically.

Okay. That was cool.

Alec was going to flip when he found out. What if he kicked her off the ranch? She was breaking one of his precious rules, after all. She tightened her hands around the steering wheel. But what kind of a friend would she be if she didn't try to help Jaret? He was one of the few friends she had.

"Stupid. Stupid."

Her only hope was that Alec wouldn't find out. She wasn't sure of the likelihood of that, considering Alec seemed to know everything. She turned right, towards Freestown. Luckily, that's the way she and Mike had come, so she knew where she was going.

She still took a couple of wrong turns, but gradually made her way to Freestown. It had taken about an hour. Jesus, she hoped Jaret was still at the 7-Eleven. Luckily, it wasn't a big city. She drove through the main shopping district, searching for the green and red sign. Damn it, she should have asked for better directions. After about fifteen minutes of driving around, she spotted one on the corner and quickly pulled into the lot.

But he didn't appear.

Had he gone? Was he still there? She bit at her lip and pulled her hood close, draping it around her face. There was no choice, she was going to have to get out and look for him. She got out of the truck.

Where the hell was he? She made her way into the store and the relief she felt as she spotted him made her feel a little light-headed.

"Jaret!" She stormed over to him.

He turned away from where he'd been perusing the slushies. "Hey there, darlin'. What are you doin' here?"

"I'm here to get you." She smacked him on the arm, then pulled her hand back shocked at herself. She never hit people.

"Oh, you weren't s'pposed to come. Alec's gonna have kittens."

"Well, I couldn't find anyone else, so I was your only option."

"What kind of slushy should I get?"

Was he kidding her?

She grabbed his arm and tugged. "Jaret, we have to go. I'll whip you up something when we get home."

"Whoop!" He turned and placed his arm over her shoulders, leaning so much of his weight on her that she stumbled. He managed to pull the hood off her face as he helped her stand.

"Damn it, Jaret."

"Sorry, darlin'. Bit unsteady on my feet."

She sighed and left the hood down as she helped him out to the truck.

"Gotta get out of here before the cops find me."

Her heart raced at those words. "What exactly did you do?"

He stumbled his way to the truck, trying to get in the driver's side. She reached out and tugged at his arm. "Jaret, you're drunk. You're not driving."

He let out a bark of laughter and gave a salute. "You are so right, darlin'. You are so right." She helped him around to the passenger side.

Somehow, even though he outweighed her by a good hundred pounds, she managed to get him inside the truck. He didn't bother to put on the belt. She grabbed it, and pulled it over him, locking it in place.

"Ah, you take such good care of me, darlin'. Wanna marry me?"

"No."

"Too bad. You've got a great ass."

She shook her head and just shut the door. She leaned against it, her legs wobbling. She was out of shape. And feeling a little weak and lightheaded. She definitely needed some more sleep and food.

"Idiot! The whole bunch of them are idiots!" She walked around to the driver's door and climbed in, turning on the truck.

"Course Alec would kill me if I made a move on you."

"Alec wouldn't care."

"Warned us all off you, course he cares. Way he looks at you, easy to see why. Like you're prime filet and he's been on a vegetarian diet for years."

"You're drunk and delusional," she muttered as she drove out of town and towards the ranch.

"Yes to the first, no to the second. Have to be blind not to see he wants you. Won't have you, though."

"Oh yeah, and why is that?" she asked.

"Cause Alec never lets himself feel anything. Not for his brothers, not for the women he fucks. And that's all he does. Fucks. Oh, he likes that dominance stuff. But he always chooses women he doesn't have to have feelings for. Cause he doesn't have feelings."

She wasn't certain about that. "Everyone has feelings."

He glanced over at her. "Sure. Unless they bury them deep. Unless they cut all ties to the people they're s'pposed to care about. He pushes everyone away. Has since . . ." his voice trailed off.

She glanced over, wanting to prod him, knowing it was none of her business. But had something happened to Alec that meant he now kept people at a distance?

"He's a bastard," she muttered more to herself than to Jaret.

"That he is. It's deliberate. If you hate him then you won't want to be around him, and he can live out his miserly existence alone."

That sounded awful. It was her worst nightmare. Having no one. And she was close to living it. But at least she had Mike.

"But he has all of you."

"Yeah, and I bet that just pisses him off. Has to keep us around. We're family. Doesn't mean he has to love us. Alec Malone doesn't love. He's loyal. He's bound by his own moral code. But he doesn't love."

She was quiet, thinking that over, and her anger against Alec dissipated. To be replaced with pity.

"Hey, this is one of the work trucks," Jaret said suddenly.

"Yeah, well, I don't have a vehicle. So I had to take one."

"No worries, darlin. Everything we have is yours."

It was a nice thought. But not true. She wasn't family. She was just an obligation.

"Just surprised to see you driving one, considering it's a stick shift. "

"I can drive a stick shift. Mike taught me when I was a teenager. So, you want to tell me what happened tonight? Did you fight with Gloria? Why would the cops be after you?"

"Gloria an' me are no more. She chose Ron Bergman over me. Can you believe that? Fucking Ron Bergman. I was trying to surprise her tonight. She wasn't 'pecting me. Walked in and there she was, fucking Ron Bergman on the table. I thought I was the only person to bend her over that table."

"Oh, Jaret. I'm so sorry."

"Nothing for you to be sorry about, darlin'." He yawned. She tried to take shallow breaths as the air in the cab became filled with the stench of whiskey. "Wasn't your fault she decided she'd rather have Ron Bergman's pencil dick over my anaconda-sized dick. Fuckin' Ron Bergman. Thinks he's a politician, you know? But he's just a forty-year-old mamma's boy. Still lives at home, for fucks sake. And, honest to God, his dick." He held up his pinky finger.

She bit back a smile. It wasn't really funny. And she knew he was using humor to hide how hurt he really was.

"What did you do?" she asked. "You didn't do anything stupid, did you?"

"Depends on your definition of stupid. May have slashed all the tires in his car and run my keys down the fancy paintwork, though."

She looked over at him in horror. "You didn't?"

"And, perhaps, written pencil deck in spray paint along the other side of his car."

Great. Shit. Her mind raced. "They're gonna know it was you."

"They have no proof," he said smugly.

"Yeah, only you just walked in on your girlfriend having sex with another man. And then that man's car gets trashed. Kind of too much of a coincidence for the cops not to put two and two together."

"Good point. All right, we need a story."

"A story? What do you mean, we need a story?"

"We just need to change the narrative. If the cops figure it out—"

"When they figure it out, they're not morons."

"Don't know about that. Two of the deputies are Bergman's cousins. So they're probably not too smart."

"Oh my God. You trashed the car of your girlfriend's lover, and two deputies on the police force are his cousins? Jaret, this is a problem."

"Never met a problem that can't be fixed," he told her. "This is what happened. I walked in on them fucking, Yelled a few insults. Stormed out of the house to get drunk. Which a number of people can corroborate. I went over to Patty's Bar. That Patty has got the best tits in the state. No offence."

"None taken," she said dryly. "Then what?"

"Well, after a few drinks I went back to Gloria's, grabbed some spray paint out of her garage and trashed his car, but we're not gonna say that."

"Good plan," she said sarcastically. "So what *are* we gonna say?"

And what the hell was this 'we' business?

"I never went to Gloria's. I called you 'cause I had too much to drink. You came and got me, drove me home, We got back at . . . " he looked blurrily at the dashboard. "What's the time?"

"You're looking at the gas gauge," she pointed out. "It's nearly midnight."

"Okay, cool, you picked me up at ten."

"And what about the clerk at the 7-Eleven? He saw us."

"Oh, I bribed him. He didn't see nothin'."

He'd bribed him? How the hell had he had the sense to do that when he could barely manage to walk on his own?

"See? All we had to do was change the narrative."

"Right. So when you say change the narrative, you mean lie. To the police."

"Exactly. Thanks, darlin'. You're the best."

He reached over and patted her thigh. She was too shocked to say anything for several long minutes. Then when she looked over at him, she realized he was sleeping. The idiot was sleeping. After everything that just happened, he decided to take a nap. He expected her to lie to the cops for him. She clenched her hands around the steering wheel as her breathing came in harsh pants. Okay, she had to get hold of herself. She pulled over to the side of the road for a minute, not trusting herself to drive while in the middle of an attack. Jaret didn't even stir as she pushed the seat of the truck back and then rested her head between her knees, trying to stop herself from passing out or vomiting. Finally, she managed to calm herself. Okay, she needed to snap out of it. Just because the police were probably going to come and talk to her, no reason to freak out. She just had to do what Jaret told her. Tell them she'd picked him up earlier than she actually had.

She could do this. She had this. He was a friend. Friends helped friends.

She was in so much trouble.

10

She was in so much trouble. Alex stormed his way out of the club. Not even bothering to answer Saxon as he called out to him. He strode his way towards his truck. She'd broken the rules.

When West had finally discovered she was missing, he'd called Saxons to tell him. What he wanted to know is why the hell she would leave the ranch? Her ass was toast. His hand itched with the need to spank her. How dare she disobey him? She'd not only put herself in danger, but she'd interrupted his scene at the club. He'd had to untie the delectable little sub he'd had bound to the St Andrews cross, and leave her with a monitor so he could grab his stuff and chase after a little brat who thought she got to disobey him.

Oh, she was going to find out very soon why it was never a good idea to go against him.

"Malone!" Saxon yelled, grabbing the door of his truck as he tried to slam it shut.

"I don't have time for this." He glared up at the club owner.

Saxon scowled. "Someone dying?"

"They will be soon," he said ominously.

Saxon spoke calmly, but there was a little twitch beside his right eye that betrayed his irritation. "You want to tell me what's going on?"

"None of your business."

Saxon crossed his arms over his chest. "You left in the middle of a scene."

"I apologized to Sarah. Find her someone else to take over. I'll make it up to her. Is that all? Couldn't we have had this conversation over the phone? I'm kind of busy."

Saxon narrowed his gaze, glaring down at him. "No, we couldn't fucking have this conversation on the phone, because you never pick up the damned phone. And I didn't come after you because I'm worried about Sarah. No doubt she's moved on by now."

Yeah. That's why he often chose her to play with. Because she never got attached. "I came out here to see if you're all right."

"Jesus, Aspen took your balls, didn't she?"

Saxon tensed. Stared down at Alec coldly. "You want to tread carefully when you talk about Aspen."

Everyone knew how protective Saxon was over his woman. Alec didn't usually back down or apologize but he did give a nod of acknowledgement. It was enough to make Saxon ease up a bit on the death stare.

"Right, now that that's solved." Alec reached out and grabbed hold of the door handle of his truck. "Get out of my way."

Saxon didn't move. Alec glared at him. "You want me to make you move?"

"Good luck with that," the other man drawled. "I know you like to do things on your own. You hold things close to your chest. But if you need some help, I'm here."

"I don't need any fucking help," Alec growled at him.

"Is that so?"

"All I need from you is for you to get out of my goddamn way."

Saxon backed off, his hands up in the air. "Fine. Go. God forbid I should offer to help the mighty Alec Malone."

Shit. "Look, it's a family matter."

Saxon nodded. "Got it. But the offer still stands. You need help. I'm here."

Alec closed the door, unsure what to say to that. He didn't make friends, deliberately kept people at arms' length. The very last thing he needed was anyone meddling in his business. And still, they offered to help him when they thought he needed it.

He left the parking lot of Saxon's and headed as fast as he dared towards the ranch. But it wasn't Saxon's problem. Or anyone else's. It was his.

And he intended to make sure she never disobeyed him again.

She made it safely home. But when she reached the ranch house, which seemed to have every light on, she found herself having to fight the urge to turn around and drive away.

"Oh, crap, what is he doing here?" She drummed her fingers against the steering wheel, staring up at the imposing figure who was standing on the porch at the top of the stairs, his hands on his hips, no doubt glaring daggers at her.

Jaret actually woke up, miracle of miracles. "We home? Thanks, darlin'."

"We're not the only ones who are home," she warned. She knew she couldn't stay there indefinitely, but it was damn tempting to try. She gulped. "I'm in big trouble."

"Huh?" Jaret asked, looking over at her. He yawned.

"You stink of whiskey," she told him.

He shrugged. "Gotta go to bed." He fumbled with his seatbelt latch then reached for the door, opening it and stumbling out onto the ground. She quickly climbed out and went around to help him.

Jaret put his arm around her shoulders and nearly toppled her over.

"A little help here?" she snapped at Alec. What was he doing, just standing there?

"Why?"

"Because I need to get him to bed and he weighs a ton," she said with exasperation. Wasn't it obvious?

"He got himself into this state, he can make his own way to bed or sleep outside. I don't care."

"Wow, you are really going for brother of the year, aren't you?"

Alec started down the steps and she gulped, standing her ground only because if she didn't, she was pretty certain Jaret was going to land on his face.

"I suggest you start rethinking the tone you use with me," Alec said in a low voice. "I am not happy with you nor him right now."

"Got that. I'm not stupid. But anytime now, there's going to be some cops turning up on your doorstep, wanting to know if Jaret destroyed the car of the guy who he caught fucking his girlfriend, and I figure it might not look good if he's found sleeping off his hangover on the front lawn. Not to mention he could get run over."

She heaved in a deep breath and tried to balance herself as Jaret rested more of his weight on her.

Alec muttered something under his breath. But he reached for Jaret and hauled him over his shoulders in a fireman's carry. Wow, he didn't appear winded at all as he carried his brother inside. He turned sideways as he moved through the front door, and she had to quickly grab Jaret's head to stop it being smashed against the doorframe. Alec obviously didn't care much about being gentle. Her fingers scrapped along the jamb and she hissed in a pained breath.

"What?" Alec half-turned.

"Nothing," she said hastily.

"Good. You've caused me enough fucking problems tonight. I don't need any more. So you do exactly what I tell you, understand me?"

"Yes. Sure." He'd always intimidated her, but right now he was scaring that shit out of her.

"Go and make some coffee and get some water. We need to sober him up." He strode off into the living room. She heard a crashing noise and winced, hoping that wasn't Jaret's head. Then she raced off to grab coffee and water.

By the time she returned to the living area, Alec had laid his brother on the couch and was pulling off his boots.

"What the fuck happened?" he demanded of her.

"Oh, um, well . . . "

"Well, what?" he asked, clearly at the end of his patience.

"I got a call from Jaret. He needed to be picked up. He was too drunk to drive and he didn't have his phone to call anyone else."

"And?"

She licked her lips. "And I couldn't find anyone. I don't have their cell numbers."

"You could have used the radio to call West."

"I did. He wouldn't go get him," she pointed out reasonably.

Alec stood, looming over her. *Stand your ground. Don't show him you're afraid.*

"And you thought it would be smart to take one of the ranch trucks and go pick him up yourself? You didn't even leave a note!"

"I didn't think anyone would notice I was gone."

He looked at her like she was an idiot.

"He needed help. He'd walked in on Gloria fucking some guy and he was torn up. So he went and got drunk and then he did something stupid . . . "

"What stupid thing did he do?" Alec asked quietly. "Please don't tell me he fucking killed him?"

Really? That's where his mind went first? To murder?

"No, he didn't kill him. He destroyed his car."

"That's all?"

That's all? That's all? That was not the response she was expecting.

Alec moved towards Jaret and then slapped him. Hard. Jaret groaned and she jumped forward, inserting himself between Alec and Jaret.

"What the hell do you think you're doing?" she yelled.

"You want to get out of my way now," Alec commanded in a low, deep voice that sent chills down her spine.

She wanted to move. Every cell in her body screamed at her to obey the very scary man glaring down at her. It would be the smart thing to do. The sensible thing to do. Instead, she shook her head.

Seemed she just wasn't that smart.

ALEC GLARED down at the tiny woman as she dared to shake her head at him. Grown men had been known to run the other way when they saw him coming. And here was this little thing standing against him? And why? To defend his brother?

"What the fuck?" Jaret's voice reached him as he continued to scowl down at Mia.

He was starting to revise her nickname. He should just call her headache. That's all she'd been to him. Oh, she'd lulled him into a false sense of security for those first couple of weeks, tiptoeing around the house, not saying boo. But as she'd settled in and felt safer, the real problems had begun.

"Who the fuck hit me?" Jaret grumbled.

"I fucking hit you, you idiot," Alec snapped at him. "And I'll do it again if you don't get some damn coffee inside you. Now. We need you sober before the cops arrive."

"What? Why? What'd I do?" He sat up then slumped back. "Fuck, too much to drink. Got to sleep."

Alec had run out of patience. He wasn't even going to ask, well demand, anymore. He simply reached out and grabbed Mia around the waist, moving her out of his way.

"Hey! Let me down, you brute!"

He set her down, turning so he loomed over her. "Brute? Honey, you haven't even seen me in brute-mode yet. Keep pushing and you will. Now, get your butt upstairs, brush your teeth, put your pajamas on and get your ass into bed and stay there."

Her hands went to her hips, her eyes sparking with temper. Damn, she was gorgeous.

"I am not a child."

"No?" he drawled. "Tell me, what rule did I give you when you came here?"

"There was so many it's hard to remember."

"Oh, you don't want to push me tonight, little one," he warned, taking delight in the way she swallowed nervously. "You know what rule I'm talking about. What was it that I expressly forbid you from doing?"

"I don't like the word forbid."

"Tough. What was the rule?"

She bit at her lip then let out a huff of breath. "You said I wasn't to leave the ranch."

"And what did you do tonight?" he asked in a dark voice.

He didn't hold back. He released the side of him he usually kept buried. The uncivilized part that had served him well in his old life. Part of him recognized it wasn't quite fair to her. She was an innocent. But the idea of her putting herself in danger made him furious. He needed to ensure that the next time she thought about disobeying him, she would stop and remember this.

"What did you do?" he repeated with a bit more of a snap.

"Alec, stop," Jaret said, sounding more sober than he'd expected.

"Stay out of this," Alec told him. "You've done more than enough damage tonight. I'll be talking to you about that later."

"I left the ranch without permission," she said in a quiet voice.

"That's right. And you put yourself in danger. What if someone had seen you? What if that someone had ties to Angelo? What happens if they turn up here looking for you?"

"The odds of that happening—"

"I didn't ask for the odds. My job is to keep you safe until the trial. Nothing more or less. You staying on this ranch is the best way to secure that. You going rogue and doing whatever the fuck you want is going to get you killed. So, get your ass upstairs and into bed."

As she turned away, he had to fight the urge to call her back. To apologize.

Instead, he let her go.

SHE WOKE up feeling worse than when she'd gone to bed. Not that she was actually in bed. She glanced around the closet she'd commandeered as a bed. She was so fucked up.

She yawned. She'd only had a few hours' sleep. And those hours had been broken up with nightmares.

She knew she'd messed up last night. But she'd been trying to help Jaret. And the likelihood of anyone seeing her had been pretty slim, let alone anyone who might have ties to Angelo. Alec hadn't needed to speak to her that way. She wasn't an idiot. She'd made a mistake, but she'd had a good reason.

She dressed and started down the stairs. She'd slept in, but it was Sunday. She didn't make breakfast on Sundays. The cops hadn't turned up last night, which had kind of surprised her. She guessed maybe Bergman hadn't seen his car yet.

She walked into the kitchen and poured herself some coffee.

"Good morning."

She gasped, turning to find Alec standing in the doorway. His face was unreadable.

"Shit. You scared me." She placed her hand on her racing heart.

"When you've had some breakfast, come to my office. I want to talk with you."

Oh. Great. That didn't sound ominous at all. And even if she'd felt like breakfast before, she didn't think she could eat now. Her stomach was in a knot. She sat the coffee down. Was he going to kick her off the ranch? He wouldn't, would he? She'd been doing Jaret a favor. She'd taken precautions. She hadn't just left to go shopping or out for coffee or anything like that.

He wouldn't make her leave. She had nowhere to go. And besides that, she felt safe there. She took a deep breath then let it out slowly.

No sense putting it off. Waiting wasn't going to change anything. Time to face the dragon in his lair. She made her way down the hall to his office. The door was slightly ajar, so she gave a small knock and stepped in.

He glanced up with a frown. "Thought I said to come after you'd had breakfast."

"I'm not hungry."

His gaze narrowed. "You're losing weight. I told you the other day that I expect you to eat more."

"You're not in charge of what I eat. I'm just a body to protect, remember? An obligation."

"You are an obligation. A responsibility. But you're wrong if you think I'm not totally in charge of you. Keeping you alive until the trial means making certain you're healthy. Body and mind."

She flushed at the reminder of her panic attack the other night. "Have the cops been here yet? How's Jaret?"

"He's still sleeping off his hangover in one of the bedrooms upstairs. The cops haven't arrived. Yet."

"What are you going to say to them? Jaret said that he wanted me to . . . um, lie and say that I picked him up earlier than I did."

"You won't be doing that," he said firmly.

"I won't? But—"

"This is not something you need to worry about. I'll take care of it. What you do need to worry about is what happens to you next."

"What do you mean?"

There was a knock on the door. West stuck his head in. "Cops are here."

Alec just nodded as West disappeared.

He stood up and started towards the door. "Stay here."

"Wait," she called out. "What should I say to them?"

He sighed and looked back at her. "You're not saying anything, because you're not going to speak to them. You were never there. You aren't even here, so how could you have been there last night?"

"That's some messed up logic," she muttered. "Malone—"

"Should have known you were gonna give me trouble first time I saw you."

"What? I haven't been any trouble." She'd done her best not to create trouble. All right, some things had happened that weren't her fault, but he couldn't hold them against her.

"Delusional too."

"Malone." She stomped her foot in frustration. She hadn't done that since she was a toddler. Felt kind of satisfying, though. Why wouldn't he give her a straight answer? Was he being deliberately annoying?

Of course he was being deliberately annoying. Why, she had no idea. Maybe he liked watching her head explode.

In what seemed like the blink of an eye he'd moved across the room and was standing in front of her. No, looming over her was more accurate. He was trying to intimidate her.

He was doing a good job.

She gulped, hoping he couldn't hear it.

"Do you know what my job is?"

How was this relevant? "Um . . . you're a rancher?"

He snorted. "Not that. What is my job when it comes to our arrangement?"

"Well, I imagine, is it to keep me alive?"

"I keep you alive. What's your job?"

"To feed your brothers?"

"Jesus, she still doesn't get it," he muttered to himself.

"There's no need to be rude."

He narrowed his gaze. "Didn't see the attitude before. Couldn't understand how you'd survived what you had, but it's there. But there's one thing you haven't learned."

"What's that?"

"Your job is to obey me. I keep you alive. You obey me. Got it?"

What she got was that he was an ass. An arrogant jerk. Handsome, sure. But that didn't make up for him being a cretin. And he thought she had attitude? He should look in the mirror. Not that she had the balls to say that to his face.

"Got it, Calamity Jane?"

She ground her teeth together. "Got it."

"You're gonna stay in here and you're gonna stay quiet. You can't do that, tell me now and I'll get my handcuffs out and cuff you to the desk."

She looked over at the enormous desk that probably weighed five times what she did. Knowing what he was, she probably wouldn't be the first woman to be handcuffed to it.

She wanted to tell herself that the hot poker that fired through her gut was disgust. But it wasn't, it was jealousy. She did not want to be jealous of any woman who had been with the macho, maddening Alec Malone.

"Don't think the cops will be too happy to find me handcuffed to your desk," she pointed out.

"They'd never find you." He turned his back on her, as though completely confident she would toe the line like a good little girl.

Which, unfortunately, was exactly what she was going to do.

"They would if I yelled," she muttered, not exactly meaning him to hear.

"What makes you think I wouldn't gag you as well?" he called back. Then he opened the door and turned to grin at her. An actual grin. One that even reached his eyes, that turned them from hard and cold into melt-in-your-mouth chocolate. "And with my reputation, babe, anyone finds you bound and gagged in my office, they're gonna think you want to be there."

He left. Shutting the door quietly behind him. And she was left standing there with absolutely no comeback to that. She was so totally out of her league.

She slumped down onto the leather sofa and looked around her. She started to feel a bit better as she realized that while she might have just been told to stay out of sight, like a naughty child not allowed to go to the adult's party, she'd also been left, alone, in the most interesting room in the house.

She shouldn't. It was wrong. It was an invasion of privacy.

But when was she ever going to have an opportunity to snoop like this again?

TWENTY MINUTES LATER, she was lying on the sofa on her back, staring at the ceiling when the door to the office opened. She didn't even turn her head as she felt him approach.

He stood next to the sofa. There was silence. A lot of silence.

Aw, shit. She hated silence. *Say something smart. Something that will show him you don't give a shit about him and his orders.*

"Your ceiling needs a coat of paint."

Hmm, that wasn't quite what she'd been aiming for.

She sighed. Then looked up at him. One eyebrow was raised as he stared down at her. There was amusement in his eyes.

Great, now she'd entertained him.

"I don't like you right now." And now she was acting like a teenager.

"So noted."

She let out a low noise of frustration. Then she swung her legs around. "Cops gone?"

"Yes."

"Anything I need to worry about?"

"I would tell you if there was." He was watching her with interest now. She didn't like it. Then she saw him take a sweeping glance around the office. She tensed. She'd left no sign of her snooping. She knew she hadn't, and yet, she almost felt like he knew.

Time to leave.

"I have some laundry to do." She tried to stand. He put his hand on her shoulder and pushed her back. It wasn't a hard push. In fact, he barely exerted any pressure. But it was very clear he wasn't ready to let her leave.

Shit.

"Malone, I—"

"Have fun snooping?" he asked.

Fuck.

When in trouble, she was fond of the ABDs. Avoid. Bluff. Deny.

"Excuse me?" she asked huffily. "I'm sure I don't know what you mean."

"You think I don't know when someone has rifled through my stuff."

She moved her gaze around the room again, coming back to meet his amused one. What did he find so funny?

"I'm insulted you think I would snoop."

He leaned in, all humor vanishing. "And I'm insulted that the woman I take into my home, putting everyone on this ranch in danger in order to protect, proceeds to disobey and lie to me."

Oh. Fuck.

It seemed all that amusement at her expense was just a front. Because he was really, really angry. Scratch that, he was furious.

"I'm sorry. I didn't find anything."

"Of course not, I'm no amateur."

She had no idea what he meant by that. Amateur what? No amateur at hiding shit? So he did have stuff to hide, she knew it. No one was as closed off as he was without a reason.

"Earth to Calamity Jane."

"Stop calling me that."

He placed his hands on his hips, still standing over her. "Do not ever go through my stuff again, understand?"

She nodded hastily.

"You want to know something, ask."

Really? Seriously? "And you'll answer?"

"Didn't say that. But then you'll know if it's something I want you to know, won't you? You don't get to know everything, haven't earned that. Likely never will. My shit is mine."

She couldn't argue with that. They were his secrets. He didn't want to share them, then that was his prerogative. They weren't in a relationship. Just because he knew all her crap didn't mean he had to reciprocate. And she got that she'd messed up. She wouldn't like it if someone went snooping around in her stuff.

"I really am sorry," she told him. "That was wrong of me."

He just gave a short nod. "On to the next topic."

She let out a breath, feeling very tired for someone who'd only gotten up a couple of hours ago.

"You broke my rule, Mia."

His voice was icy. Goosebumps covered her skin. A few days ago, that voice would have sent her running. But she'd had enough. After the night she'd had and the hell of the past few days, she'd had enough.

"And no one disobeys the mighty Alec Malone's rules. King of all he surveys," she said sarcastically.

He didn't look surprised. Didn't react at all other than to raise one imperious eyebrow. "Not if they're smart, they don't. Question is, what sort of punishment comes with breaking my law?"

Okay, so maybe she was starting to feel a little intimidated.

"You can't just punish me for breaking one of your palatine rules. I was helping your brother, for God's sake."

"My brothers can take care of themselves. They are not tiny little pixies with no sense of self-preservation. They also do not have a damn hit man chasing after their asses."

"With the shit they get up to, it's a wonder," she muttered.

This time both eyebrows rose. Uh-oh. "I am not happy with this new attitude."

"Why? Because I don't jump to do your bidding?" *Getting really brave now, aren't you?*

"No." He leaned down and grabbed her around the waist, holding her up in the air. Her feet were dangling off the ground. Holy fuck. She knew he was strong, but wow. He shook her. "Because it's going to get you damn well killed. Is that what you want?"

"Of course it's not what I want!"

He set her on her feet. "Then what the fuck were you thinking?"

Okay, yeah, not mad. He was furious. Absolutely down to his bones furious. And she didn't get why. Okay, she understood she'd disobeyed his rule. But it was her ass on the line if she got caught —unless the hit man came here and shot everyone. Then she'd be responsible for everyone's death on this ranch.

Suddenly, she wasn't feeling so self-righteous or cocky.

"It won't happen again."

"Damn straight it won't happen again. I'm going to make sure of that."

All right, she didn't like the sound of that.

"From now on, because you can no longer be trusted, the keys to all vehicles get locked away where you can't get to them. Because you can no longer be trusted, Maddox has been sent into Freestown to sort out a GPS tracker for you. Now, because you can't be trusted to follow the rules, I'm going to know where you are every minute of every day."

She scowled up at him. "You're not a damn king, you're a dictator."

"That's right, baby girl. I'm also judge, jury, and executioner. You did the crime, now you pay for it. What did I tell you would happen if you disobeyed me?"

She froze. She remembered that conversation all too clearly. Her heart stopped then raced, making her feel ill. Her head spun.

"I was helping your brother."

"They're big boys. You are not here to help them. You can feed them, befriend them, try to tame them—and good luck with that —but you do not put yourself in danger for them. They get into trouble they can't get out of, they come to me. Believe me, I'm much better equipped to handle that shit than you are."

Of that, she had no doubt.

"You weren't here."

"No. I was busy. I had a nice little sub naked and tied to a St. Andrews cross. I was about to take a flogger to her ass when I was called away because you'd disappeared. You ruined my scene, Calamity Jane."

"I'm so sorry," she said sarcastically. Who cared about his ruined scene? Only, the image he'd built in her head was a bit too hard for her to shake. Because instead of some faceless, nameless sub she'd inserted herself into that picture. It was her that was tied naked to that St. Andrews cross, about to be flogged.

Holy shit. What was she thinking? That would hurt, right?

"It wasn't my fault your scene was ruined, Jaret—"

"Was not dead, maimed, or lying in a hospital bed. Which are about the only reasons I'd leave a scene for one of my brothers. You are the reason I had to leave. And you are now going to pay the piper."

He wasn't a damn piper he was Satan in cowboy boots.

"You're going to make me leave?" She'd have to call Mike, get him to come and get her. "Okay, I'll go pack."

She felt numb. She didn't know what she was going to do. She couldn't imagine not being here. It had only been a few weeks, but it was now home. She moved past him, walking towards the door.

"I'm not kicking you out, Mia. Why would I get a GPS tracker for you if I was going to make you go?"

She twirled, the room spinning around her sickeningly. Maybe she should have had some breakfast.

"Okay . . . okay . . . that's good. I promise I won't do anything like that again. No leaving the ranch. I don't even want to leave. Didn't want to go in the first place, but Jaret was in a mess and I care about him . . . and okay, won't happen again. I promise."

"That's good to know."

She turned to walk away again. All right, maybe he wasn't the complete asshole she'd thought he was. She was getting a second chance.

"I didn't give you permission to leave, Calamity Jane."

What? For real? She swung around, holding onto her temper by a thread.

"I don't need your permission to leave a room."

He moved to his desk and leaned back against it. Why the hell did he have to look so freaking gorgeous? It was killing her.

"But you do, because I didn't say you weren't going to get punished. Your promises don't mean much since you promised to obey the rules in the first place. So now I'm going to have to do something to make sure that you remember the consequences of disobeying me."

She didn't like the sound of that.

"Oh, yeah, what you going to do? Lock me in my room?" She tried to sound tough. But the shaking in her voice betrayed her.

His smile reached his eyes this time.

"Oh, no, it's gone far beyond that. I'm going to spank you."

11

He watched as understanding dawned over her face and braced himself for impact. He expected temper. Denial. Maybe even an apology. He didn't much believe in apologies. It was all too easy to say sorry. If you fucked up and wanted to make something right, actions spoke louder than words.

But her reaction was none of those, and therefore completely unexpected.

She laughed.

Now, Alec had done a lot in his life. Seen a lot. He'd grown up in hell, figured his way out, got his brothers out and kept them alive, which was no mean feat. He was used to being in control. Everywhere. That control bled over into every aspect of his life, from sex to family to the ranch.

But with her, he didn't feel quite in control. And he didn't like it. She was a wildcard. At times, she seemed timid and shy. Although he was beginning to see that side of her less and less. His brothers had been running wild since they were born. She'd only been here a few weeks and she had them eating dinner in the dining room, taking their dirty boots off at the door, hell they even swore less when she was around.

Most women, hell, most men would cave in the face of his anger. Yet, she'd stood there and called him a dictator—which he was—and she'd stood up to him. He didn't like it. But he kind of admired it.

She wasn't his type. Yet, she filled his thoughts far more than he would have liked. And the other night, after her panic attack, when he'd held her all night . . .

Yeah, that had felt fucking good.

But girls like Mia weren't for men like him. He didn't deserve sweetness and light. He'd tarnish it. Turn it into something dark. Something he didn't deserve to be around.

And that wouldn't be fair. Mia deserved a happy ever after. To live in some cute little house in the suburbs with a puppy, three crazy kids, and a husband who lit up when she came into the room.

And that's what she'd get. This momentary shit in her life would go. He'd see to that.

Which is why he should push her out that door now.

Only, she was laughing. And much as he loved the sound, he knew it for what it was. A dare.

And no one ever dared Alec Malone.

"You think that's funny?" he growled when her laughter died down enough that she could gasp in some air. She was bent over at the waist, her hand pressed to her side as though laughing so hard had given her a stitch. Tears dripped down her cheeks. She wiped at them as she stared up at him.

"Oh, no, I don't think it's funny. I think it's fucking hilarious. You're going to spank me. Of course you are. Because I've fallen into some alternate reality where my boss and coworkers are all killed in some sort of fucking mob deal gone wrong. I should have been there, you know. That night, I should have fucking been there. But I messed up the crème brûlée. I messed up the crème brûlée and the head chef, who, by the way, was a complete fucking ass, yelled at me, then he threw the crème brûlée at me. So James, my boss, sent me home. He pretended it was a punishment to the head chef, Jacques, *Jacques* . . . like he was actually French. Oh, he liked to use a fake French accent, but I heard him talking on the phone one day while he was out back having a cigarette and that accent was pure southern."

As she talked, she strode back and forth, a bundle of energy. Her arms moved around. Even her hair came to life, bouncing along her back as she moved.

"He saw me. Think that's why he hated me. I knew his secret. Also, I can't make fucking crème brûlée. I don't know why. It just never seemed to work. Maybe I should have . . ."

"You were saying your boss sent you home?" He was loath to speak up because he was worried she'd shut down and she needed to get this shit out. It was eating her up. He knew she hadn't told Molly much. And she'd refused any Skype sessions. She needed to purge. He knew all the details already, had read all the reports even seen the video footage of her telling the detectives covering the case what had happened. But she didn't know that. And if he let her, she'd probably still be talking about damn crème brûlée twenty minutes from now.

"What? Huh, yeah, James is a nice guy." She stopped. Took a deep breath. "*Was* a good guy. Or I thought he was. He knew Jacques would make the rest of my night hell. So he sent me home. He told me to go have dinner on him and then come back tomorrow early and practice making crème brûlée. I went out, had dinner, and then I was heading home when I realized I was missing my phone. The restaurant was closed, but I knew everyone would be cleaning up for the night. I snuck in the back way, not wanting to see Jacques. Or anyone else. The quiet should have been a clue, right? It should have been a big fucking clue, but I was too stupid to figure that out."

"Enough," he told her sharply.

"Enough what?" She turned her face to him. Fuck. He didn't like the tears dripping down her cheeks, the way her freckles stood out against her pale cheeks or the dark marks under her eyes that spoke of too many sleepless nights. He didn't like that it was obvious she'd lost weight since that video footage he'd watched of her. He definitely didn't like that she'd lost weight and more sleep since coming here.

She was under his care.

Fuck. Why had he agreed to this? He should call Jardin tell him to get down here and sort his own shit out, take the responsibility off Alec's hands.

That was what he should do.

But he knew he wouldn't. Because she had attitude and backbone. And she had his brothers taking their damn dirty boots off.

He was so fucked.

"Enough putting yourself down."

"Another of your rules, oh, great one?"

"You ought to take some care, little girl," he said in a low voice that made her eyes widen. She needed to know he wasn't going to roll over and let her get away with whatever shit she wanted to. She may have done something to his brothers, but he was a whole different kettle of fish.

Whatever the fuck a kettle of fish was.

But instead of looking away or backing down, she just glared up at him. "Listen, you can tell me what to do, make me do it, but you can't tell me what to think."

We'll see about that.

"Tell me what happened when you went in to get your phone."

"I'm done talking. I have a headache; I'm going to lay down."

"I'm sorry you have a headache," he said solicitously. "You can certainly have some time to lay down, we can take care of your punishment later when you're feeling better."

She froze. "You cannot be serious."

"I am."

She ran her fingers through her hair. "What is wrong with you? What is wrong with me? Why am I staying here? Why don't I want to leave? I should hate it here. I should hate you. You go from cold to caring to cold again and now you're . . . you're threatening to spank me. What did I do to deserve this? I'm a good person. I pay my taxes on time. I don't lie. I hold the door open for people. I always use my manners. I was living a safe, boring little life until some monster who had a beef with my boss came in and shot five people in the head. Just like that. Boom! Gone."

Suddenly, she broke into hysterical laughter

And he'd had enough.

OOMPH.

He grabbed hold of her arm, pulling her into him. It took her by surprise, she hadn't even seen him move, and it took a moment for her to realize she was plastered against him, front to front. He wrapped his hand around the nape of her neck and gave a slight squeeze.

"Baby. Calm down."

Calm down? She was calm. Because rational, calm people laughed after telling someone how their coworkers had all been shot, right?

Great. He probably thought she'd lost her mind.

"Sh. Baby. It's okay."

She forced herself to quieten. Baby. She liked when he called her baby. Way better than Calamity Jane. No one wanted to be thought of as a walking calamity, causing chaos to break out wherever she went.

Although sometimes he called her babe. That was nice too. Different from baby. Baby was said in a softer voice. It made her feel like she meant something to him. Like he cared. Babe was usually said in a sexier voice. Rougher. Sometimes tinged with impatience.

And she found herself calming down. She wasn't sure if it was the touch, his words or his voice. But the tension that had her stomach tied in knots faded, her heart was still beating too fast, but for an entirely different reason.

Damn he was sexy.

He lifted one eyebrow. "Babe. You gotta stop staring at me like that."

There it was. Babe. Sexy. Yum. "Why?"

She wasn't quite sure what he meant about the way she was staring at him. She was just looking up at him. That's what you did when someone was holding you pressed against them. You looked, right?

"Because you stare at me like I'm your favorite treat and I'm gonna take up the invitation in your eyes. And I'm pretty sure you're not ready for what will happen if I do that."

"I . . . there is no invitation in my eyes."

"No?" He leaned in close, until she could feel his breath against her lips. That shouldn't be sexy. Her whole body shouldn't shiver with how close he was. "You got to learn not to dare me."

That hadn't been a dare, had it?

And then she didn't care. She didn't care because his mouth was on hers, and, dear Lord, she was certain she was having an out-of-body experience. His free hand moved to her ass, cupping it. No one had ever squeezed her butt while kissing her.

She melted against him. Her panties grew wet. Her mouth

opened on a sigh, and allowed him in. He ravished. He conquered. And, oh, did she let him. Hell, she all but wrote him an invitation.

Please, fuck me. Fuck me hard. Now.

He pulled her up onto her tiptoes, his hand under her ass. He was firmly in control and instead of freaking out, she found herself craving it. She wrapped her arms around his neck and tried to give back as good as she got. She had no doubt he was way more experienced than she was, and she wanted to do her share.

Then he smacked his hand down on her ass. She gasped. He kept kissing her. But his hand landed again.

She should knee him in the nuts. Pull away and tell him off. And maybe she would have, if each smack to her butt hadn't made her clit throb even harder. The slight warmth, only slight because she was wearing jeans after all, filled her entire body.

Okay, maybe this spanking thing wasn't so bad. What had she been arguing about? If he wanted to spank her while kissing her then maybe she wouldn't complain. Too much.

Then he drew back, staring down at her with a devilish glint in his gaze.

"And that is why you should never dare me. Now take those jeans off and bend over my desk. Grasp the other side with your hands and keep them there. Since this is your first spanking, I'm only going to use my hand on you. You can thank me later."

Wait . . . what? He'd just gone from kissing her like he wanted to devour her to barking out orders about taking off her jeans and bending over his desk and . . . she stared up at him in horror. "You want me to bend over your desk so you can spank me?"

"Yes."

The ice king was back. She didn't like it. She wanted the man who'd kissed her like she was the very breath he needed to survive.

"You just spanked me!"

He looked momentarily confused. Then understanding moved

over his face. He let out a bark of laughter. "That? Babe, that was not a spanking. And if you think it was then you are in for one hell of a shock. Did your parents never spank you as a child?"

"Certainly not."

"Hmm, so that's where things went wrong."

"There is nothing wrong with the way my parents raised me." She put her hands on her hips as she glared up at him. "And I am not bending over your desk so you can slap my ass. And I am certainly never going to thank you for it."

"Hmm, maybe I won't get the thank you. But you are getting the spanking."

No. No. No. Yes. No.

She was turning into a lunatic. Because only a lunatic would actually consider being spanked by this man. Sure, she'd kind of liked those couple of slaps to her ass. But he wasn't talking about play. This wasn't a scene in a club. This was punishment, pure and simple. And she wasn't going to agree to that.

She'd had less than a handful of lovers in her life, and not one of them had anything on Malone. Not one of them would have grabbed her and told in that low, commanding voice to calm down. They certainly wouldn't have kissed her the way he had. And no one had ever, *ever*, smacked her ass. So why the hell was that such a turn on?

Only one explanation for it. She was going insane.

"And if I say no?"

"Are you saying no?"

"I'm asking what happens if I do?"

"You go upstairs and pack up your stuff and get ready for your cousin to come and get you."

"Nice. Either I let you spank me, or you kick me out. That's blackmail."

"No, that's an ultimatum."

"Well, pardon me for getting my threats mixed up. This is not exactly a situation I'm used to. I'm not used to men who can walk into a room and shoot innocent people in the head. Men who murder an innocent woman, even if she is a rotten clothing thief, in the head. And I'm not used to men who give ultimatums like that."

"You did not just compare me to a murderer," he said coldly.

Oh. She might have. Shit. What was she going to do?

"Have you ever thought that you might need it?"

She looked over at him. She hated that he looked so at ease. As though he hadn't just laid this huge stipulation at her feet. As though she wasn't stuck between a rock and a hard place because of him.

She tried to ignore the voice in her head telling her she'd known there would be consequences when she chose to leave the ranch last night. Sure, she hadn't realized he'd want to spank her. But she knew there would be a price to pay. And knowing that, she'd still chosen to go.

Yeah, she did her best to ignore that voice.

"What do you mean I might need it? Why would you think I would need a spanking? I'm not one of your subs.

"No, you're not. They'd never dare disobey me."

Great she was just lacking all the way around, wasn't she?

"I'm talking about the fact that you're wound up tighter than a coil about to spring. Because you can't sleep, because you have panic attacks—"

"You think a spanking is going to help my PTSD? Did Molly talk to you about this? What is this? BDSM psychology 101?"

He raised an eyebrow. "You need a way to release all that tension. Someone to watch over you. Take care of you for a change. You're going to self-destruct if you can't find a way to let the pressure out. To free some of that poison building inside you."

"I don't know what you mean."

"Really? So there's not a tight knot in your stomach, a place where you've shoved all your memories of that night, your feelings, your fear?"

Oh, God. How did he know that? She couldn't answer him.

"Why haven't you agreed to another session with Molly?"

She sat on the sofa, her legs no longer able to hold her up. He came and knelt in front of her.

"Why don't you want to talk to her?"

She still didn't answer.

"Because you're afraid to let it all out? Because you're afraid of what might happen if you do? You need to talk about what happened. You could give it all to me. Give up control for a while, let me take charge, let me help you."

Jesus. His words awakened a huge desire in her. She was so close to throwing caution to the wind and saying yes. But what if she did? Gave everything to him? What would be left of her when he let her go? "I just told you what happened."

"That was only part of it, and you know it. Because you couldn't hold it in anymore. You're trying to protect yourself, but you need to stop trying to do it all on your own." His voice was soft, cajoling. This Alec was potent. Damn near irresistible.

"I don't have anyone else."

"That's bullshit."

She glared at him.

He narrowed his gaze at her, and she could see anger in those brown depths. She felt a stupid urge to try to make him smile again. To see if she could get his eyes to go back to that melting chocolate. She'd always had a weakness for chocolate.

"Why are you offering to do this? Why do you care?"

Irritation filled his face. "You think I want to care? I got enough going on in my life. I don't need trouble. I don't need some little pixie coming in and messing my life up. My brothers do enough of that. I could go to the club and have my choice of subs. They would eagerly strip and lie over my desk, without giving a hint of attitude. They'd take whatever punishment I doled out. They wouldn't dare go against me. And yet here I am, dealing with something I said I'd never deal with. Innocence. And, somehow, I don't want any of those other subs. I want sweetness. I want light. And that's never been mine to take."

"I'm not innocent," she told him.

"You're the most innocent person I've ever met, Calamity Jane."

He reached for her, pulling her close then wrapped his hand around the back of her neck and kissed her. It was a hard kiss. Possessive. He didn't hold back. He drew back and bit down on her lip. A shiver worked its way up her spine.

"Fuck me. You need someone patient and caring, who will give you time, guide you, cherish you. I can't offer any of that. I want a woman who'll let me tie her up, spank her, clamp her nipples, and take her ass. I need a woman who'll submit to me, who will obey me. Without question. And who will give herself to me whenever and however I ask it."

He reached out and lightly pinched one of her nipples. She gasped. Then he twisted it. *Ouch!* She slapped her hand over her breast to protect it. "Ow, Malone!"

"Sir."

"What?" Shit. This moving so quickly. It was hard to get her head around that he might want her. Let alone want to dominate her. She didn't know anything beyond what she'd read in books. She didn't know what she was doing.

"Call me Sir. Or better yet Master."

"I . . . I . . . please, can we slow down? This is going so fast and I can't catch my breath."

Something came over his face. Something distant. He stood. Took a step back. "Shit. Got no business doing this. This was a mistake."

"Malone—"

"Just go. Now. Before I do something we'll both regret. You get a free pass on breaking the rules. It's the only one you're going to get so don't mess up again. Now go."

Feeling like a coward, she fled.

SHE LAY on her bed and stared up at the ceiling.

Her mind was whirling, trying to work out what had just happened. He'd offered to take control and help her then he'd done a complete about-face, decided she couldn't give him what he needed, and sent her up to her room like some disobedient teenager. Just because she'd wanted to slow down? Her temper stirred. She didn't think her request had been unreasonable.

She rolled over and punched her pillow. Now he had her wondering what it would be like to give him complete control. To give him everything she held in tight lockdown, in that place deep inside her. Would it feel freeing or terrifying?

Or both?

THE DOOR to his office banged open without so much as a knock and he looked up in irritation as Beau, Tanner, and Butch barged in.

"I'm busy," he barked.

"What did you do to her?" Beau asked.

"What? Who?" He pretended to have no idea what they were talking about.

"Who?" Tanner snarled. "Like there's heaps of women around here. Mia, of course."

Mia. Even her name sent a rush of arousal through his body. Mia, who was under his protection. Mia, who was everything he didn't want or need. Mia, who kept him awake at night thinking about her soft laugh and caring smile.

Mia. Mia. Mia. Aargh.

He'd gone too far the other night. Scared her. He had no right pushing her into something she wasn't ready for.

"I don't know what you're talking about."

"Quit the bullshit and tell us what you did to her," Beau snarled at him.

"What makes you think I did anything?"

"Because you're the only one who's enough of an idiot to piss her off," Tanner told him.

"She served oatmeal for breakfast," Butch finally spoke. "Oatmeal! It's like fucking baby food."

So that explained their upset. They all worshiped Calamity Jane because she fed them.

"It's worse," Beau said mournfully. "Some baby food is tasty, like that vanilla pudding stuff that, you know, we found last spring."

Found? Found? He could feel his blood pressure rising. "You guys promised not to do that shit anymore."

"What shit?" Beau said innocently.

"No stealing. No borrowing." Didn't matter what they called it, stealing was stealing.

"Come on, Alec. It's just a little fun," Tanner moaned.

"It's a little fun that will land you in jail, and I'm not bailing you out next time!"

Christ, they'd all be the death of him

"I bet Mia would bail us out," Tanner said slyly. "She came to Jaret's rescue."

"Jaret is out on his ass if he does anything like that again. And Mia will be too." It was an empty threat. But he couldn't take it back.

"If she goes, we all go!" Tanner told him.

"At least we're not stupid enough to bite the hand that feeds us," Beau added.

"I miss her pancakes already," Butch mourned. "I'm starving here, a man can't survive on oatmeal." He glared at Alec before turning to leave.

As soon as the door slammed shut behind them, Alec turned and threw his pen against the wall. God damn it.

12

E nough was enough.

Things had gotten out of hand the other day in his office. He probably shouldn't have said the things he'd said. She wasn't his submissive. And these feelings of attraction between them, well, they'd disappear in time. He just needed to remember all the reasons she wasn't for him.

But this sulking in her room was going to stop. He'd given her all yesterday, but now his brothers were about to riot on him.

He got to her door and turned the handle. Locked. Oh, hell no. She didn't get to lock him out. This was his house.

He banged on the door. "Open this door! Right now."

He expected the door to open immediately. Boy, was he surprised.

"Open the door, Calamity Jane."

Still nothing. Worry started to eat away at him. He was certain she was in there. Nobody had seen her leave. Why wasn't she answering the door? He banged louder. Still nothing.

The door lock was one of those flimsy ones where you pressed a button on the handle. He could put his shoulder to it and crash it open. Or go get a pin, press it in the small hole on the door handle on his side and unlock it.

He didn't want to take the time to get the pin.

"If you're on the other side of the door, baby. Move back."

He took a couple of steps back and then thrust his shoulder against the door. The door pinged open. When he walked in, he was surprised to see her sitting on the bed. She looked up at him. Her face was calm.

"Why didn't you open the fucking door?" he asked in a harder voice than he'd meant to use.

"I was still thinking," she replied. There was no hint of emotion on her face. His worry increased. What was wrong with her?

"Thinking? That's the best excuse you can come up with? You were thinking?" He loomed over her, his hands on his hips.

"Yes."

"Yes? Yes? That's all you have to say?"

"I think you're right."

He sat down on the bed. He hated to admit it, but he still felt a little shaky. When she hadn't come to the door, there had been a part of him that had been worried she might have done something stupid. She was suffering from PTSD. How had he forgotten that? How could he have let her have so much time alone? The fact that he was attracted to her and didn't want to be was no excuse for not taking proper care of her.

He was supposed to be different now. He wasn't supposed to break people anymore.

"You're going to have to elaborate on that one, babe. Just what exactly was I right about?"

"I might be a sub. I don't want to be a slave. I could never give up full control. I don't want that. But there are times when it would be nice not to have to worry all the time, to think. Especially during sex. I'm not sure about the whole spanking thing. Paddles, whips, floggers, whatever else you use. I don't know about any of that. But I think I might want to try. I think you're right. I think I need to know if that's who I am."

He was having a slight problem keeping up with her.

"When I was twelve, my parents died," she said. Her voice still held very little inflection.

He knew this about her, of course. There wasn't much he didn't know about her. He was nothing if not thorough. But that didn't mean he didn't want to hear about it from her.

"But you probably know that don't you? Because a man like you doesn't let a stranger into his life, into his house, near his family, unless he knows her. I didn't get that before. I didn't get how you could look at me and see something that nobody else did. You already knew me, didn't you?"

"I didn't know you," he told her. Not at all.

For the first time she looked animated. A flash of anger filled her face. The relief he felt at seeing that was immense. Because he thought he'd changed her. Turned her into the emotionless being sitting in front of him. He thought he'd done what he'd been trying not to, that he'd tainted her with himself.

"Don't lie to me!"

"I'm not lying," he told her with a narrowed gaze. "Because no amount of looking into you could have told me that when you get mad, your eyes sparkle. And when you get tired, your eye gets a small tic above it, and that your freckles stand out even more against your skin. It couldn't have told me how infectious your laugh was, or that you'd have the balls to take on my brothers and try to teach them some manners. No background check could ever have told me that."

She was staring at him hard. "Why are you being nice to me?"

"I wasn't aware I was."

She huffed out of breath. "Is that because you don't recognize what being nice feels like?"

"No doubt," he said dryly. "Nice has never been a part of my life."

"So, you knew that my parents were dead?"

He nodded. "Killed by some drunk driver who ran through a stop light. You were sent to live with your aunt and uncle. Your dad's brother and his wife. Mike's parents."

"Do you know anything about my life there?"

He thought back to the file. Trying to think of something that might give an explanation for the shuttered look on her face.

"I know that the day you graduated you moved out. Moved into the same apartment as Mike."

She nodded. "I didn't have anything. My parents were heavily mortgaged, after their house was sold, there was nothing left. My aunt liked to tell me that all their spare money had to go towards keeping me fed and clothed or to buy school supplies. That I was the reason they never got to go on vacations overseas. I was the reason why it took them longer to pay off their mortgage then it should have. I was the reason they didn't have the life they wanted."

Shit. Enough.

He sat back on the bed, leaning against the headboard. Then he reached over and grabbed her, pulling her onto his lap. She let out a squeak of surprise, sitting rather stiffly on his lap, as though she didn't quite know what to do with herself. So he tugged her in against his chest.

He'd never wanted to kiss and cuddle and erase old hurts. Never wanted to hurt a woman quite as much as he wanted to hurt her bitch aunt.

"Baby, you know that none of that is true, right?"

She had to know. She had to know it was bullshit. That for some reason, her aunt wanted to spit venom at her. To break her down. To hurt her.

"But it was true, they'd never planned on having me. I was a burden. I tried to make myself useful. I took over all the cooking and cleaning. The cooking wasn't a hardship, I enjoyed it. I tried to make her like me. But nothing I did ever worked."

"Because she was an evil bitch," he muttered.

"The day I graduated high school, my aunt came to me and told me to get out. I didn't have anywhere to go, I didn't have any other family, so I went to Mike's. I became his burden."

Fuck me. Fuck me now. Because wasn't that exactly how he'd made her feel? How often had he been grateful she didn't complain? Or ask him for anything? Her only rebellion had been going to rescue Jaret and that had been for completely selfless reasons. She'd been taught that burdens didn't get to complain. They just had to make themselves useful.

So yeah. Fuck him.

He reached down and turned her around, so she was straddling his lap then he grabbed her chin and raised her face up. "You think that's how he saw it? That he saw you as a burden?"

"How could he not have? I didn't have anything. He had to pay for it all. My aunt was so mad about that. She asked me if I was trying to ruin her entire family. I tried to leave after that night."

"But you didn't."

"Oh, no, I did. Packed some stuff up in a duffel bag, didn't have much anyway and left. Didn't get far, though. One of Mike's friends on the force saw me, called it in to him and then the next moment I'm in a cop car being driven home and watched over until my cousin stormed back into his apartment to ask me what the hell I was doing."

"You tell him what that bitch said?"

As she spoke, she was gradually easing into his touch. And he liked it.

"No."

"Why not?"

"It would have hurt him. I love Mike. He was the one bright

spot in my life. He was protective and caring, he was everything to me, and it would have hurt him. So I never told him. He was in his last year of high school when my parents died. He was busy with baseball and getting good grades and girls. Mike was a popular guy. Besides, she never acted that way around him. She always pretended to be caring when he was there. Mike never knew. Mike can never know."

He disagreed. He should have known. He didn't give a fuck how busy he was, he should have known. And he wondered how he hadn't. Had he turned a blind eye because the bitch was his mom? Was that why he'd taken Mia in? Because he'd felt guilty knowing the way his mother had treated her?

He also wondered if that was the only reason Mia never said anything to him.

"You thought he wouldn't believe you? Or that he might take her side?"

She stiffened and he knew his guess was correct.

"She was his mom. He should have chosen her over me."

"She's dead, isn't she?"

"Yeah. Plane crash. First vacation they took after I left the house. Both of them gone at once. Mike and I are alone now."

He hated the lonely, lost note in her voice, and wanted to do anything he could to erase it.

"Where was your uncle during all this? You were his brother's kid, why didn't he stick up for you?"

Why hadn't he taught her she was worth something? That she mattered?

"He worked a lot. Long business trips away. I think that's part of the reason my aunt was so bitter. She was lonely. She told me he had to work such long hours because of me, but even after I left, he still worked long hours. I think she was lying."

"Of course she was fucking lying." Fuck. Fuck. Had everyone let this girl down? Her parents had died. Her aunt had verbally and emotionally abused her for years. And it sounded like her precious cousin and his father had both turned a blind eye to that abuse.

"You're angry," she stated. Her voice was back to that emotionless state. He hated it. "At me."

He squeezed tight. "No, baby. Not at you."

"I was never spanked as a child, but my parents did punish me. I didn't misbehave much, I was a good girl. But, still, I was grounded a few times. But my aunt, she never punished me."

He frowned at that. Sounded like she was punished constantly, just because she'd had the misfortune to end up an orphan and at that bitch's mercy.

"She never cared if I snuck out of the house or was late getting home. I never even had a curfew. I never realized why that bothered me until later. I mean, sounds like every teenager's dream. But she never gave me any boundaries because she didn't care."

She leaned back, looking up at him, that calm face giving nothing away. "I was wondering, would you care if something happened to me?"

Care? He'd fucking raze cities to the ground if anything happened to her.

Fuck. He was in too deep. Way too deep.

"I care," he said gruffly. It was as much as he could manage. As much as he could give.

"That's good, because I don't think I could do this unless you cared."

Do what?

She took a deep breath. "I think I am submissive. The other night you made that offer. And I know I messed up when I asked to slow things down—"

"You didn't mess up. I did. You were right to ask me to slow down."

"No. I just . . . I needed time to think. To work it all out. But if you think you could manage it . . . I mean only if you wanted to . . . well, maybe we could try—"

"Babe. Spit it out."

"I want you to teach me how to be a submissive. I know I don't know what I'm doing and that I don't have as much sexual experience as you do, but I'm a quick learner. I'll try my best."

He shouldn't. He should stick to his resolve not to get involved. He opened his mouth to tell her no, it wasn't a good idea. It might take her a day or two, but she'd get over it. He was doing her a favor. And she'd thank him one day when she had that house in the suburbs with the puppy that chewed her shoes, three kids who brought her joy every day and a husband that better fucking worship the ground she walked on—or he would be coming for him.

But before he could say anything, she spoke again.

"Because I don't think I can do this with anyone I don't know. And I think it really needs to be someone who knows what I went through. You know, I used to believe that everyone had good in them. Like, I honestly believed that. Stupid, huh? Because how could you kill a man who was working sixty-hour weeks washing dishes to support his four kids and a wife, who barely spoke any English? Juan had brought his family to America for a better life. And he ended up dead. Why? Juan was a good man and he died for no reason."

Her words were like punches to the gut, stealing his breath.

"How can people do that? Play fast and loose with other people's lives? How?"

She could never know what he'd been. If she did, he'd lose her instantly. He closed his eyes briefly. He was going to lose her anyway. This wasn't a relationship that could continue on, even if he did decide to train her, to show her about submission and dominance. That was where it ended.

It had to.

But maybe he could do this. Just for a while, he could have her.

"Molly offered to take me to that BDSM club you go to. She said she and her husband would watch over any scenes that I got involved with to make sure I was okay, but—"

"She said what?" he asked in a soft voice.

She had been leaning into his chest as she spoke, but, at his words, she attempted to lean back. But he pressed her face against his chest. He didn't want her to see his face right now. No doubt he looked as furious as he felt.

What the fuck was Molly thinking? Mia wasn't going to fucking Saxon's to hook up with some strange Dominant. She wasn't going anywhere. She was staying here under his watchful gaze.

"Um, she offered to take me to the club and—"

"Enough. I don't need to hear it again. You listen to me. You are not going to the club to find a stranger to fucking teach you about being a sub. Got me? Besides the fact that you aren't allowed to leave the ranch without me, you have no business walking into a BDSM club not knowing the first thing about anything, not with your background, not even with Molly," he tensed, his jaw tightening to the point of pain, "to watch over you."

"I don't want to do that, but if you won't train me—"

"I'll do it."

"Really?"

"Yes, fucking really. While you're here, for as long as we both want it, I'll train you. But you'll be trained to be the sort of sub I want. Might not always be easy on you. And there are gonna be a helluva lot more rules than you've already got. And you will obey them. Got it?"

ELATION FILLED HER. She couldn't believe that had worked. She didn't think she could do this with anyone else. She needed him.

So, fine, she'd manipulated him slightly when she'd told him about Molly's offer. She had offered, it's just that Mia would never in a million years take her up on it.

She wouldn't have the guts. Not only that, she didn't have the desire. She couldn't bear the idea of some strange man touching her. How could she ever trust someone she didn't know? How could she be attracted to him? Maybe some people didn't need those things, but she did.

"So what now?" she asked. Her heart was racing, and she could feel a mix of trepidation and excitement bubbling in her stomach. What would he order her to do? What did this involve? Would she have to get naked right away? She wasn't sure she was ready for that. Sure, this morning she'd taken an extra-long shower and made sure to shave everything. She'd rather have visited a spa and had a wax, but a girl had to work with what she had available. She'd moisturized, she'd washed her hair, she was as clean as could be.

"You eaten today?" he asked.

She looked at him in surprise "Sorry?"

"You've been in this room most of the day, haven't you? You eaten?"

"Um, Jaret dropped off a tray at breakfast."

His gaze narrowed. "You haven't eaten since breakfast?"

She shook her head.

"Where's the tray?"

"Over there." She pointed to the tray on the dresser across the room.

He looked down at the half-eaten sandwich and torn orange peel. "What the hell did he make you?"

"A sandwich and an orange. Oh, and some coffee, but I poured that out. It was horrid."

Alec muttered under his breath then lifted her off his lap and sat her on the bed. He swung his legs over the side, inspecting the food. "What kind of sandwich is this?"

"Um, chocolate."

"Chocolate? He made you a sandwich with chocolate in the middle?" He turned to gape at her.

"Chocolate sprinkles." Why it was important to point that out, she had no idea.

He just stared at her.

"It's my favorite."

"Your favorite." He shook his head and ran his hand over his face. "First rule."

She sat up straight, preparing herself. "Yes?"

"Actually, second rule. First rule, when you talk to me, you address me as Sir."

"All the time?"

"When we're playing or when I'm training you, yes. Which means right now."

"Oh, right, yes, Sir." She kind of liked the sound of that. She'd never thought she would, but it felt right.

"Good girl."

Oh, he couldn't know what those two words did to her. That they sent sparks of heat flowing through her blood. She felt the urge to do more, to hear those words of praise come from him again.

"Second rule has to do with your eating habits."

She frowned. That wasn't something she'd been expecting. What did what she ate have to do with him teaching her to be a sub?

"I don't understand, Sir. What has what I eat got to do with you training me?"

He stared at her for a moment, studied her. "If you'd come to the club, looking to be trained, Saxon would have found someone to take you on. Someone to guide and teach you. He would never choose me to be that someone, because I don't take on inexperienced subs. But none of those subs had ever been here, to the ranch. They've never met my brothers. Beyond negotiation, play, and aftercare, I don't deal with them. Don't really talk to them. I don't know about their lives, their friends, what they do. Not beyond what's in their file. I don't get involved in their lives; they don't get involved in mine."

"Never?"

"Never. We could restrict this just to play. I could teach you how to greet me. I could bind you and spank you, tie you up in rope, I could introduce you to my collection of paddles, I could stretch your ass with plugs, dress you up like a kitten and teach you about pet play. I can do all of that, and will, depending on your limits."

He wanted to dress her up as a kitten? Okay, she was a little freaked by that, and intrigued. And the freaked part became even more so when she realized how interested she was.

His mouth quirked up into a smile that reached his eyes. Warm, melted chocolate eyes stared down at her. "I can see you're a little shocked by all of that. Which also means we're gonna take this slow."

"How slow?" she asked suspiciously.

"As slow as I say, kitten."

She guessed kitten was a step up from Calamity Jane.

"But what does what I eat have to do with all of that?"

"Sir."

"Huh?"

"Remember to address me as Sir. I will give you a few warnings and then I'll start dishing out discipline to help you remember."

Okay the warm, chocolate gaze was gone. The look in his eyes was strict. Her body gave a little tremble.

"What I'm saying is that while we could just keep it to play, I don't think that's really what you need."

It wasn't?

"What you need is someone to curb those tendencies you have to put everyone else first. It's not a wrong way to be, so long as you know your limits, or you have someone watching out for you who is prepared to step in when you've reached those limits and pull you back."

"I don't put everyone else first."

He just raised an eyebrow. "Why did you learn to cook?"

"What?"

"What is it that drew you to cooking for a career? And remember how to address me."

Right. Yep. Seemed she was failing that lesson big time.

"My aunt didn't like cooking."

"And you wanted a way to make her like you."

"Didn't work," she said bitterly. "But Mike and my uncle liked my cooking."

"And they praised you."

"Yes." She added, "Sir," hastily.

"Nothing wrong with enjoying being praised or with liking to do things for others. You like to cook for my brothers?"

"Yes. I do. Even if they do have terrible table manners. I'm working on that."

"So you are." His lips twitched again. Seemed she was amusing tonight. "Brave of you."

It was.

"Do you actually like cooking?"

She straightened, realizing where this was going. "Yes, I do. I know I might have started in the hopes that my aunt," *might love me,* "well, that she might be grateful or find me useful. But I found I love it. I enjoy it."

"What would happen though if you couldn't cook? What if you couldn't be useful anymore? What if you couldn't do things for people?"

She blinked. Tapped her fingers against her leg until he reached out and lightly grabbed her hand.

"What then, baby?"

"I don't know."

"You think everyone will stop liking you?"

Maybe. "You're making me sound like a complete basket case."

He shook his head. "Not at all. You found a way to earn affection in a house where there was little to come by, even if your aunt was never won over, your cousin and uncle liked your cooking. But now, you equate being useful or needed with being wanted or loved. You make people food because it makes them feel good and that makes you feel good. And that's fine. But so long as you know that your value isn't tied up in what you can give people."

"I don't understand." Except she was worried that she did.

"Babe, you were up at two a.m. making brownies for someone who has probably said twenty words to you since you got here."

"I couldn't sleep."

"Why is that?"

She sighed. "I have trouble sleeping. Nightmares."

He drew her back onto his lap. "From now on, whenever you get a nightmare you won't be heading down to the kitchen to bake at some godforsaken hour, understand?"

"But it helps distract me," she protested.

He leaned in and kissed her. He kissed her until she relaxed in his arms and her legs dropped away from her chest. "That's my job now."

"Oh. Okay."

His lips twitched at her response.

"My brothers worship the ground you walk on. You think it's about the food, and that's all it might have been at the beginning. But not now. Now, they eat at the table and take their dirty boots off and will do whatever else you ask of them."

"They're just scared they'll get cut off from my desserts."

"Nope." He stared down at her. "They do it because they adore you. Because you mean something to them. That bitch made you feel like an interloper, like you never belonged. She taught you to keep your needs on lockdown. I'm going to have to teach you how to ask for what you need."

He was? It sounded like an impossible task.

"You go to poker nights, you know their favorite foods, you know their birthdays, you risk your life to pick their fool asses up and are ready to lie to the cops for them."

She sucked in a breath.

"And because of all of that, we do this differently. This doesn't stop at the bedroom door. My brothers have all been giving me hell because they think I did something that made you hole up in here. Sure, they miss your cooking. But they also miss you."

"Oh." It was the best she had.

"Do you understand what I'm saying?"

"I understand that you like to be in control all the time. You're also a bossy bastard."

He gave her a mock stern look. "That's Sir bossy bastard to you."

She gave him a wide smile.

"So you want to go all in? That means not all the rules that I give you are going to relate to what goes on in the bedroom. Like eating better."

It was a bit scary, kind of like jumping out of a plane with no idea how to work the parachute. She swallowed heavily. He reached over and grabbed her hand; she hadn't realized she'd been tapping her fingers nervously again. "I know it's hard to trust," he told her. "I get that. But that's why you came to me, right?"

She nodded. "I trust you. I'm trusting you with my life. I can trust you with this."

"You can. And nothing happens that you don't want to happen.

There is going to be a safe word, we're going to sit down and negotiate a contract. We do this right because you are important, Mia. Don't forget that."

Her breath caught. He really thought she was important. Okay, so she had some self-esteem issues. But he had problems with opening up. She also knew he wouldn't say anything he didn't mean.

She was important.

"So back to the eating issue."

"I don't have an eating issue." Did he think he she had some bad relationship with food or something? Where would he have gotten that idea? She loved food. It was her passion.

"I'm talking about the fact that you don't eat enough. And when you do, you eat crap like that." He nodded over to the plate.

"I'll have you know there have been studies that have shown chocolate is very good for your heart," she told him.

"How do you address me? And, just so you know, you're getting to the end of my warnings."

A little shiver went up the base of her spine. "And what happens when we reach the end of those warnings?"

"Then you discover what a Dom does to discipline his naughty little sub."

"Okay, then. Sir."

Seemed she wasn't quite brave enough to learn that just yet.

"So from now on, you start eating more than a bird does. Three meals. And I mean meals. I don't mean picking at things. And no more chocolate sprinkles in your sandwiches."

"I'm starting to rethink what I just agreed to."

He grinned later. "Poor baby, because you're going to have to eat your vegetables?"

She just glared at him. "And how are you gonna know exactly what I eat? You never eat with us."

His face froze, and she immediately regretted saying that. "Not that it matters. I mean, I know you're busy and everything."

"Do you want me to eat with you?"

She stared at him in surprise. "Only if that's what you want, Sir."

He tilted his head to one side. "It won't always be possible. Got a lot I have to do. But if it's important to you, I'll try to be there."

It wasn't a concession she'd been expecting. A wave of happiness flooded her. She found herself wrapping her arms enthusiastically around his neck. He dropped back on the bed, with her on top of him.

"Well, if I knew I'd get such a reaction I might have turned up to dinner before now," he said dryly

"What's your favorite food? I'll make it for you."

"Can you make lasagna?"

"Oh, baby, I can make a lasagna that will blow your socks off."

His eyes did that warm chocolate thing again. And she found her breath catching in her throat, she was mesmerized by him.

"While I like hearing you call me baby, I like hearing you call me Sir more. And you've just reached the end of your warnings."

Her eyes widened in alarm. He cupped her bottom. Then he grabbed the top of her pants and pulled them down over her ass. She was wearing a pair of plain, blue cotton briefs. Even though her heart was racing as trepidation flooded her, she didn't protest as he ran his hands over her panty clad bottom. He arched his neck, glancing down at her underwear.

"We're gonna have to have a chat about appropriate lingerie," he told her.

"My cousin bought me these," she replied in a breathless voice. The way he was rubbing her bottom was making her clit throb. She could feel her panties getting wet. With the feel of him against her, his scent surrounding her, the way he touched her, was it any wonder?

"I don't think he bought them with the intention of anyone seeing them," she said.

"Let's not talk about your cousin while we're in bed," he told her in a firm voice. "Kind of ruins the mood."

She tensed up. "Sorry, Sir."

"Wasn't saying that to make you feel bad," he told her in a gentle voice. "Just laying down some ground rules. Okay?"

"Okay."

"Seems we're are going to have to work on you addressing me." His hand stopped rubbing and started smacking her. He paused, rubbed the heat in. The slight sting turned into a warmth that filled her body. Okay then. If that was what discipline was like, she was going to have to be naughty more often.

His hand landed again then again. Four quick spanks before he paused to rub the heat in. Her breath came in harsh pants. She squirmed a little, trying to find some traction for her clit. His placed his arm around her firmly, holding her still.

"Uh-uh, disobedient little girls don't get to come."

"That's not fair," she groaned.

"I wouldn't complain if I were you, considering how easy I'm going on you with this spanking." As he finished speaking his hand landed five times in quick succession against her bottom. Okay, that hurt a bit more. But still her arousal grew. Became more demanding. It didn't help that she was plastered against him.

"There's a difference between a spanking given for pleasure and a spanking given as punishment," he told her. "I'm going easy on you this time, but by the end of this you'll have a nice, hot bottom. Going to make sitting for dinner an interesting experience."

He gave her another five hard spanks. Her ass was definitely beginning to burn. She pressed her legs together, hoping that would help alleviate the ache in her clit.

Three more heavy smacks. "No coming without my permission. That also means no pleasuring yourself, that's gone for you now."

She'd never been that interested in making herself come anyway. She didn't own a vibrator. She'd always thought she just wasn't that into sex. One of her ex's had called her frigid. Now she was starting to wonder if she just hadn't been getting what she needed. Because right now, there was nothing she wanted more than to feel his finger against her clit, to have him rub it, flick it, and send her soaring.

She whimpered a little as she wriggled against him.

"Poor baby," he said in a fake sympathetic voice. "You're so turned on, aren't you? This is what you need, isn't? For someone to take the control out of your hands. You don't want to be in charge of this. When we're together like this, all you have to do is what I tell you to do. You don't need to worry about anything else. Not anything that's going on. Just about doing as you're told."

"I'm good at doing what I'm told," she told him.

"Yeah? Is that why you're still owed a spanking for disobeying the rules?"

She pushed herself up slightly, so she could look into his face. He'd stopped spanking her by now. But there was still a burn in her ass that she didn't think would fade anytime soon. His hand rubbed her bottom, occasionally squeezing her cheeks, making the burn intensify.

Damned if she didn't love that.

"That was a special circumstance," she pointed out.

He cupped her face between his hands and she almost found herself begging him to put them back on her butt.

"I don't care about the circumstances; you are not to disobey that rule again. Do you understand? This is very important. This is about safety. There is nothing I take more seriously than safety."

The intensity in his gaze should have scared her. Instead, it made her feel important. Cared for.

"I won't. I promise. This time, I really won't break that promise.
"

He relaxed beneath her, and his hand drifted back down to her bottom, continuing to rub.

She rested her cheek against his chest. "Oh, that's nice."

He chuckled underneath her. "Does my baby like having her bottom played with?"

She blushed a little let the words. "No one has ever touched me there before."

"Well, you can expect to be touched there often. And I'm going to enjoy every minute."

13

She settled in at the dining table. Okay, they were still loud and boisterous, and they stole food from each other's plates, but that was who they were. They were crazy, and she loved them. She was really going to miss them when she had to leave.

But she didn't want to think about that right now. She didn't want to think about the trial coming up. That she had a hit man still after her. That, at some point, she'd have to say goodbye to the Malones. To Alec.

After that small spanking earlier and one truly amazing ass massage, which had had her squirming with arousal, he'd left her lying on her bed aching and unfulfilled.

Bastard.

Nerves stole over her as she thought about the night to come. He'd told her to come to his office after the boys were all gone. Was he going to spank her again? Would he let her come? Please let him let her come. Her clit was still aching and she'd seriously considering giving herself a little relief. But the thought of displeasing him had stopped her. It had been a damn close call, though.

Suddenly, silence fell over the room. She blinked in shock at the suddenness of it. Everyone was turned towards the door. And there stood Alec.

He gave everyone a nod then moved into the room. West walked in behind him and stepped around the table to an empty seat next to the head of the table. She expected Alec to move to the head and take a seat. This table sat twelve and she'd laid out plates for everyone.

Instead, he moved to where she was sitting, part way down the table, sandwiched between Jaret and Raid. He reached over and grabbed her plate, which was currently still empty. She'd been too busy daydreaming to put any food on it.

"Bring your cutlery," he told her. Then he turned and walked up to the head of the table. He nodded at Beau who was seated to his left. "Go sit in Mia's seat."

Okay, so obviously he wanted her to sit by him, and he wasn't in much of a mood to ask. Hell, when was he ever in the mood to ask?

Beau went without a word, but he flicked her a wink as she passed him. "You're obviously his favorite, sweetheart."

She blushed, even though he couldn't know about their conversation earlier. At least she hoped Alec hadn't told his brothers. No, he wouldn't have.

"Beau," Alec said in a low, warning voice as he held out the chair for her. Okay, so at least it seemed *he* had manners.

"What? I can totally see why she would be. She's my favorite too."

"Mine, too," Raid added quickly.

The rest of them quickly added their agreements, making her flush in pleasure.

"Sit down, Mia," Alec told her quietly. She sat, staring over at

West. He was the one brother who hadn't added his agreement, but then she hadn't expected him to. He didn't seem to like her much.

But he did give her a small nod. So, that was progress. Everyone kept eating as they passed dishes down to West. He spooned out some food before handing it over to Alec, who shocked her by filing her plate before his own.

Yep, he'd definitely gotten all the manners in the family. Well, he and West. By the time he was finished, she had an enormous plate of food in front of her.

"Um, you do know I'm a lot smaller than you are, right?" she joked, leaning towards him so she could be heard over the racket his brothers were making.

"Do the best you can," he replied. "But you don't clear at least a third of that plate, we'll be having a chat."

He gave her a firm look then glanced down to where she was shifting around on the chair, trying to find a comfortable position. She froze, felt her cheeks fill with heat. Okay, yeah, her bottom still stung from earlier.

"Whatever you don't eat, I'll finish off, doll," Maddox told her from where he sat next to her.

Shoot. There was no privacy around here. She needed to remember that. She then dodged one of his elbows as he enthusiastically dug into the pot roast. She leaned into Alec. "How come you and West have table manners and the rest of these guys . . . well . . . "

"West and I had a nanny who was a big believer in manners. She lasted longer than the rest. What? Eight years?" He glanced over at West who was clearly listening. The other man nodded. "She taught us some table manners. How to treat those that were important to us." He stared at her as he said that, and a little shiver ran over her skin.

"The next nanny who replaced her wasn't so interested in

looking after us as she was getting into the old man's pants," Maddox said.

"How do you remember that?" Alec asked. "You must have been only two when Margaret was fired and he hired Lou-Lou."

"But Lou-Lou lasted a few years. And she made an impression," Jaret interjected. "I'm only a year older than Maddox and I remember Lou-Lou clearly. She had tits out . . . " his voice trailed off as Alec frowned at him.

Then Alec turned to look around at all of them, who had amazingly stopped talking and were all listening—at the same time. Miracles did happen.

"You'll refrain from any crude remarks or swearing around Mia, understand?"

Eyes turned on her. She felt herself blushing bright red.

"Something we need to know?" Raid asked.

"Yes. Mia is mine."

A little thrill went through her. A combination of excitement and trepidation. She was his. For however long it lasted, she was his.

Lord help her.

"So you guys had nannies growing up?" she asked as she settled herself on the sofa in his office.

Alec gave her a look she couldn't decipher as he sat on the armchair next to the sofa. Shit. Should she not have asked that? Were questions about his past off the table? But he'd offered that information at dinner tonight, so how was she to know?

Suddenly he reached out and grabbed her hand, stilling the fingers she hadn't even realized had been tapping nervously against her thigh.

"You always done that?"

Asked questions about people's pasts? Wasn't that a normal thing to ask someone who you were about to enter a relationship with? Well, not a normal relationship, of course. Normal relationships involved dates and feelings and kissing, not generally hand-cuffs and blindfolds and paddles —

"Mia, you still here with me?"

"Huh?" She looked over at him in confusion. Of course she was still here. She hadn't moved.

His eyes narrowed. Then he pointed at the ground between his legs. "Here. Now."

She stood and moved between his legs. Was this part of contract negotiations? Or something he'd always want? Was she not supposed to sit on the sofa?

"Jesus, you're worrying so much it's practically coming out your pores. Kneel, kitten."

She slid down to her knees, not very gracefully. In fact, she banged her knee against the floor as she dropped, then slipped to one side, falling against his leg. But he didn't say anything about her clumsiness. She desperately wanted to rub her throbbing knee but didn't want to bring attention to it, in case he hadn't noticed.

"Okay, we need to work on that," he commented dryly.

She dropped her gaze to the floor. Shame filled her. She was never going to be one of those women whose every movement looked elegant. She wasn't some graceful swan. She was a newborn foal stumbling around on legs that didn't work properly.

"Eyes to me," he ordered.

Crap. Weren't submissives supposed to look to the floor when they were in this position? She was sure that was the case in most of the books she'd read.

"Mia. Eyes. Now."

Okay, now his voice was doing that dark and dangerous thing that made hunger pool in her stomach even as she wondered what would happen if she pushed him too far.

Not that she was going to. She raised her eyes to him.

He ran his finger down her cheek. "There you are. Keep those eyes on me. I want to see what's going on in that overactive mind of yours."

And he thought her eyes would tell him that? Was he some sort of eye-reader? He couldn't really tell her thoughts, right? They didn't teach that at Dom class, did they? Hmm, was there a Dom class?

"Kitten." He reached out and placed his hand around her ponytail, grasped it firmly, and pulled on it. The sharp tug of pain made her gasp and focus on him.

"That's better. I can see I need to work on ways to keep your attention on me and only me."

"My attention is on you." Another tug. She let out a soft gasp. It stung. Tears filled her eyes. And yet there was an answering tug on her clit. Her heart beat faster. And all those thoughts flooding her mind vanished.

"Sir."

Oh, shit. She was fucking up already. And she'd already been punished earlier for forgetting how to address him.

"Sorry, Sir."

"Better. When we play, your only focus should be on me. Obeying me. Pleasing me. When we play, you are kitten and I am Sir. Got it?"

"Okay, got it. Sir. I'm sorry. I know I'm not exactly graceful and I tend to lose focus, but I'm trying."

"Nobody expects you to be perfect, or to know what you're doing. This is all new to you." He reached down and grabbed both hands. "When you kneel between my legs, your hands are here." He placed them down on the top of his thighs. "And unless I say otherwise, I want your eyes on me."

She quickly raised her eyes from where she'd been staring at her hands on his thighs. He had nice thighs. Muscular.

"Understand?"

"Yes, Sir, is this a typical position for a sub to take?"

"This is what I require of you when you're in this position. You don't need to worry about other subs or Doms or the way they do things. This is what I want from you. Understand?"

Sort of. "So if I ever have another Dom," which was highly unlikely, "he might have different ways of doing things?"

A look crossed his face, something she couldn't decipher. But then it quickly disappeared. "Yes. The reason I want your hands on my thighs is because you have a nervous habit of tapping your fingers when you're scared or uncertain. I want you to give those feelings to me."

"Give them to you?"

"Yes. By bottling everything up, you create a poison that will eat you from the inside out. Have you ever spoken to anyone about what happened that night?"

"I told the detectives, Mike, and you."

"You were angry and you blurted things out, but you definitely didn't tell me everything. You didn't tell me how it made you feel."

"Can we talk about something else, Sir?" Part of her wanted to get up and storm away. To tell him to mind his own damn business. To point out that he wasn't exactly forthcoming. About anything. But she didn't. Partly because she knew he spoke the truth. It was a poison eating her from the inside out. And partly because she was scared that would mean this was over. And she'd never get another shot. Not with him.

"All right. For tonight, I'll let that go. You never answered me. Is tapping your fingers nervously something you've always done?"

"Um, yes. It started after my parents died. Used to drive my aunt nuts."

"I think we can agree that your aunt's opinion doesn't matter. She has no weight here, no bearing. Whenever anything she has said comes into your mind, you're going to give me that too." He tapped his finger to her forehead lightly. "I can tell a lot more goes on in here than comes out here." Now he lightly ran his finger over her lips. Her breathing grew faster. "When it's just the two of us, the only things that matter is what I say matters. What I want. So anytime something interferes with that, you are to tell me what's going on."

"You want to know everything I'm thinking?"

"If we do this right, then you'll stop thinking altogether and just be in the moment. All those dark thoughts, all those worries will disappear. Because you'll come to realize that the only important thing is pleasing me."

Okay, on the one hand that sounded nice. Not to worry or think or fret. But on the other hand, she wasn't sure she only wanted to think about pleasing him.

"Tell me what you're thinking right now."

"I'm thinking that you're pretty arrogant."

Oh, fuck. Why did I say that?

But instead of looking angry, his lips twitched. "All this time, I've been playing with subs who wouldn't dare say that to me, even if they were thinking it. And along comes Calamity Jane, rocking up my world. Seems I've been missing out."

"You . . . I . . . I'm not sure whether you want me to apologize or tell you that you're welcome." Was it a compliment or a complaint?

"Truth is, neither am I. Things seem to have quieted in your head. Let's have our chat."

She began to stand, and he squeezed one of her hands. "Did I say you could move?"

She froze. Crap. "No, Sir."

"Then why are you moving?"

Drat. Shit. "Sorry, Sir." She moved back into position. "I think I should confess that I was never good at Simon Says."

"What?"

"You know that game where you have to do what Simon says but if you move when they don't say Simon says, you're out."

He blinked for a moment then shook his head. "Yeah, I know the rules of Simon Says. There are a few differences between what we're doing and the rules of Simon Says. I'm not trying to trick you into doing the wrong thing, all right? I don't want you to mess up so you're out of the game. That's not what's happening here. You make a mistake; we talk about it. Fix it so you don't make mistakes like that again. You mess up big, and by big, I mean you lie to me, you disobey my health and safety rules, well, we'll talk about it, then I'll punish you. Like I said, I don't expect perfection. You make a mistake like moving when I didn't give you permission, I correct you. You keep making the same mistake then I might think you need something to help you remember. Like a hot ass. Or clamps on your nipples. Or a plug up your bottom."

Okay, was there something wrong with her that her heart raced at those words.

"Good. So whenever we have a talk, whether it be before or after a scene, this is the position you're going to be in, understand?"

"Yes, Sir."

"After dinner is cleared each night and my brothers have gone back to that cesspool they live in, you're going to come in here to my office. You'll strip and leave your clothes at the door. Then you will come to me. If I'm sitting, you kneel beside my chair. If I'm standing, you kneel at my feet. At those times, your hands are clasped behind your back, your head down, knees apart. Understand?"

Her heart raced at the idea of kneeling naked and waiting for him to acknowledge her.

"Yes, Sir."

"You do not speak or move from that position until I give my permission. The only exception to this is using your safeword. I would expect you to use it if you were in any pain. When you're kneeling like that, it's quiet time, understand? If you need my help reaching that silence in your head, you may get my attention by resting your head against my leg."

"Yes, Sir."

"Any questions so far?"

"So we're going to do all our play in here, Sir?"

"For the time being."

That seemed odd to her. Did that mean they wouldn't even sleep together?

"Next question, I can see it there. And this is the best time for it. Get everything out on the table so there are no misunderstandings."

Damn, maybe he *could* read what was going on inside her head?

"This will . . . I mean . . . will we sleep together?" she blurted out.

"Well, we need to discuss that. Do you want to include sex? Full penetration? Anal sex? Oral sex?"

Her mouth dropped open. Closed. Opened again.

He grinned and her heart stopped. Jesus, when he smiled, he had the power to turn her inside out.

"I can see I've rendered you speechless. Let me see if I can help. I want it all. I want to be able to lick your clit, explores your plump, sweet pussy, to make you scream as you come on my tongue. I want to train that ass to take me, to stretch it with plugs then fuck it. I want your mouth on my cock, taking me deep, swallowing down every drop I give you. And I want to take that pussy with my dick. Do you want any or all of that?"

She just nodded.

"Kitten, you need to give me more than that."

"I want that. All of that."

Satisfaction filled his face. Hunger lit his eyes. She licked her lips. Hell, yeah, she wanted all of that.

"Good," he murmured. "I'm clean. I was tested six months ago. And I always use condoms."

Um. Okay. "I was tested a year ago after my boyfriend broke up with me. I was clean. I haven't had sex since then."

"You said you got shots for birth control?"

"Yes, but I missed my last one."

"So we'll still use condoms."

"Sorry."

He cupped her chin. "Listen to me. Your job is to obey me. Your job is to please me. Your job is to tell me when you're struggling, to give me your problems so I can help you. Do you know what my job is?"

"Um, to show me what it's like to have a Dom?"

"Nope, that's our agreement. As your Dom, do you know what my job is?"

"To give me lots of orgasms?" she asked hopefully.

"No, kitten. That's a side-benefit. But I could be your Dom without there being any sexual component to it."

Her mind scrambled. "Is it to protect me?"

He nodded. "My job is to protect you. If necessary, it's to guide you, teach you, protect you and discipline you. Making certain you don't get pregnant comes under protecting you, got it?"

"Yes, Sir." Happiness filled her. Her cousin had always done his best to protect her, but she'd always felt like she wasn't giving anything in return. This felt fairer. She gave Alec what he wanted, and he took care of her.

Yeah. Nice.

"I can see that pleases you," he said dryly.

"Yes, Sir."

"Good. It pleases me too. You should know that sometimes it won't always be easy to do what I require of you. But I still expect you to do so, unless, you're overwhelmed or frightened or in pain. Then you use your safeword."

"What is my safeword?"

"We're going to use the traffic light system. Green for everything is good. Yellow when I need things to slow down. And Red for stop. And you will use them if you need to."

She licked her lips. "I don't want to disappoint you, Sir."

"Using them won't disappoint me. Not unless you try to manipulate me. And I don't believe you're the sort of sub to do that."

No, she didn't think so either.

"But I am going to teach you how to ask for what you need."

He thought she was a pushover. A doormat. She let people walk over her.

He grasped hold of her ponytail again, giving it a tug. Ouch. "That voice is back in your head, isn't it?"

She glared up at him. "Are you going to do that every time I have a thought that you don't like?"

"Yes."

"But you don't even know what I'm thinking."

"I can guess by the way you tensed up and the dark look in your eyes. Also, you should watch your tone of voice when you speak to me. Same with how you just glared at me."

Oh, crap.

"What are we going to do to address that lapse in respect, hmm?"

"Um, tell me I'm a naughty girl and then move on?"

He smiled. It wasn't a nice smile. Nope, that grin would make the Joker pause.

"Take off your top and bra."

Oh, fuck. Oh, shit. Was she ready for this?

"Every second that I have to wait for your obedience, your punishment becomes more severe," he warned.

She reached for the hem of her thin T-shirt and pulled it up over her head. It was a shirt that one of the boys had bought her in town. It was plain white with an image of red lips right over her boobs.

"I should burn that T-shirt," he grumbled. "Should have known not to send Raid to get you some stuff. Damn thing is practically see-through."

She blushed a little. She'd hoped nobody else had realized that. But, yeah, it was.

She reached behind her to unclasp her bra. It was worn and too big for her

Alec reached out and ran his finger beneath the cup of the bra, against her breast. "This doesn't fit right."

She shrugged. "I guess I've lost weight since it was bought."

He frowned. "Then should you be wearing it?"

"I've only got two bras. Don't have much choice. Not that I probably even need it, not like I've got much there."

"Bras weren't on the list of things you gave to me."

She paused. The bra was undone but she hadn't pulled it off yet. "Um, I was not about to let Raid pick out some bras for me."

"You need them."

"Can you just imagine what sort of bras he would have picked out?"

He looked thoughtful. "Go online and choose some new underwear tomorrow, then you can show me what you've chosen before our session tomorrow night and I'll get them for you."

"You-you don't have to do that."

"What's your job?"

"To obey you. Please you. But how does that please you?"

"It pleases me to have you in underwear that fits. If it makes you feel better, my favorite colors on you are teal and peach. I like lacy. And matching underwear."

"Okay." Far be it for her to argue if he wanted to see her in sexy underwear.

"Continue," he ordered with an arrogant nod of his head.

She took in a deep breath, trying not to feel too self-conscious as she pulled her bra off and placed it on top of her T-shirt.

He stared down at her breasts, not saying a word. She knew they were small. But then she guessed they were proportional. She was small all over. Some people might be envious of her size. But for her, it was a constant battle to stay in a healthy weight range and these past few months had not helped that one bit. Anytime she got anxious or nervous or afraid, the first thing she did was stop eating. She'd lost close to fifteen pounds since the night she'd walked in to find her coworkers had all been murdered. And she didn't have a hope in hell of gaining it back anytime soon. So, yeah, at the moment she was leaning towards gaunt and ill rather than svelte and sexy.

Not that she'd ever really been sexy.

"I know they're small. Even before I lost all this weight, they were small. Not much I can do about it, I guess."

She braced herself. Was he disappointed? Did he wish they were something more? Surely he'd noticed she had nothing there.

"How much weight have you lost?"

All right, that wasn't what she'd expected him to focus on. "Um, about fifteen pounds last time I checked. Might have changed since then."

"All right, then." He nodded then leaned forward and reaching out, took hold of her chin in one hand, and cupped her right breast with the other hand. "I don't care about their size or your size. So long as you're healthy. And we're going to work on that, aren't we?"

She sucked in a breath as he twisted her nipple, it was painful. But, oh, how her clit throbbed in reaction.

Holy shit. This man was dynamite to her senses. How the hell was she ever going to survive her time with him? What if he ruined her for all other men?

But, then again, she'd kick herself if she didn't give this a chance. Because tomorrow wasn't a guaranteed thing for her. So she was going to grasp everything she could today. Including having Alec Malone strip her naked and play with her nipples.

"We are, Sir?"

"We are. Or have you forgotten your new rule for eating already?" He gave her a stern look.

"No, Sir. I haven't."

"Good." He ran his thumb over her nipple. "These are gorgeous. Pink and perfect. I'm going to enjoy playing with them. I want you to stand now and go to the bottom drawer of my desk on the left-hand side. You'll see a black box in there, bring it to me."

He held out a hand to her. She put her hand in his, feeling the warmth and strength in his palm, the calluses that proved he wasn't a man who sat around in his office, making everyone else do the hard work. He helped her stand and then turned her, giving her a sharp smack on her butt to get her moving.

Felt a bit weird, walking around with no top or bra on. Thankfully, he'd already pulled the blinds, so she didn't have to worry about someone walking past and seeing her. The door to the office wasn't locked, though. She glanced over at it worriedly.

"What's your job?" he demanded suddenly.

She jumped and turned to look at him. "Um, to obey you. Please you."

"And what should you be doing?"

"Getting the black box. Sir."

"What should you not be doing?"

"Sir?"

"You don't need to worry about someone walking in here. First of all, no one would without permission. Second, you're only doing what I require of you. That's your job. To please me. So why should you worry about who sees you?"

She gave him an incredulous look. Perhaps because one of his brothers could walk in and see her boobs? What would she do? Say? How could she look them in the eye again?

"What's my role?" he demanded. "What do I do for you?"

Why did he keep talking about their roles? "Guide, teach, protect, and discipline."

"That's right. And protecting you doesn't just mean I protect your body. It means I look after your emotions and your feelings. I'm not going to let anyone disrespect you or hurt you. You're safe with me."

Safe with him? She'd never been safe with anyone. The closest she'd ever felt was with her cousin. And this was nothing like that.

"Repeat it."

She took in a deep breath. "I'm safe with you."

"Now say it like you believe it."

"I'm safe with you."

"And again."

"I'm safe with you." A feeling of peace stole over her.

"And you are doing what I require."

"I am doing what you require."

She was safe with him. She was doing what he required. No matter what happened, it was his will and he would protect her. Calm moved through her. And she walked towards the desk. She had a job and she wasn't doing what was required of her.

She opened the drawer then grabbed the small black box and turned to walk back towards him. He was watching her through heavy-lidded eyes.

"Damn, you're fucking beautiful."

They weren't the most eloquent words, not even close. But they meant the world to her. And she held her shoulders back a bit more. She could feel herself grow more confident. She might not have curves and boobs or much of an ass. But she knew Alec Malone wasn't the type to say things he didn't mean. He didn't have to. He could have anyone he wanted. But right now, he was here with her.

She knelt between his legs again and offered up the black box.

"Good girl," he told her in a soft voice.

More of those good feelings. She could get used to this. She didn't ever want to go back into the cold.

He took the box from her hand and opened it, pulling out two silver clamps. "Know what these are?"

Her breath caught in her throat. "Are they nipple clamps?"

"They are. Stand up."

She stood. Her legs trembled. "Will it hurt, Sir?"

"Yes, it likely will. Even more so when I attach the weight to them. Do you need to use your safeword?"

She thought that over for a moment. She wanted to know what this was like. She wasn't going to turn away at the first test.

"No, Sir. I can do this."

"Good kitten." He leaned in and sucked one nipple into his mouth. She gasped as the heat of his mouth surrounded her tight bud. He flicked his tongue over the tip and she nearly collapsed at his feet, so intense was the pleasure that flooded her.

"Easy, kitten. You just concentrate on standing nice and still for me." He lightly twisted her nipple.

Oh, God. Oh, hell.

"Deep breath in, baby. That's it." He placed the clamp over the nipple and tightened it. The slight pressure wasn't painful exactly. But she could definitely feel it. He moved to her other nipple, sucking it into his mouth, then he fastened the clamp to it.

Then he attached a chain to each clamp that had a small weight dangling from the end of it. The pressure increased and she hissed.

"You did so well, kitten."

Heat filled her at his words, making her tummy go all gooey.

"Now stand up and strip off the rest," he ordered. Again, he took hold of her hand, helping her up.

Nerves bounced around as she quickly stripped off her jeans and panties. She wanted to get this over and done with quickly, like pulling off a Band-Aid. When she was naked, she went to climb onto his lap, but he held up a hand, staying her. So she stood there awkwardly. Uncertain what exactly he wanted her to do.

"Beautiful. Don't look so worried. I'll tell you what I want from you. You'll never have to guess or wonder. You'll know when you're in trouble, when you've pleased me. Now, I want to look my fill first. Turn around, let me see your bottom."

Oh, dear Lord. What had she gotten herself into? But she turned obediently until her back was to him.

"Bend over, grasp your ankles with your hands and spread your legs apart."

Holy hell. This was not exactly what she'd expected. Although she hadn't been sure what she'd thought would happen. That they'd sit down and negotiate a contract and then maybe he'd spank her ass again and hopefully give her an orgasm? Possibly, but not this. Not that she would have to put herself completely on display.

"Kitten, bend over and grasp hold of your ankles. If you need to use your safewords, they're there. We can stop and talk if you need to. Otherwise get into position. I'm not going to ask again."

There wasn't really much to discuss. Other than the fact that she'd had three sexual partners in her life and they'd all been the under-the-sheets-missionary-style type. Taking a bracing breath, she bent over, spread her legs slightly, and took hold of her ankles.

The clamps on her nipples pulled as the small weights swung around. Fuck. Fuck. She might be totally out of her comfort zone, but damned if her pussy wasn't throbbing and wet.

"Good girl. I know that was hard for you and I'm pleased at how you obeyed me."

"Even though I hesitated at first, Sir?" she asked.

"Like I said, I'm not expecting perfection. I know this isn't that easy. You have your safewords if you need them. Poor baby, I noticed how difficult it was to sit tonight, does your bottom still hurt?"

She felt him move then he grasped hold of one ass cheek, squeezing.

"Yes, Sir!"

"Hmm, going to hurt worse once we get to your other spanking, isn't it?" He didn't sound the least concerned by that. Why should he? Wasn't his butt that was going to get pounded.

"Bet there was something else that was aching after I left you this afternoon, wasn't there?" He reached down and cupped her mound. Then he ran a finger along her slit, dipping the tip in between her lower lips. "Still wet. Is it from the clamps? Or because I ordered you to bend over and present for me? Or is it because I'm talking about punishment and spankings?"

She didn't say anything, she was too busy wishing he'd move his finger a bit further forward. She wouldn't need much, just a few flicks on his finger against her clit to send her soaring over the edge.

A sharp smack landed on her ass. Then another and another.

"Sir!" she cried out as he reignited the heat in her bottom.

"When I ask a question, I expect an answer, understand me?"

Oh, shit. "I'm sorry, Sir. I, well, it's all of the above, Sir."

As soon as she answered him, he stopped spanking her and his finger returned to her pussy, he pushed it slowly inside her, penetrating her.

"So warm. So wet. Damn, you're going to feel so good around my cock, aren't you, kitten? Do you want my dick here? Taking you? Fucking you?"

"Yes, Sir. Please."

"You were very naughty. I should deny you my dick as part of your punishment for breaking a rule." He was pushing his finger in and out of her pussy as he spoke. "And of course, you'd also be denied your own pleasure."

She groaned at that. "No, Sir. Please."

"Do you deny that you were naughty, kitten?"

Oh, hell. The things he said to her.

"No, Sir. I disobeyed you. I'm sorry, Sir."

"I know, baby. Unfortunately, that was a very important rule that you broke. I won't have you putting yourself in danger. Ever. Understand?"

"Yes, Sir. I understand."

"Very good." He pulled his finger out of her pussy and ran it up between her ass cheeks. "Damn, you have a beautiful ass. Round and plump. Perfect."

She'd never thought of any part of her as perfect before. But she liked it when he said it to her.

"All right, kitten, stand up. Easy." He held her steady as she rose quickly, making her head spin. When the world righted itself, she found herself blushing with embarrassment as she stared into his concerned face.

"You okay, kitten? Do you need a break? A drink of water?"

She wasn't used to being fussed over. It made her feel special.

"I'm fine, thank you, Sir. Just stood up too quickly."

He frowned. "Next time, rise more slowly, understand?"

"Yes, Sir." She was still red with embarrassment. Way to ruin the mood, Mia.

He reached out and tugged at one of the clamps. She gasped as her nipple protested the sharp, pinching pain. But then arousal flooded through her, the pain morphing into something else. Something hot and demanding.

"No bad thoughts, remember?" he told her. "Now, we're going

to sit down and talk about limits and expectations because I am very close to just bending you over the back of the sofa and fucking you."

"That sounds like fun, Sir," she said breathlessly.

He chuckled and shook his head. "No, we're going to do this properly, kitten." He turned and walked to his desk, picking up a piece of paper and a pen. Then he walked back and sat in the armchair.

"Up on my lap, straddle me, kitten."

She'd never sat on anyone's lap like that before. She wasn't sure where to put her hands or what he expected her to do.

He tugged at the chain attached to one of her nipples and pain slashed through her, clearing her mind.

"That's better," he growled. "I want your attention on me. Not worrying about everything else."

"I'm just . . . not sure what you want me to do."

He ran his finger along her breast. "You're sitting on my lap, half-naked with your nipples clamped. I would say you are doing exactly what I told you to do, are you not?"

"Yes, Sir." Calm filled her again. She liked the calm. It was a good place to be.

"That's my baby. Don't these nipples look pretty all dressed up. Going to have to get you some more nipple clamps. Maybe a clit clamp that connects to them."

Her breath caught at his words; her pulse raced.

"I can see my baby likes that idea. Clamps on your nipples and clit, a plug in your ass, your arms and feet bound, yeah, I can see how that turns you on. Tell me, if I touched your clit right now would you come?"

"I-I think so, Sir."

"Best I remind you that you're not to come without permission then," he murmured, grasping her chin and pulling her in for a kiss. "Understand?"

"Yes, Sir."

Then, as though she weren't sitting there naked on his lap with her nipples clamped, he started to calmly go through the contract in his hand. He asked her about her limits, soft and hard, went over the rules he'd made for her again.

It was the strangest conversation of her life. And it hadn't helped her gain control over her arousal one bit. In fact, by the end of it she felt so damn hot and bothered that she was practically squirming on his lap.

"Sit still," he growled at her.

She immediately froze. "Good girl. I know this isn't easy on you, but I do expect you to take this seriously."

"I am, Sir. Really."

"Is there anything you want to add then?" He looked a little mollified at her words.

"No, Sir. I don't think so."

"Climb off my lap. We'll go over to the desk to sign it."

She wiggled back off his lap. Damn it, she'd kind of been hoping he'd end negotiations with some mutual pleasure. But instead, he stood and took hold of her hand, leading her over to the desk. He placed the contract down and signed it then handed the pen to her.

"Take the time to read it over," he told her.

Even though she wanted nothing more than to get on with things, she did check everything. Then she signed her name at the bottom.

"I did it. I signed." She turned to look at him. He stood behind her, his arms crossed over his chest, a small grin on his face.

"Good. That means you're mine now." He came over then wrapped his arm around the nape of her neck. And then he kissed her. It was possessive. Hot. Wild. And she felt her legs weakening, her heart racing, her need for him so intense it might have frightened her if she were capable of holding onto a thought for more than a few seconds and at a time.

He kissed his way along her jaw then down her neck, reaching her nipple. She sucked in a breath as he reached for one nipple clamp, removing it. She let out a cry as blood rushed back into the distended nipple. Fuck! That hurt. Immediately, he took her poor nipple into his mouth, sucking gently, licking it until the pain disappeared. He moved to the other nipple, giving it the same treatment. Oh, God. Oh, God.

"Poor baby, bet that hurt, didn't it?" He sounded sympathetic, but since he'd been the one to cause the pain in the first place, she wasn't really buying it. He gave her another soft kiss then pulled back.

"Now, lean over the desk, grasp the edge with your hands and spread your legs."

14

He stood there, staring at her, one eyebrow raised imperiously. Swallowing nervously, she turned and positioned herself.

What was he going to do? Would he tell her or just do it? Shit. Shit. Shit.

A hand smacked down on her ass, making her gasp. "You're worrying, kitten. Scared?"

"A little, Sir."

"A little fear is fine. You get too scared, you use your safewords. Understand?"

"Yes. Sir?"

"Yes?" He was running his hand over her ass, and the need to press her legs together, to get some friction against her clit was almost overwhelming but she held herself still.

"What-what are you planning to do?"

He moved his hand between her thighs. "I'm not always going to tell you what's coming next, but since this is new to you, I'll go easy on you." He circled her clit in slow, lazy circles that soon had her gasping and biting down on her lip in an effort not to demand that he move his finger faster so she could come.

"First, I'm going to deal with the punishment you've got coming. It's not going to be as easy as the spanking you got earlier. No, this spanking needs to ensure that you will never disobey that rule again. It needs to show you how serious I am about your safety. And then, I'm going to spread you wide and I'm going to fuck you, right here over my desk. And if you're a very good girl I just might let you come. Don't expect that all the time after a punishment, though. Any questions?"

"N-no, Sir."

"Good girl." He moved his hand away from her and she had to bite back her protest. Probably just as well he had, since she had little faith in her ability to hold back her need to come until he gave his permission. With how on fire she felt, that just seemed like too big an ask.

His hand landed with a sharp slap on her ass cheek. Oh, God, he hadn't been joking. That one smack showed her that he meant business. Another smack landed on her other cheek. She sucked in a breath. Each slap of his hand against her ass was heavy and hard and made a very instant impression. It didn't take long until her ass was burning, a deep throb that filled her entire body. Tears dripped down her face and she clung to the desk, holding on for dear life.

Fuck. Fuck. It was too much. She couldn't take much more. Just when she thought she might have to use her safeword, he started talking.

"I don't ever . . . ever want to receive a phone call like I did the other night, understand me?" he lectured between slaps. "Do you know how my heart stopped? I didn't know what had happened to you. I didn't know where you were. You are mine to take care of. And now you're also mine to fuck, to discipline, to pleasure."

He moved his hand down to the tender skin of her thighs and

she started to bawl. Heavy sobs wracked her body. He laid several heavy, sharp smacks to her upper legs and oh, God, they hurt. They stung. And she knew she wouldn't forget this lesson for a while.

Gradually, she became aware he'd stopped. That he was lightly rubbing her lower back and making low crooning noises. Then he carefully pulled her up and took her into his arms.

He kissed her. Even though tears were still dripping down her face and she no doubt looked like a complete mess, he kissed her. It was hot. It was wild. And the pain in her bottom was soon forgotten as another more pressing need took over.

"Sir, please," she begged as he pulled back and kissed his way down her neck.

"Please what?"

She didn't say anything more. She couldn't. He drew back to look down at her, the look on his face so stern she felt a moment of worry.

"What do you need, kitten? I want you to tell me."

"Aren't you supposed to know?" she asked desperately.

"Oh, I know what you need. But I want you to ask me for it."

Christ. That was the last thing she wanted to do. He grasped her face between his large, warm hands. "And just so you know, you're not getting it until you ask."

Well, fuck. She licked her lips, opened her mouth, closed it. Why was this so damn hard for her? For some reason, tears entered her eyes and he grew all blurry.

"Baby, it's okay. You're safe here. I'm going to take care of you. Nothing bad is going to happen because you ask for what you need. I promise you that."

"I need you to take me. Fuck me. I need you to make me come. So badly. Please, Sir."

A smile crossed his face. His eyes melted, and her stomach lost that tight, knotty feeling. She'd pleased him, she could see that as clear as day. He was happy and she'd done that. She sighed happily.

"Good girl. Such a good girl. And darlin', there's nothing I want more than to fuck you." He took a step back, surprising her. If he wanted to fuck her, shouldn't he be getting closer. "Strip me, kitten."

Oh, with pleasure.

HER GAZE LOST THAT SAD, worried look as pleasure filled her face. That was better. He hated causing her any sort of stress or upset, but he was determined to ensure she knew she could make her needs known. She reached for his shirt, her hands trembling slightly. He knew how she felt; he was feeling a little unsteady himself.

She undid each button, moving so slowly it was torture, but then she spread his shirt open and tugged it the rest of the way off. And the way she stared at him, as though she wanted to lick every inch of the skin she'd revealed, well it made the wait worth it.

"Touch me," he commanded. Right then, he wanted nothing more than to feel her hands caressing him, touching him.

She ran her hands down his chest, her touch light.

"I won't break, kitten."

"Just savoring the moment, Sir. You're so gorgeous. Can I taste you?"

"Yes," he said in a tight voice. That breathless tone to her voice, the need he could hear just made him hungrier for her. She leaned in and, instead of going for his nipple as he'd expected, she bent and ran her tongue from his belly button all the way up his chest to the base of his neck. Then she laid kisses along his collar bone. Her touch was soft and gentle, yet he was more turned on than he could ever remember being. He clenched his hands into fists to keep himself from grabbing her and throwing her on the desk.

Slow. Easy.

She moved to his nipple, sucking it into her mouth. He dropped his head back, fighting his baser urges as she suckled. Fuck, what he wouldn't give to feel her mouth around his dick.

Not yet, asshole.

Build her up to it. He couldn't just lay everything on her at once. She let go of his nipple then stepped back slightly and looked up at him. Then with shaking hands, she reached for his pants. He grabbed hold of her hand without thinking. Her eyes widened with alarm.

He cleared his throat, fighting his need to order her to her knees then take her mouth.

"I thought you wanted me to strip you, Sir."

"Not yet," he told her.

Her brows came together. "Did I do something wrong?"

Shit. Stop fucking this up.

He cupped her face between his palms, watching her face shut down before him. "How can you do anything wrong when you're doing what I told you to do? If you do something wrong, I'll tell you."

"Oh." Her face cleared. "Then why, Sir?"

He clenched his teeth together, debating whether to tell her. In the end, he realized he couldn't very well demand that she give him everything while giving her nothing in return. Not that he ever intended to tell her his all his secrets. But he could give her this.

"Why do you think I like playing with experienced subs?"

A hurt look filled her face before she quickly washed it away.

"Damn it." He raised her face, but she kept her eyes averted. "Give me those eyes, kitten."

She blinked. But didn't look at him. Nope, that wasn't going to do. He reached around behind her and pulling her close to his body with one arm so she couldn't escape him, he laid a barrage of spanks on her ass. Her skin felt hot to the touch from her previous punishment and so he didn't go too hard on her. Even so, when he pulled back, tears had blurred her eyes. He reached up and caught an errant tear on his finger then brought it up to his lips.

"Kitten, when I ask a question, I want an answer. And when I tell you to give me your eyes, I expect you to look at me immediately."

"Yeah, I'm getting that," she said ruefully, reaching around to rub her ass. He caught her hands in his, pinning them behind her back.

"Uh-uh, no rubbing. Little kittens who rub their hot bottoms after a punishment get to spend some time in the corner with their ass on display and their hands bound behind them."

He noticed the flush that ran up her cheeks. Embarrassment at the idea of being on display? Of being treated like a naughty child? Was that a hint of arousal as well?

"Well? Why do you think I play with experienced subs?"

"Because you want someone who knows what they're doing? Who submits fully and without causing you any problems?"

Okay, she read him better than he'd thought. But she hadn't gotten it all.

"I do like that. Or thought I did. I must say, there's something to be said for a little kitten who pushes her boundaries. Not sure when the last time I put a naughty subbie in the corner was and I find myself looking forward to the next time you provide me with that opportunity."

She shook her head. "That's not going to happen."

He tugged at her hair. "Sir."

"That's not going to happen, Sir. I'm not going to do anything that will make you . . . make you put me in the corner."

He cupped the side of her face, staring down at her with a

mixture of amusement and affection. He hadn't played with anyone he'd cared about this much before. It made this a very different experience.

"You know if I actually believed that I might be a little disappointed," he told her. "Which goes against your reasoning, doesn't it? I mean, why would I look forward to punishing you when I usually play with subs who never disobey me, never push their boundaries, where the only pain I inflict is for pleasure—theirs or mine?"

"They enjoy pain?"

"Some do. To varying degrees. You telling me that spanking didn't turn you on a little? And before you answer, you should know there's a penalty for lying."

She glanced down.

"Eyes, kitten," he growled.

Her eyes went immediately up to meet his. "It hurt. But there was also some pleasure. Especially . . . " she trailed off.

"Especially?"

"The spanking you gave me earlier in my bedroom, when you rubbed my bottom, I got turned on by that."

He leaned in and kissed her lightly. "Thank you for being honest. Honesty and communication are very big between a Dom and sub. I can't read your mind. I'm pretty good with body language but when I ask questions, I need honest answers, understand?"

She nodded. "Yes, Sir."

"There's another reason I don't play with newbies," he told her.

"What's that, Sir?"

"I have needs that might scare someone who doesn't share my desires. I like my sex rough, kitten. I like to fuck. Hard. I enjoy mixing pain with my pleasure. And I only choose partners who enjoy that as well."

Her eyes had grown wide as she stared up at him.

"Don't look so scared. I'm not telling you this to frighten you, but because I want you to know why I might need to slow things down sometimes, like not removing my jeans right now. It gives me a minute to calm things down. To remind me that I can't just shove you against a wall and take you. That I have to take care. That I have to be gentle."

"Why?"

He blinked. That wasn't the response he'd expected. Actually, he'd half-expected her to call things off, and he wouldn't have blamed her.

"What do you mean, why?"

"Why do you have to be gentle? I mean, maybe this first time I wouldn't want to try it, but I don't want you to curtail your needs because of me."

"Mia—"

"No, just listen. Please, Sir," she said hastily, no doubt seeing his face darken as she interrupted him. "You seem to have this idea that I'm completely innocent, but I've had sex before—"

"Not sex like I want," he interrupted.

"No, I've never done anything like this before," she admitted. "But how do I know I wouldn't like things rough if I've never tried? I think I might like to try that."

"Really?" he drawled. "You'd be happy for me to bend you over whatever piece of furniture was closest and fuck you when the need comes over me? To go around without panties on so when desire strikes, I can just flip up your skirt or pull your pants down and fuck you? Or paddle you? Or take off my belt and lay stripe after stripe on your skin? You'd be happy for me to order you to your knees to give me a blow job? For me to wrap your hair around my hand and fuck your mouth? To push as far as I could until you found yourself struggling to take me? That's what you want to try? Because there wouldn't always be a warm-up. There wouldn't always be pleasure for you."

. . .

HER NIPPLES WERE hard and aching by the time he finished talking, and her heart was racing so hard she actually felt a little ill.

"Well?" he demanded harshly. She knew he was trying to scare her off, but he'd just stirred her curiosity. Every word he'd said had ratcheted up her arousal.

"I wouldn't want anyone to see me," she stipulated.

"People are going to see you if we're at the club."

Sadness filled her for a moment. "But we can't go to the club."

His eyes were hard, merciless, his jaw could have been cut from granite. She reached up and cupped his face, worried he might push her hand away or reject her. She wasn't certain she could take his rejection. But he remained still. She ran a finger over his mouth, and he opened his lips and took it into his mouth, sucking strongly.

"I wouldn't want any of your brothers to see us."

"All right," he said immediately.

"I don't have any experience to call on to know whether I'd like any of that stuff or not. But you like it, and I want to try."

"I don't want you doing anything that you hate or makes you scared because you think I need it. Because this arrangement isn't about what I need. It's about showing you what you need. About teaching you to ask for what you need. It's showing you your submissive side."

She didn't like that. It sounded entirely too one-sided. She wanted him to get what he needed as well. She didn't want to be some charity case he'd taken on.

Poor little orphaned girl.

He reached out and squeezed one nipple, making her squeak and go up on her toes.

"What was that thought?" he growled.

Shit. He could read her too well. How did he do that? She guessed from years of being a Dom.

"I don't want to be some sort of charity case to you," she told him. The pain in her nipple brought tears to her eyes. He eased up as she spoke. "I've spent enough of my life being an obligation. I want to give to you."

"You will." His eyes warmed. "Don't worry about that. But we'll do things my way."

She opened her mouth to protest and he placed his hand over her lips. "At least until I decide otherwise. And if I decide you're ready, then we'll see just whether you can handle my dark side."

She shivered a little at his words.

"For now, we've got to deal with the fact that you've forgotten how to address me."

Oh, fuck. He wasn't going to spank her again, was he? She wasn't sure how much more her poor ass could take.

"You've never taken anything in your ass? Never been fucked there? Had your asshole played with?"

She shook her head.

"Words, kitten."

"No, Sir. Never." Anal sex has been on her list of things to try.

A smile crossed his face. "Good."

15

Ah, there was nothing like having a nervous little subbie waiting to find out what you were going to do to her next. He glanced over to where he'd placed Mia over the back of the armchair. Her hands were down on the seat of the chair, balancing herself. The back of the chair was low, so even though she was short, she could still touch the floor. And it put her at the perfect height for him to fuck her.

Soon.

Right now, he was running coating a small butt plug in lube. He'd ordered a set online, each one bigger than the last. He was doing it out of her eyesight so she wouldn't realize what he was about to do. He grinned as he walked up behind her.

"That is one pretty, pink ass," he murmured, reaching out to grab one ass cheek to squeeze it. "Spread your legs nice and wide."

She let out a sound of protest that soon turned to a moan of pleasure as he lightly massaged the cheek he'd just abused.

"Yeah, my baby likes her bottom to be touched and squeezed and played with, doesn't she?" He moved his hand down her ass to her pussy. "Did you shave this just for me?"

He heard her swallow.

"Yes," she said quietly.

He smacked his hand against her pussy, and she went up onto her tiptoes with a squeak of surprise.

"Yes, what?"

"Yes, Sir. Sorry, Sir. I'm sorry I keep forgetting."

"Sh," he soothed, hearing a note of true distress. He had to remember that she had a deep need to please. He didn't want her too stressed. Certainly, she needed to remember how to address him. But not to the point that she worked herself up about it. "We're gonna work on that. Every time you need a reminder, I will be only too pleased to provide one."

"I'll bet," she muttered.

"What was that?" he asked with another smack to her pussy.

"Nothing, Sir."

He reached up with his hand and spread her ass cheeks. She tensed.

"Easy, little subbie," he soothed. "I'm not going to do anything that will harm you." He ran the tip of the plug over her puckered hole. "It might feel uncomfortable, there might be a little pain at first, but it won't cause you any damage. This plug is very small. Especially in comparison to me. And I definitely intend to take you here at some stage."

"Oh, God," she groaned as he pressed the tip into her bottom.

"Take a nice deep breath in," he told her in a low, commanding voice. "That's it, now let it out slowly and work on relaxing."

"That is not a simple thing to do, Sir," she told him.

"Hmm, well, luckily you're going to get lots of practice since I intend to play with you here. A lot. And maybe having something up your bottom will help you focus and remember how to address me."

"Yes, Sir." She took in a deep breath and as she started to let it out, he pressed the plug inside her, pushing it gently but relent-lessly past the tight ring of muscle until it was fully seated inside her.

He tapped the end of it, listening to her groan. "See? That wasn't so bad, was it?"

"Have you ever had a plug in your ass, Sir?"

"Yes, I have."

She turned to look back at him, giving him a startled glance.

He raised an eyebrow. "Surprises you?"

"Well, yes, Sir. Why?"

"I like to experience things before I inflict them on others. There isn't much I haven't tried." He smiled bitterly. "Eyes down, subbie. I didn't say you could look back at me."

She turned her head around. "Sorry, Sir."

"How does that plug feel? Squeeze your ass around it." As he spoke, he ran his hands down her thighs then reached around to find her pussy wet and warm. He flicked his finger across her clit, hearing her groan.

"It's a little weird, Sir. But it feels better when you do that."

He had to grin at the hope in her voice. "Aw, is my little kitten in need of an orgasm? Has it been hard for you, having to go all afternoon without any pleasure? Has your clit been swollen and aching since that session in your bedroom?" As he spoke, he played with her clit, circling it then flicked at it firmly.

Her breath came in sharp pants as she pressed back against his hand. But to her credit, she didn't move out of position.

"Yes, Sir. It was so hard. Oh, Sir, please . . . "

"Please what?" he asked in a low voice.

"Please. Please . . . "

He started to withdraw his fingers.

"Please make me come, Sir!" she said quickly.

"Good girl," he murmured. "Such a good girl to ask for what

you need. And you asked so prettily that I'm not going to stop at just one orgasm."

With two fingers of his other hand, he penetrated her, pushing deep. She clenched down around him. Jesus, she was tight. So tight that he worried he shouldn't take her this first time with a plug inside her. But the plug wasn't that big and damn, she was going to feel good around him.

"That's right, clench down on me. This is exactly what you're going to do when my dick is inside you, when I'm taking you. You're going to suck me in, you're going to welcome me into this tight sheath, aren't you?"

"Yes, Sir."

"Stay in position. I want you to stay nice and still while I make you come. But you're not to hold anything back, understand me? You're not to smother any noises." He leaned over her. "Sir wants to hear you scream."

"Yes, Sir."

He drew back into his previous position and brushed his finger against her clit, moving it faster and with more pressure, driving her higher and higher.

"Come for me, kitten. Come nice and hard."

It didn't take much more. Just a few flicks of his finger against her clit until she came. Her pussy pulsed around his fingers, her cries of pleasure filled the room and he knew he couldn't wait much more to have her.

But he brought her down slowly, still gently rubbing her clit as he pulled his fingers free. He brought them up to his mouth and tasted her.

"Damn, you taste fucking delicious."

A SHIVER RAN up her spine at his words. Then she felt him move away from her and she had to work hard not to turn and look at what he was doing. She heard some rustling. Then what sounded like a drawer opening.

Then he moved up behind her, placing soft kisses up the inside of her thigh. Was he? Oh, God, he was . . . she groaned as he moved to her pussy and his tongue ran along her slickened lips.

"Sir," she groaned.

"You don't like having your pussy licked?" he asked.

Oh, no, she liked it all right. And as his tongue flicked against her clit, she discovered she liked it very much.

"No, Sir. I mean, I like it. But, do you?"

"Baby, with the way you taste and smell you can bet your ass you're going to have trouble keeping my mouth away from this pretty, plump pussy."

Shit. The things he said to her. It sent more waves of arousal flooding through her and she let out a low moan as she felt his tongue enter her passage. It was decadent. It was stunning. Somehow, she didn't think he would spend so much time on her pleasure. Her breath came in sharp pants as he used his thumb to toy with her clit while his tongue thrust in and out of her passage.

"Sir! Oh, Sir!"

She was so close to coming again. How was that possible? She'd never had one orgasm after another. And there she was, close to that cliff again in a matter of minutes since her last orgasm.

She had to fight the urge to fall over, knowing she wasn't allowed to reach that peak without his permission. God, that was hard. But she wanted to please him, wanted to be what he needed. When he drew away from her, it was a shock and she let out a noise of protest.

"Fuck, yes, baby. You need to come again, don't you?" He placed his hands on her hips and she felt his cock nudge at her entrance. Oh, God, was he going to fuck her while the plug was still inside her? She hadn't seen his dick, but she had a good idea he wasn't going to be on the small side.

He slowly drove himself inside her, pausing to let her adjust. A sweat broke out over her skin, her body trembling with a combination of need and trepidation, because she knew by the feel of him that he wasn't small at all. In fact, he was stretching her almost to the point of pain.

If she hadn't been so slick from her orgasm, it might have been more of a struggle.

And you want him to get rough with you? To fuck you without giving you pleasure in return?

Well, that had been before she'd felt how big he was. But even knowing his size, she knew she'd still want to try. Because it was who he was. And she wanted to show him that she loved who he was. That she could be what he needed.

A hand wrapped around her hair and tugged. Fuck, he was a bit too fond of doing that. But the sharp pain definitely brought her focus back onto him.

"You're thinking too much. When you're with me, when my hands are on you, there is only kitten and Sir, understand?"

"Yes, Sir," she gasped as he thrust deep, seating himself inside her. Oh, the burn. It was delicious and painful all at once.

And she wanted more.

Luckily, he wasn't in the mood to make her wait. He drew back and drove forward. He fucked her. There was no other word for it. She just held on for the ride. Tried to keep her position as best she could. And she took him. Over and over.

Never had sex been like this before. So raw. So hot. So all-consuming.

"You're going to come with me, kitten," he commanded, reaching down with one hand to play with her clit.

Oh, God, she couldn't. Could she? But her body told her otherwise, her need building with an intensity that took her breath away.

"Come with me, baby. Now!"

She rushed over the edge, her head spinning, crying and bucking against him as she heard him give his own shout of satisfaction and he followed her over.

16

S he was lying on his desk on her back, her feet were flat on the surface, her knees were bent and her wrists had been tied to her ankles. She had a ball gag in her mouth, smothering any noises of pleasure and pain.

And there were plenty of both.

Before he'd ordered her onto his desk, he'd had her bend over it and he'd inserted a butt plug. This was the biggest one he'd given her yet and, oh, God, it had burned. And then the burn had become a hot ache in her pussy.

She held a squeaky toy in one hand, a substitute for her safe word, he'd told her.

Five days had passed since they'd signed that contract and she now found herself in this position, naked, bound and plugged on his desk because she was being punished.

But perhaps even worse than all that was the deep throbbing in her clit. She needed to come so badly. And that bastard kept pushing her to the edge and then pulling her back.

Who knew being so turned on could actually be a punishment?

Not looking away from his computer screen, he reached out and ran a finger through her slick lips then pushed it deep into her pussy. He just kept it there, not moving it.

"You've been a very naughty girl, haven't you, kitten?"

He pressed another finger deep. And kept them still. It was torture. She longed to move her hips, to find any sort of friction. But she knew doing so would just result in him spanking her. She knew that for sure, since that was had happened when she'd tried earlier.

How long had she been lying there? How long was he going to continue to torture her?

"What was my rule about your necklace? You are to wear it at all times, aren't you? When you take it off to shower you put it on as soon as you get out. That was the rule, wasn't it, kitten? Not such a hard rule to follow. So why is the second time I've had to remind you to put it on?"

Christ. Why hadn't she remembered to put the thing back on this morning? He was right, it was the second time it had happened. The first time, he'd given her a firm scolding. This time, it seemed he was determined to drive her insane.

The necklace was a simple locket. But inside the locket was a GPS tracking chip he insisted she wear. She thought he was being overprotective. He disagreed.

"Isn't that right, kitten?"

She nodded. He pulled his fingers out, drove them in deep. In and out. His movements grew faster, harder and her breath became harsh, haggard pants as she pulled on her control.

She couldn't come. She couldn't come.

She didn't know what he would do to punish her if she did, but she was certain she wouldn't like it. He was strict. But fair. If she messed up, he always explained to her what she'd done wrong. Often, she got a free pass the first time but if it happened again, well, things like becoming a naked desk ornament happened.

She couldn't believe how much she needed his dominance. How quickly she'd come to crave it. And how well her body responded. She was never as calm, or her head never as quiet as after a session with him. It was like he cleared everything away. Because she only had to do as he told her.

Her one issue, and it was becoming bigger every day, was she knew he was holding back. He still hadn't shown her that darker side. She got it. She was new at this. She should be thankful for his control.

But she couldn't help but want more than what they had for a couple of hours each day, in his office.

You can't ask for more, Mia. You know better than that.

Suddenly his fingers withdrew from her pussy and then they smacked down on her clit. She groaned and arched.

"I seem to have lost your attention," he drawled in a low voice.

Oh, shit.

She shook her head as he stood and loomed over her.

"No? Are you sure? Perhaps I need to bring you back to me." He moved his laptop to one side then turned her so she lay along the edge of his desk. Then he undid his jeans, drawing them and his black boxers down to reveal his thick, hard erection.

Then he removed her ball gag. But before she had time to say anything. To do anything more than swallow hastily, he was pressing his dick against her mouth.

"Open up, kitten. Time to apologize for being so naughty."

Oh, she had no problem with that. She'd learned that she thoroughly enjoyed sucking him off. Giving him pleasure. It made her insides bubble with happiness.

She licked her way around his head as he'd taught her, then took him deep into her mouth. He did most of the work, slowly fucking her mouth. But there was control in every movement. She looked up at him, noted the tension in his jaw and just wished he'd give in.

Give it all to her.

Then he reached down and flicked at her clit with his finger. Fuck. Fuck. She was on fire in seconds, whimpering around his dick in her mouth, so desperate to come that she thought she was just going to have to take the discipline he'd dish out for coming without permission when he suddenly drew his cock out of her mouth.

"Got to have that slick pussy." He drew his fingers up to his mouth, sucking of them. "Fucking delicious.

"Please, Sir. Please let me come," she begged.

"Are you going to forget to wear your necklace again?" he asked.

"No, Sir. I promise."

He moved her around again, so her ass was at the edge of the desk. Then he leaned over her, his dick nudging at her entrance.

"Please. Please."

"I like listening to you beg. I should make you go to bed with your clit throbbing and your ass on fire."

No. No, he wouldn't.

But she knew he would.

"Please, Sir. I promise."

He reached into a drawer, grabbed a condom and sheathed himself. Then he pressed his cock against her entrance once more then thrust deep. She let out a cry and he stilled. "Kitten? Okay?"

Okay? She was anything but okay. She felt amazing. "More, Sir. Please. So good."

The tension in his face melted away. He pulled back, thrust deep. Each deep thrust nudged the plug in her ass, and it felt fucking amazing. He kept his movements slow to begin with. Then faster. Harder.

"Sir. Sir! Feels so good."

"Fuck yeah, it does. Christ, you're so tight, especially with that plug in your ass." He pressed his thumb against her clit, just holding it there.

She whimpered. He had to let her come. He had to. She couldn't take it. How could she hold herself back? He leaned over her and sucked one of her nipples into his mouth. Each pull sent a ripple through her body to pool in her swollen clit.

It was too much. And yet, not enough.

"Please, Sir. I need to come so badly. Please."

He straightened up, and grabbed both of her hips, holding her steady as he fucked her.

"All right, kitten. You can come. But you ever forget not to wear your necklace again and you'll be going a week without an orgasm. Understand me?"

She gasped. A whole week? She'd never survive.

Jesus. This from a girl who'd gone months without an orgasm without blinking. He was spoiling her.

Then he rubbed his thumb against her clit and all thoughts fled her mind. All she could concentrate on was the sensation of his rough thumb against her tender clit. She clenched around his dick and the plug as a wave of sensation washed over her. A small orgasm rocked her.

Not enough, not nearly enough. But then a second wave came. And a third. And then her whole body tightened as she reached that cliff and dived over it. She panted, her head thrashing back and forth as he kept playing with her clit.

"No, no," she cried out. She was too sensitive. She couldn't go there again.

"One more, baby. You give me one more before I give in. That's it. I know you have it."

She wailed aloud as she came again. It shocked her, the noise that was part pain, but mostly pleasure. Then he grasped hold of her hips once more and fucked her deeply. He leaned slightly over her, staring down at her.

"Fuck yeah, baby. You feel so good." He gave two more thrusts then with a groan he came. His head was thrown back, the muscles in his neck tight as he found his release. Satisfaction swirled through her. She lay there in a happy daze.

She barely felt him untie her and wipe her clean. Then she was in his arms and he carried her up to her bedroom. He tucked her under the covers, made certain the bathroom light was on, and laid a kiss on her forehead.

It was all very pleasant, almost sweet.

Then he left her. Alone. Like every other night. She wrapped the blankets around her and tried to tell herself it wasn't a rejection. That it didn't matter he couldn't or wouldn't sleep with her. That she didn't care.

Even though she knew she did.

SHE HESITATED as she laid her hand on the door handle leading to his office. She wasn't sure exactly why. She'd been coming to his office at this same time for the last eight nights.

And, yet, tonight she hesitated. Why? She knew there would be pleasure. And pain. And she knew she would enjoy herself. Hell, she fucking loved everything he did to her. Even when she couldn't walk very easily the next day. But he was holding back.

He wasn't using her in the way she knew he enjoyed. He was still treating her with kid gloves. Well, that wasn't exactly true. She spent plenty of her time with a sore ass, her nipples and clit clamped, her bottom plugged. Last night, she'd even spent some time in the corner, her arms bound behind her, her painfully sore butt on display as she'd been made to stick it out, her nose pressed to the corner.

Yeah, she was in no hurry to repeat that. Unfortunately, for her, she'd made the mistake of saying something disparaging about her non-existent boobs and he'd taken exception.

But still, there was something missing. And she wasn't certain how to bring it up.

You should ask him.

What? Ask him to take her roughly? What if she didn't like it? Then what? She rubbed her aching head. And what if he didn't want to do that with her? What if she was lacking somehow? What if the reason things hadn't progressed was because of her?

They had their little routine. She'd head to his office each evening after his brothers left. They'd play for a while. Then after each session, he took her back up to her bedroom, carrying her if necessary, and tucked her gently into bed. Like a child.

The orgasms were awesome. Amazing. Like nothing she'd ever had. It was just . . . it was starting to feel like she was being placed into this box. Like she was an appointment on his schedule.

From nine to eleven, fuck and dominate Mia.

Okay, she needed to stop being stupid. She should be glad he didn't want to sleep with her, last thing she needed was to wake him up with one of her nightmares. She'd hoped the nightmares might ease off with how exhausted she was when she tumbled into bed after a session. And she had to admit, she was falling asleep easier these days—almost before he even left the room.

But if anything, the nightmares were getting worse. And she knew it was because the trial was getting closer. She'd spoken to Mike a week ago about going back to New York. She'd had her first Skype session with the assistant DA just that morning. She'd felt so ill afterwards she'd thrown up. Thankfully, she'd been alone so no one else had heard her. But if talking about it with the lawyer had made her ill, how was she going to cope with testifying while Angelo was in the room.

Frankie Angelo.

She shuddered. Okay, she had to stop talking thinking about

this or she was going to make herself ill again. Taking a deep breath, she knocked once on the door then entered as she heard him call out a greeting.

As soon as the door was shut, she locked it then started to strip, folding her clothes and placing them on the floor by the door.

Then she strode over to where he was working at his desk. He didn't look up. Mostly, that never bothered her. But tonight, it made her feel icky inside. Unwanted.

Stop it, Mia.

She knelt at his feet, placed her hands palm up on her thighs and spread her legs wide, straightened her spine, and kept her head down. She didn't much like this position. She preferred when she was between his legs, with her hands on his thighs. It felt more intimate. But right now, he was working. So she needed to wait.

Normally, she enjoyed the peace. She liked taking a moment to center herself. It helped her go from the Mia outside to the one in here. She fidgeted around, unable to stay still. Too much was going on inside her head to find any sort of calm.

He immediately wrapped his hand around the nape of her neck, the gesture both comforting and commanding.

"What's going on, kitten?"

"Nothing, Sir." She didn't want to talk about any of the shit going on inside her head. She was a mess. Her thoughts jumbled, jumping from one worry to another with lightning speed. Nausea bubbled low in her stomach.

He moved his hand away from her neck and she sat back. He turned his chair to face her, but she kept her gaze lowered. "Sorry, Sir, I didn't mean to interrupt your work."

"Eyes to me, kitten."

She let out a quiet sigh. Damn it. The man saw too much. But she raised her eyes to meet his gaze, knowing she didn't have much choice.

He cupped her chin in the palm of his hand. "What is the rule when I ask you a question?"

Drat. "You expect an honest answer, Sir."

"Did you just give me an honest answer?"

"No, Sir."

"Well?"

"I don't want to talk about it, Sir."

He sighed and gave her a disappointed look. Shit. She hated when he looked at her like that. That icky feeling grew.

"Go to the cupboard and get a paddle. The rectangular black one."

Oh, crap. She really didn't want to do that. She'd seen his collection of paddles. It was vast. And for some reason, he kept them mounted in a big cupboard in his office. But she got up and walked over and opened the door. Each paddle was on a hook attached to the back of the cupboard. She reached out and picked up the one he'd requested then she shut the doors and turned, heading reluctantly back to him.

He pointed between his feet and she knelt and offered up the paddle. He took it from her and set it on the desk. She placed her hands on his thighs as he required in this position. Then forced herself to look up at him.

"Want to change your answer and tell me what's going on in your head, kitten?"

"If I do, does it mean I won't get paddled?" she asked hopefully.

"No, it just means I won't go as hard on you as I will if you don't answer me."

Well, since she really didn't want to talk to him about what she'd been thinking she guessed she was going to have to handle having a sore, flaming ass.

"I don't want to change my answer, Sir."

His gaze narrowed. "I don't like that you're holding back, kitten."

"You and me both, Sir."

"What's that supposed to mean?"

She remained stubbornly silent.

"All right. If that's how you want to play it. Over my lap."

He was upset with her. She hated when he was upset with her. But she still didn't say anything, just stood and positioned herself on his lap.

"Make sure those hands stay down," he warned.

She wrapped them around his calf as he reached for the paddle. It descended on her ass without warning. Fire broke out across her cheeks, making her gasp.

Fuck. Fuck.

"Want to change your mind now, kitten?"

"No."

Another smack of the paddle. Oh, God, how was she going to survive this. The pain was already immense, and she'd only had two smacks of the paddle.

"What's going on, kitten?" Another smack. "And before you tell me nothing, remember I have a whole collection of paddles I can use on this ass."

He wouldn't. At least she didn't think he would. But she had to give him something to make sure that wouldn't happen.

"I spoke to the assistant DA on my case today," she blurted out.

"What? I thought that was set for tomorrow."

"They moved it up a day. You weren't here so West set me up on your computer. Hope that's okay."

"Of course it's okay." He'd stopped paddling her, at least, and was even rubbing her ass. The pain morphed into something far more pleasant and she started to relax even though she was still lying over his lap.

"I'm sorry I wasn't here, baby. It didn't go well?"

"I . . . I think it went okay. But afterward . . . " Shit. She hadn't meant to mention afterward.

"Yes?" he pressed. He held the paddle against her ass when she didn't answer. Shit.

"Afterwards I threw up," she whispered.

Something fell against the floor. The paddle. And then she was right-side up in his lap. She winced as her hot ass met his hard lap.

"What? What did he say to you? Did he scare you? Give me his name."

"What? Why?" She gaped at him.

"Because I'm going to call him and rip him a new one." His eyes had darkened nearly to black, his jaw tense with anger.

She melted. "I'm okay, Sir. He didn't scare me."

He remained tense for a moment then he ran his fingers through the strands of her hair. "What made you feel ill?"

She shrugged, even though she knew he wasn't going to accept that as an answer. "Talking about it all over again was a lot harder than I thought. I've spent so much of my time trying to forget. The other day when I told you, well, I was so angry it just came out. But he asked so many questions, making me think about it over and over. If I can't handle just talking about it with him how am I going to handle it with Angelo in the same room with me?"

"Fuck. This is my fault."

Okay, that wasn't what she'd been expecting him to say. She leaned back to look up at him in puzzlement. "Um, I'm not sure how any of this could be your fault, Sir."

"You have panic attacks and nightmares. You won't agree to any more sessions with Molly. It's eating you up, keeping it all locked up inside you. And yet I haven't pushed you to talk about it. I didn't do that, and it's gotten to the point of making you physically ill."

She shook her head. "You didn't do this. You didn't shoot my coworkers. You're not the one trying to put a bullet in my brain. You didn't murder my neighbor thinking it was me. You didn't do any of that, Sir."

He cupped the side of her face in his hand. "This is always going to be with you. A part of you, there's no getting away from it. But you can't let it eat you alive. You can't let it darken who you are."

Like something had to him? Because while she didn't know much about his life, she got the sense that he was talking from prior experience. God, she wished she was brave enough to ask him. But she was too scared he'd tell her to get lost.

"This isn't on you, Sir. It's on me. I have to learn how to deal with this. I don't like talking about it. I thought if I didn't think about it then I could live with it."

"Trust me, that's no way to live. I know."

"Something bad happened to you, didn't it?" she whispered bravely.

He snorted. "If only it was one thing. But I don't talk about that shit. And look at me. Look at what I've become. This is not what you want."

"It isn't? You have a family that worships the ground you walk on and would do anything for you." Didn't he know what he had? And how she'd kill for that?

He looked a little surprised at her words. Then his face closed down. "We're not here to discuss me or my family."

"No, you get to keep your secrets, but I'm expected to lay myself bare. Because you don't want me to become as dark and twisted as you are? News flash, I'm not seeing much of the dark and twisted. Lonely and a little bitter, yes."

"You want to watch what you say to me right now, little girl," he told her in a dangerous voice that very nearly had her begging for forgiveness.

"You can spank me for it later," she snapped back, uncaring for once. "You're the one who keeps telling me to ask for what I need."

"I don't see much asking. I don't see much respect for your Dom. I'm being lenient on you right now because you had a hard day, but I'm warning you not to push me any further."

Why was she pushing at him like this? This wasn't her. She didn't like confrontation. She should be grateful to him. He was trying to help her.

It wasn't his fault he didn't care about her as much as she did him. It wasn't his fault he didn't love her.

Oh fuck.

She wanted his love. She wanted it all. She wanted to live here in this house, with him, to sleep in his bed each night, to have him fuck her, dominate her, and cherish her.

And she'd never have it. She had no right to want more. To get angry at him because he couldn't give that to her. They had a contract that would end when she left. This wasn't a happy ever after situation. She might be a bit pissed that he wanted her to confess every thought in her head while he gave her little back, but he was doing it to help her.

And that was all it was. It wasn't a relationship. Not a real one. He wasn't her boyfriend. Wasn't even her lover. He didn't sleep with her because they didn't have a relationship—they had an arrangement.

"I'm sorry, Sir. I had no right to say that to you. I know you're just trying to help me. You're under no obligation to tell me anything in return. I'm so sorry." She felt close to tears. There was a huge knot in her stomach that burned.

Sometimes she thought she was destined to always be on the outside, looking in. But in these circumstances, it wasn't fair for her to complain. He was giving her exactly what he'd promised. He was showing her what it was like to submit. He gave her a few hours each day where everything went silent and she could just be.

She should be thanking him, not trying to make him angry.

"So sorry. So sorry." She kept her gaze lowered.

"Sh, easy, baby. Hey, it's okay."

"I'm sorry. I'm a terrible submissive. I shouldn't have said any of that. I'm—"

"Enough," he growled. "No more apologies, understand? There are just things I can't tell you. Things you can't know."

"It's okay, Sir. You don't need to explain." She clenched her hands together. "I understand." She needed to get out of there. To leave before she lost it. Or before he could tell her to go. She didn't think she could bear that. For him to tell her it was over.

"I wish I'd known the appointment had been changed so I could have been there with you."

She was happy to have him think that was the only reason she was upset. She certainly didn't want to have to explain that it was more than that. That she knew she wasn't enough for him and that was why he didn't want to sleep with her. Why he didn't take more from her.

Never enough. Never right.

Oh, God, she needed to shut off the voice before he realized there was more going on there. She needed to get away from him.

"I had to do it on my own," she told him, forcing a small smile for his benefit.

His gaze narrowed. Obviously, she wasn't doing a very good job of pretending to be okay.

"You won't be there at the trial. I have to be able to do this on my own. Without anyone holding my hand."

"Maybe. But I could have been there for you afterwards. You should have called me."

She blinked.

"It didn't even occur to you, did it?" he asked darkly. "To call me and tell me you were struggling."

"Alec—"

He was angry, but she wasn't exactly sure why.

Doubts bubbled around inside her. "I have a headache." It wasn't a lie. Her head was pounding. But it was also a good excuse to get away from him. She needed some space.

"What?"

She reached up to rub her temple. "My head really hurts. I think I just need a good night's sleep. Do you think we could skip tonight, and I could go to bed?"

"Of course." He reached up and brushed her hand away, massaging her temple. "Have you drunk plenty of water today? Did you eat some dinner?"

He hadn't come to dinner tonight. He'd only made one other dinner since that first night. Nobody else thought anything of it. Except for her.

"I ate dinner," she reassured him. "I think it's just everything that happened today catching up with me."

He slid her off his lap, holding her for a moment to make sure she was steady before standing then swinging her up into his arms.

She wrapped her arms around his neck. "I can walk."

"You can. You won't, though." He carried her up the stairs, buck-naked. His brothers didn't hang around after dinner anymore. She didn't know what he'd said to them, and she didn't want to know. No one had said anything to her, though. Thank God, or she'd probably have died of mortification.

When he reached her bedroom, he set her down. "Go do what you to need to do, babe. I'll wait for you."

He turned away and started to pull down the bed. She slipped into the bathroom. She took a migraine pill first because it felt like it was building towards a bad one. Then she brushed her teeth and flossed, used the toilet before pulling on the large T-shirt she slept in.

She moved back into the bedroom.

"You take some medicine?" he asked from where he stood next to the bed.

"Yes."

"Good." He walked over to her then gently tipped her chin up. His eyes studied her. "Too pale. Dark patches under your eyes. Definitely in pain."

She didn't think he required an answer and she didn't feel much like talking. She just wanted to crawl into bed and pull the covers over her head and try to forget this day ever happened.

"Think you should sleep with me tonight, babe."

Okay, that was unexpected. She'd only slept with him the night of her panic attack. So he'd sleep with her if he thought she needed watching? Not because he wanted to.

Damn, when did she get so bitter?

"I'm all right."

"You're definitely not all right and I don't like it." His voice was a low growl of discontent. She thought about pointing out that he was off the clock, so to speak. But she figured she'd already pushed her luck far enough tonight.

"I'll be okay. Best thing to do is sleep someplace quiet and dark. If I slept with you, you'd probably just disturb me."

No way in hell. Because she wanted nothing more than to feel his arms around her. But she wanted that for the right reasons. Not out of a sense of obligation.

She didn't want to be anyone's obligation anymore. She wanted to be wanted. For who she was. Not what she could do for someone. She wanted to be someone's everything. To be loved.

She deserved that, right? Yes, she deserved that.

The words settled inside her. She deserved more.

Well, all right then. Took her long enough to figure that one out. She guessed she owed that to him. Loving someone who didn't love you back sucked. Big time.

"All right then, baby. Come on, lie down before you fall down. I'll come check on you later."

"No," she said quickly. Too quickly. He frowned down at her.

"I'm just better being alone." She also didn't want him coming in in case she was no longer in the bed. She moved the blankets and light out of the closet each morning, putting them back so he didn't have a chance to notice when he brought her up to bed. But if he popped in at any time ... yeah, not good.

"Okay, baby. You just rest." He tucked her in and leaned over to kiss her. And if there was a note of disappointment in his voice, well, she just told herself she'd imagined it.

HE WAS FUCKING THIS UP.

Fucking up royally.

Shit. Shit. Shit.

He paced back and forth across his office, unable to stay still. No point in going back to his paperwork or trying to go to bed to sleep. His mind was taken up with her.

Her pale face as she stared up at him, her eyes filled with hope then disappointment then pain. Damn it. When had she become more than a project? That's the way he'd tried to think of her. Someone to teach. To guide. To help. These past few nights she'd given him her submission. Her desires. Her obedience.

And what had he given her? A few fucking orgasms and a sore ass.

There was a knock on the door and he frowned. Was it Mia? "Yes?"

The door opened and West stood there.

"What are you doing here?" he demanded. "Thought I told you guys to stay out after dinner."

"You did. But I left something in the kitchen and I saw you walk down the stairs alone so I figured the coast was clear. I wanted to talk to you. About Mia."

"What about Mia?"

"Look, it's none of my business, but I just want to check that you know what you're doing."

"You're right. It's none of your business."

She's not like the women at the club you play with. She feels something for you."

"Since when did you become so protective of Mia?"

West watched him warily. "I might not have agreed with letting her come here. Might not have appreciated the way she's changed things around here, but that was before."

"Before what?"

"Before I saw the way she affected you. You love her, don't you?"

"I don't love anyone."

West snorted, moved over to the whiskey, and poured them both a drink. He handed one over to Alec. "You might like to tell yourself that, but it ain't true. You love us."

"Wanna bet?" Alec asked churlishly.

West sighed, finished his drink, and turned away.

"Where are you going?" Alec demanded.

"There's no talking to you right now. Not when you're brooding and feeling sorry for yourself."

"Fuck off, I'm not brooding."

West turned back to look at him. "No? Why are you here alone? I thought you spent every evening in here with Mia, tying her up and fucking her?"

"She's not feeling well."

"She had a hard day. She's one of us now, Alec. You might want to keep that in mind."

"What the fuck does that mean?"

"It means that I get why you push her away with one hand and pull her close with another, but that doesn't mean that we'll stand by and let you hurt her."

"I'm not fucking hurting her. She consented. There's a contract—"

West gave him a disgusted look. "I'm not talking about BDSM, Alec. I'm talking about the fact that you're only giving her a very limited part of yourself when she deserves everything. That woman loves you."

"She doesn't."

"Yeah. She does. And you love her, you're just too stubborn to admit it. You think you have to punish yourself because of everything you did when we were younger."

"I'm not punishing myself."

"You forget who you're talking to. I know all about punishing yourself for past sins."

Alec studied his brother. "You did what you had to. He was evil. He deserved what he got."

"Yeah, well, now I'm getting what I deserve. Because there's a price for everything, right? My price is living my life without the person I love most. But you don't have to pay that price, the person you love is right here. And you're fucking everything up. You're pushing her away because you think you can't have her. You think you don't deserve her. You think you have to live in the dark when you can live in the light. Her light. If you just fucking open your eyes and see it, you can have it all. You think I wouldn't kill to have my light back just for a few minutes? To hold her? To see her smile? To kiss her? I'd give anything. But I can't have the woman I love. And you, you asshole, you're just going to throw yours away."

The words struck deep. "I can't give her everything. I can't tell her all of it. I expect her to give me everything and I'm not willing to do the same in return. So how can that work?"

"It can work if you want it badly enough. But I think you're selling her short. Under that sweet, fragile exterior that woman has the heart of a lion. And she's loyal to the core. You want her to give you her shit, well, let her take on yours. You need to let that out, bro."

"And if she can't take it? If she can't handle it?"

"Then she's not right for you. But I think she can. I think Mia is the woman who could give it all to you if you'd just let her in. She needs you, Alec. She needs you to hold her when she's scared. She needs your protection. Your possession. And, obviously, she needs the kinky shit the two of you get up to, since I've never seen a woman wear a more satisfied smile than she has these last few days. But you also need her. And if you let her go without trying, you'll never forgive yourself."

17

As he climbed into bed, West's words beat at him.

If you let her go without trying, you'll never forgive yourself.

He didn't want to think about her leaving. Couldn't without feeling ill. He knew West was right. He expected everything from her yet held her at a distance.

Because he didn't believe she could handle his past? Or was West right? Was he still punishing himself for past sins and part of that was to deny himself anything that made him happy?

He'd done things he shouldn't have in his youth. And for years he hadn't allowed himself much of anything that would make him happy. Kept his brothers at a distance. He only played at the club a few times a year.

Fuck. He hated to admit it, but West was right. Not that he'd ever admit it to him; he'd never hear the end of it. Question was, what to do about it? Did he open up? Tell her everything? She had enough on her plate right now, he couldn't add to that. But maybe once the trial was over . . . yeah, maybe then he'd tell her all of it and see if she could still love a deeply flawed man.

A CLAP of thunder sounded in the distance. Shit. He'd forgotten all about that storm rolling in tonight. Sometimes the power went out during these storms, which is why they had a generator. But it took a few minutes to kick in and during that time, they'd be without power.

Mia didn't like the dark.

Fuck. Another clap of thunder sounded. It was coming in fast. He didn't want to wake her if she was sleeping. Hadn't she said that was the best thing for her migraine, to sleep it off? But what if the storm woke her and the power going out frightened her? What if she had another panic attack?

He threw off the blankets as another clap sounded. Far closer this time. The power flickered then went out. And he took off towards Mia's bedroom. He didn't know what it was, some instinct, but it was screaming at him to get to her.

That she was in trouble.

Another clap of thunder sounded as he reached her bedroom. He stormed inside and moved towards the bed.

Only she wasn't there.

His heart raced. Where was she?

"Mia! Mia!"

The lights suddenly flickered on. The generator had kicked in. The light he'd left on in the bathroom came on, and he immediately spotted the extension cord lying along the floor.

It led to the closet. What on earth?

Suddenly it hit him, and he raced over, opening the closet door without thought. The small figure curled under a blanket in the corner of the closet shied back with a cry.

Oh, baby. Oh, his poor baby.

"Mia! Mia, baby. It's okay. It's me. It's Alec." He crouched down, realizing that looming over her probably wasn't the way to make her feel more at ease. "Baby?"

"A-Alec?"

"It's me, sweetheart. You're safe. You're safe now." What was she doing in there? "Did you get scared because of the storm? Is that why you're in here?" But that made little sense, she'd had to have already have the extension cord ready to get the lamp in there . . . unless . . .

"Oh, baby, how often do you sleep in here?" he asked.

Another clap of thunder sounded, and she cried out. Her legs were curled up to her chest in a protective gesture. He needed to get her out of there. As much for his own peace of mind as for hers. But he couldn't just grab her and risk frightening her further.

"Baby girl, I'm going to pick you up, okay?" he said in a low voice. "You know it's me. It's Alec."

"Sir," she said suddenly.

"What?"

"Be Sir. I think I can get out if you're Sir."

He felt as far from Sir as possible, the idea of dominating her in order to get her out of the closet felt wrong so on many levels. But if this is what she needed.

He straightened. "Kitten, I want you to get out of there. Now."

Her arms dropped down from where they had been anchoring her legs to her chest.

"Kitten. Out. Now. Kneel here." Fuck, he felt like the world's biggest jerk. But she came out, crawled her way out to kneel at his feet. And then that was enough. More than fucking enough as far as he was concerned. He was going to hold her.

And he was going to tell her she was safe.

That she'd always be safe. With him.

He crouched down. "Baby, I'm going to pick you up now. Because I need to hold you. Badly."

"You need to hold me?" she asked in a shaky voice, looking up at him.

"Like you wouldn't believe."

"O-okay." She held out her thin arms to him and he scooped her up, standing with her held tightly in his arms. He carried her to the bed and laid her down. She let out a startled cry, clinging to him. "Don't leave."

He lay down beside her, gathering her in tight, and placing a kiss on her forehead. "I'm going nowhere, baby. Not ever. And neither are you." She was trembling against him. She startled in fright at another clap of thunder. "Jesus, baby. How often have you been sleeping in the closet?"

"I know it seems weird. You must think I'm a headcase—"

"Sh. I don't think that at all. I do think that I damn well should have known you were sleeping in a fucking closet."

She let out a small cry and buried her face against his chest and he suddenly realized she thought he was angry at her. He grasped her chin, pulling her face firmly up. He could see her clearly with the light from the bathroom shining down on her frightened features.

"Listen to me, baby girl. I am not angry at you."

"I'm a mess."

"You're not a mess," he said firmly.

She gave him a look of disbelief. "I'm a mess."

"All right. You're a bit of a mess. But if you're a mess, I'm a fucking disaster."

She sucked in a breath. "What do you mean?"

"First of all, I want you to know that I am not angry with you that you're sleeping in a closet, I'm angry at me for not knowing about it. How often, Mia?"

She licked her lips. "Most nights. I feel safer in the small space. I know that's silly—"

He placed a finger on her lips. "That's not silly, baby. Not at all. I wish you'd told me, though. I could have helped you."

"I didn't want to talk to Molly."

"What?"

"When you found out that I have panic attacks you made me see Molly. I like Molly. But I didn't want to talk to her again. I didn't want to talk to anyone about what happened. I just wanted to forget. But I can't. I can't get it out of my mind. It's never going to go away. I tried to bury it, but it keeps resurfacing in my night-mares. The only time I ever feel calm is when we're in the office together. When you take charge. And tonight, I ruined that."

"Listen to me. You did not ruin that."

"I tried to push for more."

"Which you had every right to do," he said fiercely.

"No." She shook her head. "No, it wasn't fair of me. I know what this is between us—"

"Do you?" he questioned. "Because I only just figured it out."

"What? What do you mean, you just figured what out?"

"I only just figured out that I love you."

She was still. Then she stared up at him. "What?"

"I love you, Mia Alcott."

"No, you don't."

He raised both eyebrows at her vehement tone of voice. "You want to run that by me again?"

SHE LICKED HER DRY LIPS. Okay, so, soft and warm Alec was gone, replaced by harder, sterner Sir. Her tummy bubbled with leftover fear and a good dose of nerves.

"I know I overstepped earlier," she told him. "I went too far. It wasn't my place—"

"Not your place?" he whispered.

"I'm not your girlfriend. Not your full-time sub. I'm just

someone you're training. We have our couple of hours a day and that's all. We don't sleep together. We don't eat together. We don't discuss our day. Well, you don't discuss yours. I get that you ask me about mine because you feel obliged to help me. I'm messed up; you think you can fix me. That's kind, but you can't." She waved her hand towards the closet. "As you can see, I'm more fucked up than you thought."

He cupped her face between his hands. "Refer to yourself as fucked up one more time and I'm going to forget that I just found you sleeping in a fucking closet and I'm going to go get one of my paddles and beat your ass, understand?"

Her breath caught. He suddenly lay on his back with a groan, placing his arm over his eyes. "Fuck! Fuck!"

"What is it? Are you okay?" He sounded like he was in pain.

"No. No, I'm not okay. I just told the woman I love that I love her, and she doesn't believe me. That was not how I was expecting this to go. I've never told anyone I loved them. Not even my brothers."

Another clap of thunder, further away this time. The storm was moving away. The wind rattled at the windows. Thunderstorms had never been her favorite. When the power had gone out, she'd been terrified. And then he'd come. He'd come for her.

"I keep them at a distance," he continued. "I keep this barrier between us. Do you know why?"

"No. Why?"

"Because I love them. Because I love them, I keep them away. Makes no sense, right?" He moved his arm away and rolled onto his side to look at her.

"Not really." The knot in her stomach started to unravel slightly at his words.

"I know it makes no sense, but I still do it. I had a fucked-up youth. Like, really messed up. I did things, so many things I'm not proud of. I didn't really want to do any of them, but I still did them. Because if I didn't, I knew Marceras would hurt my brothers. Love makes you do things for people. Love makes you weak. I didn't want them pulled down into the dark with me, though. So I did what he wanted. And still nearly took one of my brothers from me anyway."

"Who is Marceras?" She could scarcely believe he was telling her any of this.

"Tony Marceras. Head of the Marceras family. Ran a crime syndicate in Detroit. My father was his numbers man. Dad was an accountant with a taste for gambling. He got in deep, too deep to get out and so Tony offered him a way out. He started working for the Marceras family, which suited him fine. They provided him with what he needed to be happy. Women, booze, and drugs. And he cooked their books. He hid their money, laundered it. When I turned sixteen, Tony pulled me into his office. He told me it was time I started giving back to "the family." You know, since they'd given so much to me. I told him no. I thought he might threaten me, have me beaten. Instead he dragged Beau in from another room and he cut off his finger. Right in front of me. Told me he'd keep hurting him until I agreed. That I had plenty of brothers for him to move onto once Beau was dead."

"Oh, Alec." She couldn't even imagine. It was so horrific. She ran her hand over his chest, trying to comfort him the only way she knew how.

"I told him I'd do it. I started by pushing drugs, worked my way up the food chain. I knew if I wanted to keep my brothers safe, I had to become indispensable to the family, so I could keep them out of it as much as possible. Didn't exactly work. Especially when West fell in love with Marceras's oldest daughter."

"What?" she breathed out. It was like something out of a novel.

"Lana. She was gorgeous. And so sweet, especially considering where she'd come from. Marceras saw West's interest in her, used it to lure him into the family business. West went willingly, even though I tried to reach him he wouldn't listen. He was blinded by her."

"What happened?"

"Marceras married her off to one of his enforcers. A sick son of a bitch who beat her. Who raped her. Who ended up killing her."

"Oh no." She placed her hand over her mouth.

"Yeah," Alec said grimly. "West went crazy. I've never seen him so out of it. He stormed off and I couldn't find him. I didn't know what he was going to do. I only knew that whatever happened wouldn't be pretty."

Her heart beat fast. She couldn't even imagine West's pain. "What happened?"

"Well, West couldn't go after the enforcer, because Marceras had killed the bastard. Apparently, the beatings and rapes were okay, but killing her went too far."

"Jesus. Jesus." She'd thought she'd known evil but to do that to your own daughter . . . it made her feel sick.

"So, West went after the only person left for him to punish."

"Marceras?" she asked.

"Yes."

"What did he do?" she whispered.

"He killed him."

"Oh, God. Oh, God. How . . . I mean . . . how is West not dead?" Or in jail? Would the Marceras family not have retaliated?

"Because I'd been working against Tony in the background. His oldest son, Mateo wasn't happy with the way the old man ran things and he wanted to take over. But he couldn't do it without my help. By then I was practically the old man's right-hand man."

He let out a shuddering sigh. "Shit. Can't believe I'm telling you this."

"You don't have to," she whispered, even though she was dying to know.

"I made a bargain with Mateo," he whispered back. "Basically,

I'd kill his father if he let my brothers go. Free and clear of the family."

"What about you?" she asked.

He had grown rigid. "Figured I wasn't going to make it out. But at least they would."

"Oh, Alec."

He had been prepared to sacrifice himself for his brothers.

"You're a good man."

He barked out a laugh. "Baby, I was going to kill a man."

"A bad man. He chopped off Beau's finger," she said fiercely.

"Yeah, he was a bad man. Doesn't make me a good man, though."

"I say you are." He'd done everything he had for family. "And I won't hear anyone say anything differently."

"Jesus," he muttered. "You're supposed to be disgusted. Horrified."

"Family first, right? No one messes with the Malones."

He kissed the top of her head. "No one messes with the Malones, but baby that still doesn't mean that I—"

She reached up and placed her hand over his mouth, scowling. "I said no one was allowed to say you aren't a good man and I meant it."

He shook his head.

"What happened next?" she asked, done with debating this.

"Mateo stepped into his place and we disappeared. I paid a fortune to have our birth certificates all changed so we shared my mother's last name. Only West, Jaret and I have the same mother. I bought this spread, I'd saved a fuck load of money working for Marceras and I'd invested it wisely. I brought my brothers here. I kept them safe."

"And your father?"

"I don't know where he went to. Slunk off somewhere in the middle of the night. Good riddance."

"Is that why West doesn't leave the ranch? Is he worried someone will recognize him?"

Alec shook his head. "Mateo covered it up. No one knows it was West except for us and Mateo. And our old life shouldn't follow us here. I don't like that Mateo knows but so far he hasn't used that knowledge against us. I've tried to tell West that no one is coming for him. That it looks more suspicious, him hiding out from everyone, personally I think it has more to do with him punishing himself for Lana's death or some such shit. He was never a people person anyway."

She snorted. "That's an understatement."

"I'm not a good person, Mia." He rolled onto his side to face her. "I don't deserve you. I don't deserve any sort of happiness. That's why I tried to keep you at a distance. It wasn't fair of me. My only excuse is that I was afraid that if you knew the truth, I wouldn't even have our sessions in the office. But I've hurt you and I don't ever want to hurt you, Mia. I don't deserve to be loved. But I want it. I want your love. I want it all. But I understand if you can't love me."

She stared at him for a long moment. "You love me."

"I love you."

"You kept me at a distance because you didn't think you deserved me."

"I don't deserve you."

She launched herself at him. "If I ever hear you say that again, Alec Malone, I'm going to take a paddle to your ass, because I love you."

"You love me?" He wrapped his arms around her, holding her tightly.

"I love you. And I don't care who you were in the past. That's not who you are now. You're a bit of a jerk at times, utterly bossy at others, but you're my man. And I say you're a good man."

"I'm not, but I'm glad you think so."

"I know so," she said fiercely. "No more punishing yourself."

"No more punishing myself," he agreed. "No more sleeping in closets."

She nodded. "All right. No more keeping me and your brothers and everyone else at a distance. You let us love you."

"I'll let you love me. My brothers, we'll see. If I spend too much time with them, I might kill them."

"You can handle dinners," she told him. "We'll go from there."

He cupped her face. "We'll go from there. You'll tell me every-thing about that night."

"I'll tell you." A haunted look came over her face. "I still have the trial to get through."

"Not without me, you won't. I'm going to be there for you. Through all of it."

That knot inside her was almost completely gone.

"After the trial, you're coming here with me. To your home." He stared at her intently. "Understand me? This is your home. Where people love you."

She placed her hand over his. "Home. I like the sound of that. I didn't think I'd ever have one."

"Your aunt was an abusive old bitch. She didn't know the trea-sure she had. She should have cherished you. Loved you."

She looked at him, her eyes glistening with tears. "I can't believe this. I can't believe that such a horrific thing led to me finding you. Is it fair that I have happiness, when they can't?"

"You think any of them would want to live the rest of your life in misery? Alone? Or do you think they'd want you to live your life to the fullest? You were given a second chance, baby. If you'd been there, you'd be dead too. But you're not. You owe it to them and to yourself to live."

"They'd want that. Well, maybe not Jacques, he was a complete bastard. But Juan, Sophie, Lucas, Marion, and James, they'd want that for me."

He leaned in to kiss her. His lips had just touched hers when she heard the first shout. He stilled. Then pulled back. Suddenly, he climbed to his feet. She frowned as she heard an agonized cry. Her gut tightened. Something was in pain. Fear. He raced over to the window.

"Fuck! The stables are on fire. I need clothes."

"What? Oh, God." She stood and reached for her clothes. He turned back to her, pointing to her. "You stay in the house, understand me? Do not leave the house. I won't be able to concentrate unless I know you're safe."

"I won't. Just go." He shouldn't be worrying about her. He needed to get outside. She got dressed and headed downstairs. She might not be able to help, but the least she could do was make coffee and food.

She stepped into the kitchen, reaching over to switch on the light. She never even heard someone sneak up on her. She was suddenly pulled back against a hard body, a heavy hand slamming on her mouth to stifle her scream. Before she could even fight, there was a prick at her neck.

And then she knew nothing.

18

M ia woke up slowly, blinking to try and clear the cobwebs in her brain. Where was she? Why was she lying on the floor? What was going on? Did she fall? She frowned, trying to think back . . . then it came to her.

Someone had grabbed her as she'd entered the kitchen. She hadn't even had time to scream. Had they . . . had they drugged her? She gasped in a breath, fear flooding through her as the very man who featured in her nightmares came to stand over her. He pulled back his foot then kicked out, catching her in the stomach, making the air rush from her lungs. Winded and in agony, she curled up into a ball. Another blow landed. She closed her eyes. He must have moved because another burst of pain broke out in her back. She gasped for breath. Her side burned. Her ribs. Had he broken her ribs?

"Boss. Boss, you got to stop, we want her alive, remember?" someone said.

"I'm not going to kill her. Just want to punish the bitch a bit." Another blow landed on her lower back; she couldn't help but let out a cry of pain. "That's it, cry, bitch. Scream. I like it when they scream."

"Hey. Hey," another voice spoke. This one high-pitched. Scared. "You didn't say you were going to hurt her."

"What's it got to do with you, Osborne? You're gonna get your part of the bargain, what do you care if I make the bitch hurt?" Angelo asked.

Osborne? Alec's next-door neighbor? What did he have to do with this? Was he working with Angelo? Where were they? How had they known where she was?

"You said you'd get me Malone's ranch. So far, I haven't seen much evidence of that. All I see is you beating on a defenseless female half your size."

Wrong move. Even she knew that. She moved her head and spotted the man she guessed was Osborne, since he didn't look like one of Angelo's goons. She glanced around the room. Heads of dead animals were mounted on the rich red walls. She shuddered. The red reminded her of blood. The carpet beneath her was cream. The furniture brown leather. It was a grotesque combination.

"You'll get your precious ranch, Osborne. You have to be fucking patient."

"You promised to kill Alec and his miserable brothers," Osborne whined.

"And I will. As soon as they give me what I want."

Her heart raced. Kill Alec? And his brothers? And what could Angelo possibly want from Alec?

"She better not be bleeding. Blood will be hell to get out of this carpet. This wasn't part of the agreement," Osborne whined.

"Jesus fucking Christ, I can't take it anymore," Angelo complained.

She heard a *ping*. She gasped in horror as she saw blood appear on Osborne's chest. Trembles rocked her body as she turned to look up at Angelo and saw the gun he lowered. "Now, *that* blood is going to be hard to get out of the carpet." Angelo said as Osborne collapsed. His goons laughed.

Oh, God. Oh, God. Panic filled her. She had to fight hard to stop herself from vomiting. Osborne's face turned towards her, his lifeless eyes stared straight at her, and it was all that was needed to send her spiraling back into the past.

It was the quiet that got to her first as she stepped into the back room. Even though the restaurant was now closed, there should have been noise from everyone cleaning up. Of Jacques ordering everyone around in his loud voice. But there was just this weird thudding noise.

She was moving quietly. She didn't want to alert anyone that she was here. She walked to her locker and retrieved her phone. And she wanted to know what that noise was.

As she moved out of the back room towards the kitchen, she nearly tripped over a pair of legs. At first, she thought it was some sort of sick joke, that the blood on his chest was just paint. But then she realized his chest wasn't moving . . . that his eyes were staring sightlessly at the ceiling. She hadn't liked Jacques, but she'd never wished him dead.

She knew she should leave. But she must have been in shock, because she crept her way forward, peered around the corner and into the kitchen. They must have dragged a chair into the center of the room and tied him to it. Not that he needed to be bound, as beaten as he was, he wasn't going anywhere. The man looming over him smiled down the man. It was an evil, twisted sort of smile. At least now she knew what that sound had been, someone beating up her boss.

"You never should have double-crossed me, James."

James didn't move. She didn't even know if he was still conscious. She hoped he wasn't as she saw the man standing in front of him lift his gun and pull the trigger.

Smack! A foot landed against her shoulder, sending her sprawling forward, bringing her back to the present. Angelo just laughed. Like he had that night.

He was going to kill her. Just like he'd killed them.

Oh, Alec, where are you?

HE STARED at the still smoldering stables. At least the fire hadn't had a chance to spread. And they'd rescued all the horses, even if several of the animals had bad burns. He coughed and wiped at his streaming eyes.

"Beau," he called out as one of his brothers approached. "Do me a favor and go check on Mia."

Beau gave him a nod, not even attempting to give a smart-aleck remark before turning and running off towards the house.

Christ. What a fucking mess. How the hell had this happened? Was it lightning?

"Alec."

He looked over as Haven's sheriff approached. He'd sent Tanner down to let the fire service and Jake through the gates earlier.

"Jake."

"All the horses okay?" Jake asked.

"Yeah, gonna have to get a couple looked at." He ran his hand through his hair. Something about this didn't feel right.

"Alec! Alec!"

He turned back, fear filling him as he saw Beau racing towards him.

"Alec, she's not there."

"What do you mean she's not there? I told her to stay inside."

"I looked everywhere, couldn't find her anywhere."

"Easy," Jake said calmly. "She's bound to be around here some-where. We'll all look for her."

"I've got a better idea; she was wearing her locket when I last saw her. We'll track her." He made his way to his office, Beau and Jake on his heels.

"Track her?" Jake asked.

"He makes her wear a GPS tracker," Beau told him.

"Jesus, you guys really are fucking crazy. And paranoid."

Five minutes later, as he stared at her location on his computer screen, he knew his paranoia was justified.

"What the fuck is she doing at Osborne's?" Beau asked. "And how did she get there?"

"Beau, go get the rest of the boys and arm up," he told his brother.

"Alec—" Jake started.

Fuck. Just his luck the damn sheriff was here. He turned to him but was interrupted as his phone rang. He looked at the caller ID.

"Osborne," he told Jake before he answered it. "Osborne, what the fuck are you doing with my woman?"

He ignored Jake's surprised look.

"This isn't Osborne. And your woman has a big mouth." He froze, moved his gaze to Jake then set the phone away from his ear and put it on speaker, but still held the receiver close to his mouth. "Who is this?"

Jake's eyes narrowed in understanding.

"This is Frankie Angelo."

He sucked in a breath. Fuck. Angelo. How had he gotten to Mia? "Don't you fucking harm her."

"I see you know who I am. Good. That should make this easier. I was just going to kill the girl, you know. Until I discovered who'd given her refuge. I was shocked to discover she was living with Tony Marceras's right-hand man."

Okay, now he really wished Jake wasn't there.

"What do you want?" Because he obviously wanted something from him.

"I want a meet with Mateo."

"That's gonna take me some time to set up," he warned. It wasn't actually going to happen at all. But it didn't have to, since he already knew where Mia was.

"You have twenty-four hours or the bitch dies. Either way, I'm happy." The call ended.

Alec slammed his fist down on his desk. "Fuck. Shit."

"You want to explain what's going on?" Jake asked as he stood and headed towards the door.

"You should stay here," he told Jake. "What's going to happen, you don't want to be involved in."

"Oh, I think that's exactly why I need to be there," Jake countered. "To make sure that you don't do something stupid."

"A mob boss has my woman. My woman, who is the star witness in a case against him for murder. And I'm going to get her back."

"I'll help you," Jake said grimly. "Although, I wish to fuck you'd told me about all this before."

Alec smiled. It wasn't a pleasant smile. "We don't like cops much in my family."

Jake snorted. "Far as I can tell, you guys don't like anyone. But, right now, I'm here to help you. Afterwards you can explain all of this to me."

TWENTY MINUTES LATER, he was stationed outside Osborne's place, using a pair of high-powered night-vision binoculars to figure out what the fuck was going on. He could see clearly into the large living room. Angelo and three goons stood around the room. Combined with the three guards posted outside the house, that made for seven men to take down. Osborne was lying on the floor, not moving.

That news had made Jake start cursing, even more than when he'd seen the arsenal the brothers had brought with them. He'd given Alec a dark look, meaning he was going to have a lot of explaining to do later.

Not that he gave a fuck. So long as later, he had Mia back, safe in his arms. Mia was also lying on the floor. His heart had stopped when he'd seen that. He'd almost lost his shit until he'd seen her move.

They were all in place now. His brothers had the place surrounded, waiting for his signal to go in. Thank fuck, he'd gotten her that GPS tracker.

"Think Angelo set the fire?" West asked.

He nodded. *Yep, as a diversion.* He guessed whoever had taken her had slipped into the house when the power was down so as not to set off any alarms, which made him think that had been deliberate and not due to the storm. That had just provided some cover.

Fuck.

"I should have guarded her better. I should never have left her on your own."

"We're gonna get her back, brother," West told him. "Nobody messes with the Malones. Course you're gonna have to make it official so people know not to mess with her."

"Oh, I'll be making it official." There was going to be no doubt in anyone's mind who she belonged to.

"About fucking time, thought I was gonna have to marry her myself," Raid said. Alec turned to glare at him. "What? Only way to make sure she keeps us fed."

"What's the plan?" West asked.

"Raid and Tanner are going to take out the three guards outside. I'm going to go in there and have a talk with him and the rest of you, except for Tanner who's taking watch, will wait for my signal, then come in hot."

"You sure that's a good idea?" Jake asked. "He could shoot you on sight."

"He won't. He needs me to get to Mateo. But I need to be in there to protect Mia." He didn't like how she'd curled up into herself on the floor. Had that bastard hurt her? He'd kill him.

"Just remember, we only shoot as a last resort. And we don't shoot to kill," Jake warned.

Alec nodded, but if his baby had been hurt then all bets were off.

MIA COULDN'T BELIEVE he was just walking through the front door like nothing was amiss. Like he was walking into a business meeting. She wanted to scream at him to run, to get out of there. Only, she knew he wouldn't. He wouldn't leave her. He'd never leave her.

Tears filled her eyes. She couldn't get him killed. She just couldn't.

His gaze immediately went to her and he studied her intently. She wished she could sit up, but last time she'd tried, the pain had been agonizing. Alec's gaze turned to look at each of the men standing around her. His fury filled the room, so cold she shivered.

"Who hurt her?"

"What are you doing here?" Angelo asked, looking panicked. "How did you find us? Where are my guards?"

"Who. Hurt. Her."

The worry cleared from Angelo's face as he realized he had the upper hand. Or thought he did. One of his goons had his gun aimed on her, as though they'd been worried she'd make a run for it. She could barely breathe from the pain; she was hardly in any condition to run. "She must have gotten bruised while being transported."

"How did you find her?"

Angelo shrugged. "Bugged her cousin's house. Heard his call to her a week ago, arranging to transport her back to New York. I sent my boys down first to scout around. They found Osborne here sniffing around your place. He was very helpful. We came to an agreement. Osborne wanted you gone. He wanted your land and was more than willing to let us use his place as our base. Unfortunately, Osborne also had a use-by date."

Alec glanced down at Osborne then away, his expression not changing. This was the Alec who'd done terrible things that she knew he'd probably never talk about. This was the Alec who was going to make Angelo wish he'd never been born. Thank God. She relaxed as she realized he wouldn't be here without a plan.

"So? Did you contact Mateo?" Angelo asked impatiently.

Alec tilted his head. "How did you know who I was?"

"Osborne had photos of you all. I recognized you. You don't remember me, do you?"

"He only remembers the things that are important," Mia said quietly.

Angelo glared at her. "Shut up, bitch."

Alec took a step towards him. All of Angelo's men turned their guns on him and she stiffened, wishing she'd never said anything. "You want to watch how you talk to my woman."

Angelo swallowed loudly. "I saw you once when you were working for Marceras. My father was good friends with Marceras. They had a business arrangement. Until Mateo took over and cut him off. Now that I'm in charge, I'm looking to recreate those ties."

"And you didn't think to just call him like a fucking normal person?"

"Watch your tone," Angelo said silkily. "Or I might have to hurt her." He moved towards her. Pulled back his leg as though to kick her.

And that was when Alec yelled out, "Go!" Then the leash was off, and Alec erupted. He grabbed Angelo, yanked him away from her as around her she heard glass breaking and thunderous yelling. But her attention wasn't on anyone or anything but Alec. He had Angelo on the ground and was pummeling him.

Someone tried to pull him off. Someone in a sheriff's uniform. Shit. The police were here. That meant she had to stop Alec before he killed Angelo. Too bad.

"Alec, Alec, stop! You're going to kill him!" the sheriff yelled out.

"Alec," she called. She forced herself to sit up, breathing through the pain. She placed one hand on her ribs. "Alec! Alec, stop!"

She rolled to her knees. Christ, why was this so hard? "Alec, I need you!" She attempted to stand. But the room spun around her. Then gentle hands grabbed hold of her, pulling her against a warm, hard chest.

Alec. His face was still a dark mask of fury, but he was under control again. And she could have wept in relief.

"Alec." She tried to reach for him. Winced at the pain in her shoulder and back. Her ribs.

"Easy, baby girl. Let's get you seated." He carefully led her over to a large sofa. "It's okay, you're safe now."

She glanced around her, shocked as she saw all his brothers were there. Angelo's goons all had their hands on their head and were kneeling in the middle of the room. Raid and Butch stood over them.

Butch caught her looking, and she expected him to wink, send her a smart remark, but his face was filled with worry and fury.

Alec was running his hands over her, searching for where she was hurt. The handsome looking man in a sheriff's uniform was kneeling over Angelo. Was that Jake? Molly's Jake?

"We need an ambulance for him," the sheriff said in a tight voice.

"We need an ambulance for Mia first, Jake," Alec said. "He can wait."

Jake didn't protest, instead he stood and moved over to her and Alec. West moved up to cover Angelo, his gun pointed straight at the other man's head. She swallowed heavily.

"Is she all right?" the sheriff asked.

"Of course she's not all right," Alec replied.

"What's wrong with her?" Raid asked.

"Anything broken?" Beau added.

"Fuck, she's such a little thing," West said then he drew his foot back and kicked Angelo in the gut.

"Hey!" Jake snapped as Alec finished up his examination.

"What?" West snapped.

The sheriff looked at Alec. But he didn't look away from Mia. "What? He deserved it."

"Fucking ass wipe deserves a lot more," Raid said. He walked over to Angelo and spat on him. "Nobody messes with the Malones, fuckwit, and Mia is a Malone."

What? No, she wasn't.

"I'm not," she whispered.

"What, baby?" Alec's gaze gentled as he looked down at her.

"I'm not a Malone."

Alec straightened and looked around him. "Looks to me like you are."

"What did she say?" Butch asked.

"She doesn't think she's a Malone," Alec told them just as they heard sirens approaching.

"Fuck, if you're not a Malone, Mia, then how come we didn't get to kill anyone?" Maddox asked sulkily.

"We didn't even beat on any of these dicks 'cause we didn't think you'd like it," Beau added.

"We held back 'cause of you, Mia," Jaret told her gently as he walked over and looked down at her. "We're here because you're a Malone and nobody fucks with the Malones."

Warmth filled her. Tears entered her eyes as she looked around at them all. "I'm a Malone."

"Hell yes, you are." Alec cupped her face between his hands. "And as soon as you're better, I'm making it official."

"You did not just propose to her now." The sheriff looked at him in shock. "You cannot ask someone to marry you when she's just been kidnapped and beaten."

"Of course not," Alec told him. "I didn't fucking ask at all."

Jake shook his head. "All of you are insane."

She just smiled at Alec. "I'm a fucking Malone."

He leaned in and kissed her. "You are, baby. You definitely are."

EPILOGUE

She was going to kill the bastards.

She'd just finished planting the last of the flowers and the place was starting to look presentable. It had taken her a long time to get over her trauma. And she wasn't talking about her physical injuries. Things had gotten worse before they'd gotten better. Her screams during the night had been enough to wake the boys in the bunkhouse. Jaret and West had started sleeping in the house, so they could be close in case Alec needed them for anything.

At first, she'd been embarrassed by that. But they'd never treated her any differently than they had when she first moved there. They still flirted, up to a point. And, if they ever went past that point, Alec let them know, in no uncertain terms.

He'd let down a number of his shields. He now ate dinner with them each night. He watched games with his brothers sometimes. And he was killing it at poker night.

Slowly, but surely, with Molly's help, and Alec's love, she'd started to get the nightmares and panic attacks under control. The panic attacks had gone from three or four a day to twice a week, to where she hadn't had one in weeks.

She'd slowly started making changes to the house. Slowly, because West didn't react well to change. He'd bellowed for days when she'd painted one of the walls in the living room a dark blue. That had brought back old insecurities until everyone else had come to her defense. A shouting match had ensued, which somehow, she'd ended up in the middle of—having the time of her life.

They were starting to corrupt her.

Through it all, Alec had been by her side, loving her, caring for her, holding her through all the nightmares, and bringing her back to him when a panic attack gripped her.

He was everything.

And she'd never been happier in her life.

Except for right at that moment. Because she was going to commit murder. She'd just gone to fetch the hose to water her newly planted pansies when she came back to find them wrestling on the ground, trying to throw punches, each attempting to get the best of the other. She stood there, just glaring at them. Pair of idiots. Raid slammed his fist against Butch's nose. Then Butch punched Raid in the side.

She was turning to go and get Alec, although, he'd probably just let them fight it out, when they rolled closer to her flower patch.

Oh, no, they didn't! She'd spent far too long planting and tending to those flowers; no way were those idiots going to ruin them. Just as Raid rolled, squashing some of her newly planted pansies, she remembered the hose in her hand. Twisting the nozzle, she turned it to full throttle and aimed it at them.

They both came apart with yells loud enough to wake the dead. Men came running from all directions. And she just stared down at the two soaking wet men. One with blood dripping down his face, the other holding his side.

"What the hell is going on here?" Alec boomed from behind her.

Oh, drat.

"Mia sprayed us with the hose," Butch complained.

"We were just having a bit of fun, Mia," Raid added.

She turned the hose, which she'd had pointed at the ground, back on them. They held up their hands to protect their faces, spluttering and protesting. Suddenly an arm reached over and plucked the hose from her hand, before turning the nozzle off.

"Hey!" she cried out. She turned to look at Alec. "I told them not to go near my flower patch. Now look at them, they trampled my pansies." She pointed over at the flowers. Then she turned back to Butch and Raid. "Apologize. Now."

"You two better apologize or she'll cut you off from dessert," Jaret said. His tone was teasing, but his smile didn't reach his eyes. He'd been more serious since Gloria had cheated on him.

She nodded. "Yep. Instead of getting lemon meringue pie like everyone else, you'll be getting an orange. If you're lucky."

"You're mean," Raid said. But he smiled as he said that. "Gotta admire that."

"Sure do," Butch added. "And we did trample on her weeds."

She gritted her teeth against pointing out that they weren't damn weeds. They knew that, they were just needling her.

"Sorry, Mia," Butch said.

"Yeah, forgot how much those weeds mean to you," Raid added.

"Won't happen again."

They stood and shuffled off, the others following, already teasing them.

She turned to look at Alec. He stared down at her sternly. "Are you going to turn the hose on my brothers every time they do something you don't like?"

"Yes," she replied promptly. "You got a problem with that?"

He broke into a smile. She liked that he smiled more now. Then he leaned in and kissed her. "Not at all."

He pulled back before the kiss could deepen. Frustration bit at her. Everything in her life was perfect. She'd been worried when Jake and Alec had secluded themselves in his office for hours. But Jake hadn't arrested anyone, so she guessed everything was okay. All Alec would tell her was not to worry. Even Angelo had done the decent thing and gotten himself shanked in prison, so she didn't have to testify. Yep, everything was perfect except for one thing. Alec was still holding back. In fact, he was worse than he'd been before. Oh, he'd given her a couple of fun spankings. He'd even tied her up the other night. But it wasn't like before.

Somehow, she had to convince him she wasn't broken. That she could take all of him. She'd asked Molly what she thought she should do. She'd had a number of crazy suggestions but none of them felt right. Mia wasn't one to play games.

As Alec turned away, she looked down at the hose on the ground and picked it up. Well, if it was good enough for his brothers . . . she turned it on full blast and aimed it at his back.

He let out a yell and turned to look at her. And the look on his face had her dropping the hose and turning to run. She didn't get far before she was picked up and thrown over his shoulder. She let out a screech, and he immediately froze and lowered her to the ground. Gently.

"Are you okay? Did I hurt you?"

"God damn it. No, you didn't hurt me. Don't stop!"

"What?"

She was aware of their gathering audience, but she didn't care. "I said, don't stop."

He frowned. "Why did you turn the hose on me?"

"Because I wanted to get your attention."

His eyebrows rose. "If you wanted some attention, you could have just asked to talk to me."

"But I don't want to talk to you. I am sick of talking. I've talked so much I'm tired of my own voice. I want you to fuck me. I want you to take me over your knee and spank me for getting you all wet. Then I want you to get me all wet."

Alec looked around at his brothers. "All of you. Go."

"Oh, man, he's always ruining our fun," Maddox complained.

"You tell him, Mia," Butch added.

"And if you don't get what you want from him, you know where to find me," Tanner said. He avoided West, who'd aimed a hand at the back of his head in reprimand.

When they were gone, Alec turned back to her. "Kneel."

She knelt on the grass, trepidation making her heart race. Fuck. What had she been thinking? You didn't challenge a Dom like that. She licked her dry lips.

"Eyes on me."

She raised her gaze to his.

"Now talk."

"Could we go into your office?" she asked. Even though he'd told his brothers to go, that didn't mean they'd stay away forever.

"No, you started this out here. You finish it."

"Okay, well, I want to resume our, um, activities."

"You're gonna have to do better than that," he growled.

"I want to be your submissive again," she blurted out. "I know you have this idea that I'm fragile and I need to be handled gently. But I'm doing much better. I've healed physically, I'm having fewer panic attacks and nightmares. I want you to dominate me again."

"Is that so? And to tell me that you had to turn a hose on me?"

She shrugged. "I tried talking to you, but you weren't listening."

"You'll have to forgive me for taking some time to adjust after my woman was kidnapped, taken from my protection, and beaten. Given a whole new set of nightmares to add to the old ones."

She softened. "I'm sorry, Alec. You're right. I forgot this wasn't just about me."

He reached down, raised her chin. "But that doesn't mean that you're going to go unpunished for what you just did. Clearly, you're in need of a firmer hand. And luckily, I'm ready to give that to you."

"And you won't hold back any longer," she blurted out hopefully.

"What?" He frowned.

"I know you've always held back a bit because you didn't think I could handle it, or you're worried about scaring me. But I know who you are, Alec. I saw you. You. That night you rescued me. I saw your darker side, and do you know what I thought when I did?"

"No," he whispered.

"I thought, thank God. Because here was the man who would do whatever it took to take care of me, protect me. Please, Alec. I want all of you. I need all of you."

He didn't answer for a long moment, and she thought she'd done the wrong thing.

"Go into the office and strip then lie over my desk."

"To your office? Not the bedroom?" Disappointment filled her. She'd hoped things would be different.

"I don't like to play in the bedroom. At least not now while you still have nightmares. I want that to be the place where you have my softer side."

"Oh." She could deal with that. And she took the hand he held out to her and let him pull her up.

❧

TEN MINUTES later she let out a cry of pain as he brought the crop down on her ass. It hurt. God damn, it hurt.

He certainly wasn't holding anything back. Which was exactly what she wanted. And yet . . . ouch.

"Next time you want my attention, kitten, what are you going to do?" he asked in a silky voice. Oh, he was seriously displeased.

"I'll come and respectfully ask for it, Sir."

The crop landed. Fiery pain erupted. "Try again."

"I-I'll come kneel next to you and wait until you give me permission to speak."

The crop stopped and she breathed in on a sob. "Good girl. That's a good girl. Bet you're starting to wish you hadn't picked up that hose now, aren't you?"

"Yes, Sir," she sobbed out.

"Master."

"What?" She turned her head to look behind her. His gaze was shuttered, his face giving nothing away.

"You want all of me, kitten, then you'll get all of me. And you'll call me Master."

"Yes, Master."

"Good, kitten. Roll over and put your feet flat on the desk, spread yourself wide."

She rolled, wincing as her hot ass came into contact with the desk. She bent her legs, putting her feet on the wooden surface. She was open, vulnerable and a shiver of anticipation went up her spine. Then the crop landed with a smack on her pussy and she let out a howl. Her feet slipped and she dropped her hand to cover her mound.

Fuck. Jesus.

"Move your hand," he growled.

She let out another sob but drew her hand back.

"Get back into position. If you can't keep in position, I'll have to bind you."

"I'll try, Master."

He granted her a small smile. "Good girl." He landed the crop again, but before she even had a chance to scream, he had dropped his mouth to her clit, sucking on the abused nub gently. Oh, fuck. It was sensation overload. Her clit was on fire. And yet, she couldn't help but want more. Another smack of the crop with his mouth sucking on her gently, and she realized he wasn't hitting her nearly as hard as had on her bottom.

Thank God.

Another smack. More sucking. And the pain was erupting into a deeper hunger. Two more times the crop landed. She wanted more now. She needed more. She let out a groan of protest as he put the crop to one side.

He quickly stripped out of his clothes, obviously in a rush as he yanked at them. Then he leaned over and kissed her. His tongue toyed with hers as he took command of her mouth.

"I need you," he murmured.

"Yes. Please."

He kissed his way down her body, swirling his tongue around each of her nipples.

"I cannot wait. I have to take you. Tell me you want me. That you're ready for me."

Ready for him? She was on fire. It burned. It made her ache. He reached her pussy and lapped at her clit until she was panting, her need for him so great she trembled.

"I need you. I'm ready. Please, take me, Master."

"I do like to hear you beg." He straightened, pulled her ass to the very edge of the desk then he thrust deep. She screamed. Oh, God. It was too much. Nerve endings flared to life. But he didn't give her time to adjust. He wasn't holding back, just like she'd demanded of him. And the way he took her was like nothing she'd experienced before.

He drew back, rolled her over and drove back into her. She

could only cling to the desk and hold on for the ride. He grabbed hold of her hips, slamming her onto his thick, wide dick. He stretched her. He fucked her. And she reveled in the wildness.

A hand smacked against her ass, awakening the heat there. She cried out. "Master!"

"Say, fuck me, Master!"

"Fuck me, Master!" she cried out.

"Tell me that you're mine."

"Please, Master. You own me. I've always been yours. Always. Please."

He reached around and rubbed this thumb against her clit. He wasn't gentle. Wasn't hesitant. He drove her up into a hot, hard orgasm and kept going.

"No, Master. No!"

"Yes. You're going to come again. Are you allowed to disobey me?"

"No!"

"Then come again, kitten!"

She screamed out her next orgasm. Fuck! She hoped none of his brothers heard that and came running. But then he gave a few more hard thrusts and let out his own shout of satisfaction.

She lay panting against the desk for a moment, unable to move, unable to do anything except try to breathe. Sweat coated her body. Had she ever done anything so invigorating?

He leaned over the back of her. "You okay, kitten?"

"I don't think I've ever been better. But I might have to wait a bit for round two, okay?" she murmured sleepily.

He let out a chuckle. "We've got the rest of our lives for round two, baby."

Yeah. She sure did like the sound of that.

.   .   .

I HOPE you enjoyed reading Mastered by Malone and meeting those Malone boys! Read on for an excerpt from Daddy Bear.

EXCERPT FROM DADDY BEAR

"So, you want to tell me what's going on? This isn't like you. Why are you being so snappy and rude?"

To her horror, and his, she guessed by the look on his face, she burst into tears. He immediately pulled her into his arms, rocking her gently. Which just made her cry all the more.

"How can you be so nice to me when I'm being so horrid?" she wailed. "I'm an awful, terrible person."

"No, you're not. And I don't like hearing you say such mean things about yourself."

"But it's true, I'm being so awful to you and you've been nothing but nice to me. You've taken care of me, done everything for me and I...I..."

"Yes?"

"I just feel so grouchy. I don't know what's wrong with me."

"Shh. Shh. Let it all out." He rubbed his hand up and down her back soothingly until she'd quieted down. Then he lay her back down and got up. She had to fight the urge to call him back to her. It was ridiculous, he only went as far as the bathroom and he quickly returned with a roll of toilet paper in his hand.

"Going to run out of this stuff soon if we're not careful," he told her with a grin as he wiped her face then held it to her nose. "Blow."

"I can do that myself." Sheesh, she might have been ill but she wasn't an invalid.

He gave her a stern look. "Put your hand down, little one, and blow."

She blew her nose and he wiped her clean, turning to throw the used tissue in a trash can. Then he turned back and gave her a stern look. "Now. I know you're feeling better. Might be you're itching to get out of that bed and that's what's got you so out of sorts."

"Maybe," she whispered. "I guess."

"You guess?" He looked thoughtful. "You know, I've been thinking about how much you've slept these past few days. Had me really worried about you."

"I...I'm sorry?" Was he upset about that? But he was the one who was keeping her in bed, so it couldn't be that.

"Nothing to be sorry about. I'm just wondering if there was more to it than your head injury."

And now she felt even worse. "I'm sorry, Bear. I really am a horrible, selfish person for treating you like this when you've been nothing but kind."

"That's one," he told her.

"What?"

"I've given you plenty of warnings about not putting yourself down. So that's one spanking you've earned."

Her eyes widened and she gaped at him. "You...you're going to spank me?"

Printed in Great Britain
by Amazon

44928958R00158